D1737712

KIDNAPPED IN PARADISE

PARADISE SERIES

BOOK 7

DEBORAH BROWN

KIDNAPPED IN PARADISE
All Rights Reserved
Copyright © 2015 Deborah Brown

ISBN-13: 978-0-9903166-5-7

Cover: Natasha Brown

PRINTED IN THE UNITED STATES OF AMERICA

KIDNAPPED IN PARADISE

Chapter One

We took a sharp turn, tires squealing around the corner of the quiet residential street. Had we been in a smaller vehicle, the tires would have left the road. Or worse, caused a roll-over; then we would have skidded through someone's living room window. The demon in the driver's seat turned the wheel hard, blew past the wrought-iron gate into the courtyard, and managed to leave the paint job on her black convertible Mercedes intact.

The two-story white Key West-style house was located on the outskirts of Tarpon Cove, the first exit going south off the Overseas Highway in the Florida Keys. An inviting veranda wrapped around the upper level, with tropical flowers of all varieties in brightly colored pots lining the courtyard.

I inherited the house from my aunt Elizabeth. It had taken me a long time to put my personal stamp on the interior. For a long time I felt like a guest, much like when my brother Brad and I would come and spend summers with my aunt. After applying a fresh coat of paint, moving in my own furniture, and recovering a piece or two of Aunt Elizabeth's furniture, it now felt like my home. I made the patio an extension of the house. It was a large entertainment area with comfortable furniture and an outdoor kitchen, a place that Aunt Elizabeth would be happy to find regularly filled with family and friends.

"Give me my keys," I demanded, holding my hand out to my best friend and roommate, Fabiana Merceau.

Her blue eyes held a hint of humor.

"No." She flung her long brown hair over her shoulder. "Who does all the driving? I do!" She poked her chest with her finger. "I need to keep the keys to make sure you don't trick me and get behind the wheel."

Fab and I met when she broke into my house and made herself at home, spoiling my cat.

We hopped out of the convertible black Hummer that I scored in a deal from our on-again, off-again employer, Brick Famosa. Brick owned a variety of businesses, including a car dealership in South Miami. Where I'd paid for my ride, Fab negotiated a trade in exchange for her high-end sports car. Neither of them discussed the details, but it left Fab far more obligated to Brick's sleazy ways than I would ever have allowed for myself.

"I bet I have a better driving record — one ticket, ever. And you?" I snickered as I took the lead down the so-called 'secret path', a bare strip leading around the side of the house that had once been overgrown with weeds. The path ran along the side of the house to the back patio and pool. I had it cleaned out and paver bricks put down. How it retained the 'secret path' name I wasn't sure, since everyone who'd ever been to the house knew about it.

"Aww, yes. Madison Westin, the slowest driver ever. Was your ticket for driving too slow?" Fab yanked on one of my red curls.

"Ha! Speeding." I shot her a smirk before stopping at the back of the house, puzzled. The French doors that led into the living room, which always stood open in a welcoming gesture, were closed. This was especially strange since both of our boyfriends' cars were parked out front.

"I can't believe that one of the guys closed these doors in the middle of the day, even though I worry that the neighbors will walk in."

"Trust me, word has gotten around that we shoot people." Fab walked over to the pool and ran her hand through the water, testing the temperature. She passed by me, flicking water at my face. I ignored her and stared off in the distance, listening for the sounds of the ocean. I never got tired of life at the beach.

Fab slid her lock pick from the back pocket of her jeans. In seconds, she'd handily opened the door.

I sighed as I watched Fab. As usual, I felt unprepared. I only wore skirts, and the only ones with pockets were denim, which I reserved for jobs where running for our lives was involved.

Standing in the doorway, Fab burst out laughing. I followed, curiosity pulling me across the threshold into the living room.

The last thing I expected to see was Jax, tied to a straight back chair next to the coffee table, his long tan legs extended out in front of him.

"Madison... Hi, Honey." Jax made the word sound like *hon-knee*. "Can you explain to these two assholes who I am and get me untied?"

It had been a while since I'd seen Jackson Devereaux, aka Jax. He looked like he'd just rolled off the beach in his white shorts and tropical shirt. The last time I'd laid eyes on him, he had one foot out of town, feeding me a vague promise to never return.

"He says he's your husband?" snapped Creole. Creole's blue eyes were frigid, his expression forbidding.

Creole, born Luc Baptiste, went by the street name that he used as an undercover detective with Miami's finest. I never tired of looking at his caramel-colored skin, strong bone structure, and dark shoulder-length hair. His defined jaw, covered in day-old stubble, always made me want to rub my cheek along his.

Fab laughed and dropped onto the couch, draping herself on her boyfriend's lap. Didier, no last name, was a male model who graced billboards and was as sought after as any

Hollywood star. Both of them were French, sizzling sexy, and they liked to fight in their native language, effectively cutting off eavesdropping.

"He left off the '*ex*' part." I smiled at Creole. Creole and Didier glared at Jax, so I knew he'd been a pain in the ass. "Why is he tied to the chair?"

"Because they're both dicks," Jax snapped, tossing his head in their direction.

Didier's pale blue eyes stared icily as his foot shot out and kicked Jax's chair.

"Don't leave out the part where you tried to break in like a common, vulgar criminal." Didier's black hair was disheveled and standing on end, though it only made him sexier, if that were possible.

"Babe..." Jax winked and slowly perused my body, stopping to ogle my breasts before returning to my eyes. "I'm still tied up."

Creole snarled at him.

"Please," I mouthed to Creole. I really didn't want any ass-kicking going on in my living room.

"Oh, brother," Jax rolled his eyes. "What the heck has happened to you? I thought the last boyfriend was a jerk, but this Neanderthal... Your taste in men has gone downhill since our split."

I couldn't help myself. I laughed at his audacity. Jax must have forgotten that his husband skills completely blew, the cheating not the least of it.

"You might want to keep in mind you're not untied yet," I said, crossing my arms.

Fab jumped up and jerked open a drawer in a side table, removing a switchblade knife.

"Let me," she said with an unnerving grin. She closed the space between her and Jax, holding the knife out and running her finger along the blade for him to inspect.

"You're crazy!" he yelled. He tried to lean away and tottered in the chair, barely saving himself from falling to the floor and taking the chair with him. "Why aren't you on medication?"

"No blood on my hardwood floor," I admonished Fab.

Fab handed me the knife, and I sliced through the rope with no mess.

"Now that I'm back," Jax said, shaking his arms to get the blood circulating again, "we should talk reconciliation. We've missed you."

"We?" Creole raised his brow and looked around.

Fab snickered.

"He named his...uh..." she pointed downward. "Mr. Sir."

Both Creole and Didier laughed.

Knowing Jax was about to give Fab provocation to kick his ass, I jumped in front of him.

"How's your family?" Without waiting for an

answer, I said, "Let's go outside and sit by the pool."

"Sit down," Creole bellowed and pointed at Jax. "I want to know why you were lurking around and what you want. Even better, I want to know when you're leaving."

Jax sneered at both men and made himself at home on the daybed/couch, stretching out. At six feet, he was the shortest of the three men. His brown hair was sun bleached and lighter than I remembered.

Jax scooped up my hundred-year-old, long-haired black cat, Jazz, who'd just sauntered in from his food bowl. The cat stretched out on his chest and went to sleep. Animals and children loved Jax. He'd wanted custody of Jazz in the divorce, and I laughed in his face.

Jax would have gotten bored the first time the cat showed him his tail, showing off how insufferably spoiled he'd become from having the four of us to do his bidding. Jazz had certain expectations that had to be met or howling would ensue. The loud racket turned out to be quite an effective motivator.

Creole lowered his voice, explaining to Fab and me that Jax had woken Didier while he'd been lying on the couch. Jax had jerked the handles of the French doors and tried to force open the windows.

"Too stupid to notice they had locks," Didier said with a smirk. The model had his best friend and workout partner on speed dial; he'd called Creole to ask whether he should wait until the prowler got in the house to shoot him. Creole told Didier to hold off unless the prowler actually got inside and promised that he'd be there in under five minutes.

At first Didier had been resistant to learning how to shoot. Then Fab bribed Didier to go to the gun range for target practice, and he quickly became her star pupil.

Jax blew me a kiss and patted the space next to him. I ignored him and sat in the chair he'd vacated.

"Are you in trouble?" I asked, knowing the answer had to be yes. Although we had remained amicable, helped along by rarely speaking to one another, I suspected his reason for being here was because my most appealing trait to him was that I could be helpful in a tight spot.

"I'm back in the Keys on a business deal. Thought I'd stop by," he said, his eyes gauging the reaction of everyone in the room.

I could feel Fab's eyes rolling, but I refrained from looking at her. Creole and Didier didn't know him but I'd bet his slow response, as though he had to think up an answer, wouldn't pass Creole's detective sniff test.

"Let me translate: a drug deal or some other illegal deal went bad. You're being hunted, and you need a place to hide out. Does that sum it up?" I smiled sweetly at him, knowing he wasn't selling hymnals door to door.

"You know I turned my life around. No drinking, no drugs. Been sober for a while and I like it that way." He reached out to touch me and I twisted away. He managed to grasp a lock of my hair that I wrestled away. My long red hair looked good today, and I had low humidity to thank.

"I do need a place to stay for a few days," he continued.

Creole had paid attention to every word out of Jax's mouth, but at the last he shot to his feet in protest.

"Not happening! Sleep in your car, under your bicycle, or on the beach, I don't care. Don't step one foot on this property again without an invitation."

Jax rolled his eyes down Creole's torn jeans, coming to rest on his dirty feet.

"He's disgusting," Jax said.

When one consorted with drug dealers for a living, dress was casual and precluded him from wearing a suit to sit in a dark, seedy bar working out the details for an illegal transaction. Often times he got arrested, and one of the detectives on his team would give him a free ride back to his office in a warehouse at an undisclosed location.

"You made a friend or two the last time you were here. Go stay with one of them." I walked over and sat next to Creole and put my hand on his thigh, a gentle reminder that bodily harm to Jax wasn't worth it.

Jax set Jazz aside, letting him have the pillow, as he stood.

"I really would like to talk to you..." he paused, looking around, "alone. Can we go outside?"

I looked at Creole. His expression said that he didn't like the idea, but nodded anyway.

"Text me where you are staying and I'll come by in the morning," I whispered, looping my arm in Jax's and walked him to the front door. We stood on the front step. "Are you okay?"

"Yeah." He smiled, his dimple deepening. "I just need a friend. I'll see you tomorrow."

He started down the driveway, then came back and hugged me. "It's really good to see you."

He disappeared down the driveway. I stood for a moment and heard a car start a house or two away. The hairs on the back of my neck tingled...always a bad sign that I tried not to ignore.

I walked back in the house, shutting the door. I found Fab standing there, apparently spying through the peephole. She pulled me into the living room. The look on her face told me she hadn't heard a word.

Creole raised his eyebrows. I hated that everyone stared at me.

"He didn't say anything." I practically sprinted into Creole's open arms.

Fab broke the silence. "I know what will make you feel better. Tomorrow, I have a surprise for you," she said, eluding Didier as he reached for her, a frown on his face.

Creole groaned and I wrinkled my nose.

"No, thanks. You know I hate surprises."

Didier managed to drag Fab back onto his lap and whisper something in her ear, which she ignored.

"This one you're going to love."

"If that were the truth, you'd tell me now."

Chapter Two

Fab and I sat at the power table on the sidewalk at The Bakery Café; the last table at the far end of the walkway, where we could watch everything that happened. I informed Fab that I would need a large caffeinated drink to fortify myself for her surprise. Both of us kicked back in our work attire, enjoying the last of a cinnamon roll. For me, "work attire" included a short skirt, just long enough to cover the Glock holstered at my thigh. For Fab, mid-thigh shorts, showing off her ridiculously long legs. Plenty of room for the Walther shoved into the back of her waistband.

"Where did Creole go so early?" Fab asked, checking out every single person walking by as though they were wanted with a big reward posted.

"Work-related. He got a text and left. It's pretty annoying, since I had plans to start the morning in a different way."

Fab laughed at me without an ounce of compassion. She reached in her pocket and pushed a business card across the table.

"FM Associates," she told me, even as I read the words.

She had finally decided to make it official; she was starting her own business. She'd had a private investigator license for longer than I'd known her. I worked under Brick's license, not yet having accumulated enough hours for my own. When we worked for Brick, all the good jobs, which meant guns and danger, went to Fab. Brick funneled the missing dog jobs, and the occasional misplaced remains of a loved one, my way. My main function was to serve as back-up and try to put the brakes on anything ridiculously dangerous. So far I had so-so success with reining in my daredevil friend.

"Is this your surprise?" I asked, admiring the black card with gold lettering.

The two of us had business cards, but we could never come up with a name. All it had was a phone number, which meant the cards garnered quite a few unprofessional comments.

"There's more. Come on." She pulled me out of my chair and back to the SUV parked at the curb.

Fab drove like a maniac, but as usual she managed to get us everywhere in one piece. It surprised me when she turned into the parking lot of Jake's, a bar that I owned, along with the rest of the block, on the south side of the road through town. I bought out the bar's namesake as he was fleeing the Keys, a handful of debt collectors that wanted him dead on his heels. It didn't matter that Jake couldn't pay; the collector would use his death as a teaching tool. An occasional grisly death served as a deterrent to other non-payers.

Jake's was a tiki-themed dive bar that served the best Mexican food in the Cove. The rest of the block consisted of the recently remodeled Trailer Court, an old deserted gas station, and Twinkie Princesses — a roach coach that served fried food, or so the sign said. I'd never seen it open for business, but they paid their rent on time.

My eyes shot to the far side of the property, and my mouth dropped open at the sight of an old lighthouse sitting where a car wash used to be.

"What in the hell?" I shrieked. "Where did that come from?"

I pointed to the tall cylindrical building with the red rooftop.

"Surprise!" Fab cried. "That's my new office." She noticed my look of complete shock and added, "You said I could have that empty space for my office."

"How did it get here?" This wasn't the small house converted into office space I had imagined.

"It arrived on the back of a flat-bed late yesterday afternoon." She ran around and opened my door, tapping her foot impatiently as I slowly got out of the car.

I was rarely rendered speechless, but this was one of those moments. Fab took my hand and dragged me over to the structure.

"There are three levels," Fab explained as she unlocked the door. "I'll make the top space the office because it's all windows."

I had one foot over the threshold and jumped back.

"Who died in here?" A strong stench permeated the air around us. "The body's not still in there, is it?"

I pinched my nostrils and walked backward, not wanting the stink on my clothes.

"I'll give you the number of the crime scene cleaner." I frowned as I thought of the weird business owner who'd told me once I was his only repeat, non-law enforcement customer. "Mention my name, tell him you're family, and you might get a discount."

"Older buildings sometimes have scents," Fab sniffed.

The sound of a motorcycle roared up. I turned, happy to get away.

"What's he doing here?"

Gunz hefted his large body off his Harley, wearing his signature tropical shorts and boat shoes. Big and bald, he had a fondness for spray-on hair when the mood suited him. He'd built his reputation on supplying forged paperwork for a price, having started out with phony identities and then branching out to complete packages.

"More surprises," Fab whispered. "Be nice, he's painting his hair on again."

He waved, big sunglasses covering his face,

making his arrogance less noticeable. "I got a guy coming over to see about hooking us up to plumbing and electrical. Already hired a crew to do the repairs, power wash, and paint. We should be ready to move-in in about a week. I made it clear, no excuses."

Due to his illegal entrepreneurial spirit, Gunz kept a very low profile. His only weakness was dating certifiable, crazy girlfriends who enjoyed "jungle sex," as I'd once heard him call it. That was one of the few times I minded my own business and didn't ask for him to elaborate.

"I hate to be the party crasher here, but are you two going into business together?" I wagged my finger between the two of them. "You're a criminal," I hissed at Gunz before turning on Fab. "You assured me you'd only be taking jobs on the up and up."

Gunz cleared his throat and glared at me. "I'm reformed."

If he didn't look so sincere, I would've laughed.

He pulled himself up to his full height of six and a half feet tall. "I sold off the lucrative paper business. I only kept my police department account. I'm now a banker. I arrange loans and repayment plans," he smiled with a flash of teeth.

"So you're a loan shark," I huffed.

He growled and started to speak, but I cut him off.

"Listen you two: you both are now under my two-sheriff call limit. The second time you're under investigation or arrest, you're both out. And a second rule: if there is even a whiff of a maimed or dead body—out," I pointed to the street. "The lighthouse stays and becomes a seashell store."

Fab scowled at me. She hated my shell obsession. I brought buckets full home from the beach and occasionally forced her to stop at the Beach Shack so I could snag a bag. I used them for mulch in my potted plants, as they didn't attract families of bugs.

"Now that we're agreed," Fab said, as she glared at Gunz.

Gunz's phone rang and he went out of earshot to answer it.

Fab turned to me, saying, "I've got my first corporate account and I need you for back-up tonight."

"What's the job?" I asked.

"Nice neighborhood, which will satisfy your boyfriend. You stay in the car, wait for me to come back. Like the old days. Anything goes wrong, you drive away."

Creole and Didier were both adamant that we not take jobs in criminal neighborhoods. Creole had gone so far as to place a tracking device in the Hummer, though Fab regularly disconnected it and always chalked it up to faulty equipment. Recently he'd found a way to affix the offending device so that she could no longer remove it, pound the hell out of it, and toss it in the back of his truck. Nor could she expect to avoid the wrath of Didier.

"I would never leave you, and you know that." I looked at the lighthouse in a new light now that I'd gotten over the shock. "I love it. Is it stolen?"

"Who in the heck steals something that big?" she sniffed.

Most people wouldn't notice that she didn't answer the question, but I did.

"I wouldn't get too comfortable until big brother Brad okays this unholy twosome of yours. He put hours of sweat turning the run-down dump of a trailer park into a tourist destination, and he's not going to allow anything to mess it up," I warned her.

Chapter Three

I heard a shrill whistle and turned to find my brother Brad, and hopefully soon-to-be step-son Liam, waving from the entrance to the Trailer Court.

Brad was getting serious these days with Liam's mother, Julie. They were talking about buying a house. That level of commitment would be a first for my brother. It surprised me that our mother hadn't ambushed the two of them with a surprise wedding, a fact which I bet had more to do with her boyfriend putting his foot down, rather than her exercising patience. Brad spent a lot of time with teenaged Liam; he somehow mastered that fine line of adult good influence and friend. When I hung out with Liam, it made me think that maybe I wouldn't suck at motherhood...someday.

Gunz grunted something to Fab that only she could understand. Before jumping back on his bike, he nodded to me, which I interpreted as, 'See ya'. I walked across the driveway to Jake's, leaving Fab behind in an animated conversation with the big man.

"Why do you two look so shifty?" I asked Brad and Liam.

"We just stopped cleaning up for a cigarette and a beer before the reporter gets here," Liam told me with a straight face.

I kissed Brad on the cheek.

"You two get in trouble and it will be my fault, you know. Then I'll blame Mother. And what reporter? Please don't tell me someone died and it made the news."

Brad, muscled and tan from all the time he spent on the water with his commercial fishing business, leaned his six-foot frame against the picket fence. While his boat had been docked for repairs, he'd personally undertaken the renovation of the Trailer Court. It sat at the back of the property I owned, adjacent to Jake's and barely visible behind a row of trees.

He bulldozed the old trailer park, once a crumbling eyesore, and it was now fast becoming a favorite place to stay. I had to admit that the genius of his plan escaped me at first. Brad was enthusiastic, so I went along with his ideas. It sounded better than an empty lot, and I had no intention of selling it to condo-building vultures.

Brad rescued a handful of Airstreams from the property, and he'd found a place on the Atlantic coast to help restore the dirt pile into a 1950's-style tourist destination. Each vintage aluminum travel trailer was restored with all of the comforts of home and available for overnight stays, by the day or week.

He had each Airstream shell expanded in length and rebuilt from the chassis up, complete custom floor plans, each with a fully-equipped kitchen, bedroom, living space, and small but luxurious bathrooms.

The interiors were done in rich woods and highly-polished aluminum, mimicking the original 1950s design. Outside, each trailer had its own faux-grass lawn, which didn't look bad but had an odd feel under one's feet.

It had been my job to scour South Florida for authentic decor and accessories, or as close as I could get. All the old picnic tables I found were termite infested, so I settled for new ones and had them painted in a variety of art deco colors. The chaise lounges were also new, comfortable seating for visitors to enjoy the warm, balmy breezes of the Florida Keys. Fab had done her part by haggling every flea market vendor and antiques dealer down to the last nickel.

Every trailer had a theme and era-appropriate pieces—televisions, radios, and books. I had a hard time ferreting out original kitchen appliances that actually worked. I lucked out and located a man out of state who specialized in replica appliances—all shiny and new and working perfectly. Each trailer came fully furnished with dishes and linens. I cheated a little by going to a factory outlet, where I spent an afternoon mixing and matching dinnerware.

"We're getting a mention in a national travel magazine. We've jumped from local news to the big time," Brad said. He and Liam high-fived.

Fab snuck up on Brad from behind.

"Notice my lighthouse?" She tugged on Liam's hair and they did a secret handshake. I'd watched their convoluted hand routine several times, and I still didn't get it.

"Hard to miss," he chuckled. "I made sure that the paperwork was legal before it got off-loaded. I saw hair-in-a-can guy hanging around earlier. I told Gunz his reputation preceded him, and given the slightest provocation I'd toss his ass in the Gulf. He took it well. Reassured me of his all-legal status."

"I told Gunz no screwing this up," Fab said. "He needs office space to project his new corporate image."

I took a breath and kept my mouth shut about what I thought of his chances for success. Even if he could sustain legality, he'd get bored. He reveled in life on the edge.

I pulled on the end of Fab's hair to get her attention.

"When you're out there on the curb," I pointed to the road, "that lighthouse is all mine. I'd like it if you could get rid of the smell first."

"Could you be anymore unsupportive?" Fab sniffed.

"Probably."

Liam and I laughed.

"Where's Crum?" I asked. "He's usually hanging around, eager to eavesdrop."

Liam spoke up.

"He left here throwing around the 'F' word, looking uncomfortable in a pair of long pants for his appearance in court."

"Pants? I'm surprised he owns a pair."

The retired college professor wandered around in his tighty whities and rubber boots; for dress-up, he preferred boxers.

Liam continued to laugh.

"The pants were a half-foot too short."

"Sort of felt sorry for him," Brad said. "He looked a mess. He had a stained white dress shirt to go with his flood pants, and worn loafers so big they banged the concrete when he walked. I'd say he was trash diving again and couldn't find everything in one can."

"Court date? Did you help him get bail?" Fab asked me.

I shook my head, having no clue what they were talking about. I was just happy that my phone hadn't rung in the middle of the night, with Crum on the other end asking for a ride home. I'd already informed the regular jail-goers that free rides from lockup were now during business hours only.

"Stupid ass!" Brad snorted, then explained to me. "Crum decided to lie on a bench in the boat launch area off Hyacinth, reading last week's newspaper. The sheriff drove up and asked for

ID, which he didn't have. Despite being early afternoon, he got written up for loitering. Either Crum didn't know he was sitting on the drug dealer bench, or he copped his infamous snotty attitude, and the sheriff didn't like being treated like gum on his boot."

"I warned him not to cop a 'tude with the judge and remain calm," Liam said.

"Gave Crum my number in case he gets locked up and needs bail," Brad elbowed me lightly. "If you can pick your drunk friends up, how hard can it be?"

"Good to know. I'll start referring the middle-of-the-night calls to you," I said.

"I told the professor that if he gets locked up, he should put my name on his approved visitors list. How cool would that be?" Liam looked excited.

I knew he wanted to go visit the jail, since he found out I'd done it more than a few times. I never mentioned that I could arrange a visit; his mother would flip.

"I'm leaving tomorrow, going out on a short run on the boat," Brad said.

Liam didn't look happy.

"I'm thinking about hanging up my nets," he continued, giving Liam a teasing glance. "If we're going to be a family, I'll have to take on the job of making sure you don't get in any trouble, so I'll need to be around."

"You can also keep Mother out of trouble," I laughed.

Since all of us Westins had relocated to Florida, we were closer than ever, which meant, for the most part, that we meddled in each other's love lives.

"Now that we're getting good write-ups, the reservations are rolling in," Brad said. "Crum deals with the day-to-day, keeps the place cleaned up. He's forbidden to fix anything, though, after I caught him trying to fix a leaky pipe with tape. He has to call my handyman. Best of all, he doesn't take any crap. We had a couple of loud, drunken guests. Twice he told them to shut it up, and then manhandled them off the property. He's eccentric, but the guests tolerate him and don't seem to notice that he stomps around in his underwear."

"Crum gets someone he can't handle, tell him to call me," Fab offered. "I'll come over and shoot them. Problem solved."

She made a finger gun, giving Brad a wink. As long as I've known Fab, she rarely resorted to shooting a person—she always had something much more clever planned.

"Mother and I both would love to have you around all the time. Give you a chance to bond with Spoon," I said to Brad.

Jimmy Spoon was Mother's younger boyfriend by ten years; a reformed bad boy. She told me he always listened and made her laugh.

Brad would have to get over the fact that he was hot and sexy and not a retired businessman with a paunch.

Brad grimaced. "I'm busy bonding with Creole and Didier. Your boyfriends don't fool around when it comes to their workouts. I thought I'd puke after the last bike ride. Smartass that I am, I said, 'Sure I'm good for fifty miles,' instead of admitting it had been a while since I'd been on bike other than to ride around the beach."

An SUV blew into the driveway, skidding up to where we stood. An attractive blonde jumped out with tape recorder and camera in hand.

"So much for journalists being dumpy old men with a pencil behind their ear," I whispered to Brad.

"Behave," he shushed me. "You're watching the black and white movies again."

"Nice legs," Liam checked her out.

"I noticed that," Brad said.

"So sorry, we have to leave." I waited for a response but Brad and Liam had turned their attention to their guest.

* * *

"Hey, Boss!" Phil, the bartender, waved when I walked through the door of Jake's.

As soon as I bought out the previous owner, number one on the to-do list was having the run-

down bar disinfected. Then I'd tı
attention to making it a fun place to ɯ...
eat, adding big screen televisions, a juke box, and
a game room, which was currently used for
poker by Mother and her friends. She had total
control and a strict invitation-only policy and, as
long as it made money for the house, I didn't feel
compelled to complain.

All the seats at the bar were currently
occupied by locals, mostly men who hung on the
curvy, blonde bartender's every word. Two
women sat on the end in front of video game
machines that Mother had brought in. The
machines were an instant hit.

I put a tray together with glasses, ice, and a
pitcher of tea for Fab and me. While she stayed in
the driveway smiling at her phone and speaking
in French, I checked my cell phone for any
missed messages and went out to the deck. I
sought out my favorite corner table, the one with
the best view of the inlet of water that ran along
the property's edge.

I wondered about Jax and why I hadn't heard
from him; silence from him wasn't a good thing. I
called his number, but it went straight to
voicemail. I didn't know how much trouble he
was in, but sometimes the best choice was to
pack up and clear the state line before anyone
came looking. He wouldn't be the first person to
choose that problem-solving technique.

Fab blew in like a mini hurricane. Most of the

men stopped mid-sip to look at her lithe body, not realizing those legs could kick a man to the ground in the blink of an eye, and that they'd be lucky if that was all she did. She wouldn't think twice about kneeing them between the legs.

I poured her a glass of tea.

"So we're divorcing?"

"You're my new assistant." She gave me one of her creepy smiles; it no longer bothered me, but most people found the look unnerving.

"An assistant you keep in the dark," I sniffed. "I want overtime, hazard pay, and paid vacation."

"Just as long as you know who's boss."

I laughed at her. When she started getting in trouble, I'd be easy compared to Didier and Creole.

She scowled at me.

"Don't worry about Gunz. You won't be seeing him around much. I told him if he gets caught doing anything illegal, he's out."

She tapped my glass with hers and smiled.

Chapter Four

"Since this is your first 'corporate' client," I said as I made air quotes, "why are we skulking around in the middle of the night?"

Fab stared intently at the road as she flew up the interstate, getting closer to Fort Lauderdale. It hadn't been hard for the two of us to leave the house at almost midnight without questions. Creole worked erratic hours, mostly at night, and Didier had a business meeting in New York and wouldn't be home until the morning.

Fab blasted her horn at a car wanting to slide in and share the same lane.

"My client had the hot idea of me subbing in for the receptionist who's going on vacation. No amount of explanation could convince him I would suck at the job. Mostly, I didn't want to be humiliated by getting fired on the first day," she grimaced. "So I decided to take care of business before I got stuck reporting for a desk job."

I bit down on my lip to keep from laughing. Fab sucked at customer service. It wouldn't take long for her to turn surly and rude.

"So whatever we're doing is Plan B?"

She nodded.

"I tweaked the game plan a little. Thought I would tell the client after I got the job done. Once I get tossed as the worst temp ever, it will be difficult to come back and snoop around."

Fab cut around an old junker car, coming a hair's breadth from removing what was left of the front bumper. The driver, a twenty-something, was either incredibly short or scrunched down in his seat, his head barely clearing the top of the steering wheel. Apparently, he had no sense of humor; he stuck his middle finger out the window.

"You showed him whose is bigger," I chuckled.

"Back to business," she snapped her finger. "I've already staked out the office and the entire building. The surrounding area is all high-rise office buildings, restaurants, and a dead zone on the weekends. Their security system is lame. I can bypass it in seconds after picking the lock. I'll be in and out in less than a half hour. They'll never know I snooped through their offices."

Fab suffered insomnia when Didier left town, which made this a perfect opportunity to do some night-time sleuthing.

As we drove, Fab told me that her client was a commercial real estate developer who'd lost every deal he tried to put together in the last year. In some cases, he'd been outbid by as little as a few hundred dollars, always to the same broker and his client, an anonymous corporation.

Not a man to believe in coincidence, Fab's client felt certain it had to be someone from his office feeding the crucial information, and he wanted proof. If it wasn't a mole, then he still wanted the person responsible. There were only three other people that had access to the confidential information, all believed to be trusted colleagues.

Fab was dressed like a burglar in form-fitting blue jeans, a long-sleeved shirt, and tennis shoes. She had her long hair tucked under a plain baseball cap. And then there were her accessories: Fab never left home without her lock pick and her Walther.

Surprisingly, Fab didn't do her usual driving trick of waiting until the last second to exit the freeway before cutting diagonally across three lanes of traffic. Once we were off the ramp, she maneuvered the deserted streets. She found the place with ease and parked around the corner on the opposite side of the street.

"Wait here," Fab directed. "If the cops or anyone else shows up, text me, and you get out of here. When I get to a safe place, I'll call you."

I slid across the seat and moved the SUV closer to the corner, giving me an unobstructed view of the two intersecting streets in both directions. I whipped a paper map out of the console and created a cover story to memorize for why I would be sitting in a darkened auto in the middle of the night. I would blame it on the surly voice of the GPS woman—she was in a bad mood and had given me bad directions.

I tried not to check the time every few minutes, but I couldn't resist. I managed to keep my eyes on the five-story building across the street. Eighteen long minutes later, Fab darted out of the building on the far side, a young man in a security guard uniform giving chase right behind her.

How did she not know about him? I wondered.

Good thing Fab was in excellent physical shape and not a bad runner. I watched as her hat flew off and her hair cascaded out behind her, but she just continued to pound the pavement. We'd made a pact to stay out of jail, so getting arrested and being charged with breaking and entering, or worse, couldn't happen.

Just as she was about to sprint around the corner, she stumbled, going down flat on her face. In the next breath, she jumped back on her feet and launched herself forward, the guard still in pursuit. She disappeared from sight onto a side street.

I started the engine and jammed my foot on the gas pedal, making the tires squeal. I rounded the corner to see that the guard had gained ground and was within arm's length of Fab; his hand snaked out to grab her and came up with air. The next time, she might not be so lucky. I sped up, shining the high beams and laying on the horn. After startling the guard, I maneuvered the car into the space between Fab and the guard and released the door locks.

The passenger door flew open and Fab hurled herself inside, landing in a sprawl across the seat. I glanced in my mirror to make sure I hadn't miscalculated and that the guard was still standing several feet away. I stepped on the accelerator and sped away as the guard fumbled in his pocket. Fab, out of breath, gulped in huge breaths.

She lowered the back of the passenger seat and crawled off the console so that she was lying face down, her butt sticking up awkwardly in the air.

I took off into the night, turning randomly down darkened streets, not sure where I was going. At the light, I recognized the name of the street, knowing it would take us back to the interstate. After making the turn, I kept to the speed limit, not wanting to attract any attention.

Fab's breathing slowly returned to normal.

"It didn't take long to find the information," she said at last. "I had finished snooping when I heard someone in the hall. Surprise, and it was on me—a security guard! I scouted this location twice, including the general area, going over every single inch of the building and no guard, and none of the other buildings on this block have one. My client also made a point of telling me that there was no guard. He threw open the door, flipped on the light, and asked, 'What the hell are you doing in here?'"

She paused. "I recovered first from the mutual shock, head butted him, and during those few seconds it took him to stay on his feet, I ran. I kicked open the door to the stairwell and caught a glimpse of him out of the corner of my eye, he was coming fast. Thank goodness for tennis shoes, not my usual strappy sandals, or I would have been running barefoot and been caught for sure."

Fab's ability to get out of tight spots had always amazed me. I unscrewed the top off my water bottle and handed it to her.

"All the practice I've had sliding down banisters and jumping steps came in handy. I raced down two flights of stairs and jumped the last section banging out the exit," Fab said, laughing to herself.

I merged onto the interstate and breathed a sigh of relief that we were headed south back to the Cove. And mostly because there were no flashing lights behind us.

Fab downed the water and pitched the bottle into the back seat.

"Thinking this job would be a piece of cake, I didn't plan an alternate getaway. Last time I ignore that detail! I hit the pavement, not sure of my direction, and focused on not letting the damn guard catch me. You'll be proud of me. I only thought briefly about shooting him and was relieved when it registered that the furious honking wasn't sirens. I knew it had to be you, kind of happy you don't follow directions."

I grimaced. "I guess breaking into an office building isn't the sure thing that it used to be. Did you get what you needed? Hopefully you don't have to go back."

Fab grinned at me and retrieved the micro camera she'd tucked into her pocket. She pulled up several images of memos and emails she'd found in a file, which were barely visible from my vantage point.

"I believe I found the mole. Stupid woman left a paper trail."

"Was it someone in the inner circle?"

Fab shook her head as she continued to admire her handiwork.

"The VP's executive assistant. She's been with him for ten years, and she's also his mistress. She fed the numbers to his competitor, who in turn set up dummy corporations to cover their tracks. According to one memo she'd sent to her co-conspirators, the guard had been hired two days ago. She'd been ballsy enough to hold late night meetings at the office. I wonder what made the company decide to hire a guard?"

"Maybe to keep someone from doing what you just did." I looked over at her, assessing her torn pants, scraped-up hands and knees, and bleeding arm. "How badly are you hurt?"

Fab shook her head. "Not much. Actually, I'm feeling pretty good."

"It's the adrenaline rush that's got you

pumped up. That's why nothing hurts. It's why your mouth is dry, your hands are shaking, and why you're obsessing on the details instead of looking me in the eye." I shoved more water at her. "Drink this. Put your seat back again. Just lay there and breathe slowly."

"I see no reason to tell the guys about this, do you?" Fab worried.

"My new policy: I won't rat us out—but if Creole asks, I'm not lying."

"Then you'll give me a heads-up, right?"

Fab hadn't realized yet that Creole always found out and then shared details with Didier. That man could convince a jury to give a life sentence for littering.

Just once, couldn't she fess up? I wondered.

"How do you plan to hide your injuries?" I asked. "Do you need a doctor? I know one I can call in the middle of the night, and there's always our favorite nurse."

"Why?" she looked puzzled.

"You must have hit your head, because you're not complaining about my driving."

Chapter Five

The screaming woke me up. I sat upright, disoriented, and looked around, calming somewhat when I realized that I was in my own bed. The morning sunshine streamed through the bedroom window. It took me a minute to realize that I wasn't dreaming, and in fact it was Mother screaming my name. Fab's bedroom door hit the wall and footsteps sounded in the hall. I tugged on my sweat pants and pulled on a t-shirt before I retrieved my Glock, opened the door, and raced for the stairs.

In the entryway, Didier had his arms around Mother, who was mumbling incoherently. Fab had her Walther cocked as she headed for the front door. She cracked it open, took a peek, and slammed it shut.

"Don't go out there," she ordered as she flew back upstairs.

"Why not?" I yelled after her.

Mother looked at me, her cheeks drained of color and her brown eyes round and frightened. "Call Creole. Tell him to get his ass over here now. He'll know what to do."

Didier walked Mother over to the couch and I

followed. He gave me a brief shake of his head, letting me know he had her under control, and stood with his arms around her. I took a deep breath, trying to control myself.

"What is going on?" I asked.

Maybe the peep hole had answers. I crossed to the front door and looked out into the courtyard, but I didn't see anything amiss. I picked Mother's phone up off the floor from where she'd dropped it and texted Creole: *9-1-1*.

The phone rang in my hand just as Fab raced by me and out the door.

"Mother said to get your ass over here," I told Creole before he could say a word.

I knew his next question would be the same as mine, and I wasn't going to sound stupid with a lame answer of, "I don't know." I pulled open the door. First I looked at Fab and then I looked down. Then I screamed.

"Madison, answer me!" Creole yelled.

Fab pushed me back into the house and kicked the door shut, taking the phone from my hand and commandeering the conversation.

"Madison is fine. There's a severed head on the front doorstep. The rest of the body appears to be missing." She hesitated and then handed me back the phone. "He hung up without even a good-bye."

Fab went outside again and this time came back laden with pink bakery boxes from The Bakery Café that Mother had dropped outside.

They appeared to have survived the abuse of being dumped on the ground. I caught the scent of egg soufflé that drifted out of one box. If I knew my mother, the other box had an assortment of breakfast pastries. Everyone had lost their appetites now, but they'd make great leftovers.

I slid onto a stool at the kitchen counter and put my head down. "Anyone we know?" I asked faintly. I'd seen a dead body or two, but nothing prepared you for the sight of one, and certainly not just the head.

The phone rang again, and this time a photo of Mother's boyfriend, Jimmy Spoon, came up on the screen. I handed the phone to Fab, as this was her area of expertise — imparting gruesome news. I noticed the miniature camera dangling out of her pocket and knew she'd been taking pictures of the deceased.

"You know everyone in town; maybe you could get over here pronto and ID the body," she barked at Spoon over the phone.

I winced, knowing that Spoon, the local badass, didn't tolerate being ordered around. Since Fab was now just staring at the phone in her hand, he must have hung up on her.

Fab jerked on my arm, and we both went into the living room. We sat on the daybed across from Mother and Didier. He still had his arm around her, but she looked less sickly and more coherent.

Fab looked at me. "Since we have no clue as to the identity of John Doe, we have no answer for why he's on our doorstep."

"Have we screwed anybody over lately?" I whispered.

"There's no one in my past that would send that kind of message. And that's what it is—a message," she whispered back.

Creole burst through the French doors in work attire of rumpled shorts and shirt, his eyes a deep blue, canvassing the room.

"What's going on? Nothing you say ever makes sense," he barked at Fab.

She pointed her finger toward the door he just entered. "Go back out the way you came in, and come back in the front door."

Creole looked about ready to tell her to take a hike, when Didier gave Creole a nod, some kind of guy shorthand taking place.

Creole whooshed out a long breath. "Don't go anywhere," he said as he pointed at me.

"He's going to have questions. Go answer them, and be nice," I said to Fab.

"I'm always nice," she said, giving me a deranged smile. "This time I'll speak slowly so he can understand."

I bit back a laugh. As soon as she stood, I stretched out on the daybed and began stacking the pillows under my head. Jazz, seeing a good opportunity for a nap partner, jumped from the chair to the table and then right beside me, nudging my hand for a head scratch before he settled down.

Everyone turned toward the front door at the sound of Spoon's voice. Mother bounced up, but Didier caught her by the back of her shirt and pulled her back down, saying something to her in annoyed French. Although she didn't understand him, she stayed seated.

"Stay here," Didier said as he stood up. "If you go outside, I'll tell Spoon you were quite naughty."

I covered my mouth to keep from laughing. The look of annoyance on Mother's face was priceless. She must have decided it wasn't worth arguing over, because she sank back against the cushions, clutching one to her mid-section. I stayed with her. Unlike Fab, who had a fascination with gruesome crime scenes, I didn't feel the need to see the head — again.

"Make yourself comfortable, Mother. I don't think we're going anywhere until after the sheriff and coroner leave, whenever that is." I wrinkled my nose.

"Do you have any idea where... well... *he* came from?" Mother pointed to the front door.

I shook my head, but I noticed that more than once since the discovery Jax had popped into my head. I couldn't help but wonder if he could supply any answers. Before mentioning his name, I planned to speak to him, on the chance I was wrong. I hadn't even told Mother he'd arrived in town. Could there be a correlation in Jax's situation and the corpse-less head on our front stoop?

The door opened and everyone trooped back inside, Fab in the rear. She looked at me and shook her head, giving no indication she had anything newsworthy.

Creole crooked his finger at me. His blue eyes, dark and intense, checked me over, his mouth twisted and hard. I returned his stare but focused on the day-old beard that begged me to run my cheeks across the whiskers.

He sighed at my hesitation and crossed the room, hooking my arm around his neck and scooping me into his arms.

"I can walk," I whispered, then licked the stubble on his cheek.

"Behave yourself," he whispered back and carried me through the doors out to the far corner of the pool. He sat on a chaise and put me on his lap.

At first I thought he would kiss me, but instead he looked down my top. "I called Kevin; he should be here in a few minutes. Spoon ID'd the head as belonging to an ambitious, low-level drug dealer, Jones Graw. Spoon thought he moved north a long time ago. Big question is, why is he dead and how did end up on your doorstep? I don't like the message that's being sent."

Neither did Fab, I thought.

"Maybe he got delivered to the wrong door." I wrapped my arms around his neck and pushed myself against him, making a kissy face.

His lips found mine, sparking chemistry. The kiss grew demanding, consuming, lips and tongues dancing. Creole's arms encircled me as I dissolved into him. After a long moment, I finally pressed my face against his chest, breathing heavily.

"Break it up, you two," Fab said cheerfully, as she rattled a deck chair against the concrete.

I glared at her. "You couldn't just call out from the door?"

She scooped her hair off her neck and pulled it into a ponytail. "No, I couldn't," she laughed and walked away.

Creole's hands cupped my face. "I have to go. I don't want you to worry. I called in a few favors, and your house will be under constant surveillance."

"Don't you think I need a personal body guard? Someone who never leaves my side? Sexy and funny is a must." I smiled up at him.

"Got that covered. I'll be back," Creole said as he gave me a quick kiss. "I'll see you later."

I watched as he disappeared onto the path in the direction of the beach.

Chapter Six

The last place I wanted to be was inside my house, but guilt led me back. I peeked through the doors before entering. Mother sat on the couch with Kevin Cory, a local sheriff, next to her. He'd be my brother-in-law when my brother Brad marries his sister. He only tolerated the Westin women, and I heard him tell my brother it would be nice if we didn't go off 'half-cocked' all the time.

Kevin was minus a partner these days and wouldn't have another one anytime soon, due to cut backs. His last one asked for a transfer 'out of this dickwater' town. Kevin said she'd complained incessantly about the dull-witted people. Lucky her, she got sent to Gainesville, a college town in the middle of the state with no beach view.

Three other uniformed local sheriffs that I didn't recognize milled around. I looked at the stairs, wondering if I could sneak up them unnoticed and hide in my bedroom, but I didn't think that would be supportive of Mother. Spoon sat next to her and had her anchored to his side.

Brad didn't approve of their relationship, due

to Spoon's colorful past. I reminded him that the man had reformed and become a somewhat-scary pillar of the community. I also pointed out that, although younger, at least Spoon wasn't our age or 'fresh out of high school' as we liked to tease Mother. What hadn't escaped Brad's notice was that Spoon made Mother happy.

Mother was in her sixties, but lied about her age. They were an attractive couple. She was always well-dressed. Not long ago, her blonde hair would have never be out of place. Now she sported a wind-whipped look. She'd been a good influence on Spoon. He seemed less intimidating somehow and smiled more often. Mother had a hand in upgrading his wardrobe, but still kept it beach-casual.

I slipped into the kitchen and sat at the island. Because of the open floor plan, from here I could survey the living room, yet not be an easy target for relentless questioning.

Fab slipped onto the stool across from me. "The coroner just left with a metal box in hand."

"Did you overhear anything?" I shuddered, pushing away gruesome images.

Fab looked around before answering. "You know I'm not allowed to eavesdrop anymore."

I rolled my eyes. "That may be, but you do it anyway." I'd seen Didier disappear upstairs. "I'm going to have a talk with Didier about changing you into someone totally unfun. Thank goodness you only listen when it suits you."

"How long before you can get Weirdo, the crime scene cleaner, over here?"

"Is there a big mess out there?" I squeezed my eyes closed. "You have to stop calling him that, or I'll never remember his name. And it's not 'Weirdo.'"

We looked at one another and laughed. We both knew that giving people rude nicknames was juvenile and a habit we needed to break.

I stood up, walked over to the kitchen garden window, and stretched across the sink as I checked out the courtyard. Nothing appeared out of place. The only sign of a crime was a piece of yellow tape tossed on the driveway.

"It will be a long time before I use the front door again," I said.

"Just think of it as an excuse to drag home second-hand stuff and plant it with flowers," she smirked.

"It has me thinking about redoing the front step. Hire someone hunky to pour a skim coat of concrete over the death scene, and I'll embed it with seashells."

Fab had more patience for my shelling hobby of late. She had zero patience for walking on the beach and having to slow down so I could bend over every other step. Now she helped me fill the bucket to the top, then we'd hide it and finish our walk. I had been banned from sneaking off on my own to find shells, which annoyed Fab because it took her longer to find me, and she liked knowing where everyone was.

Fab snorted.

"I heard that. I've got to leave. There's an emergency at The Cottages," I said. I didn't look at her to sell my lie, but thought it sounded convincing.

The whole dead body—well, the severed head—and all its implications made me squeamish. If I could put distance between me and the doorstep, I could pretend for a little while it never happened.

Fab put her finger under my chin and turned my face up.

"I don't like saying I don't believe you, but I don't."

"Be a best friend and take care of things here." I jumped up to leave. I'd barely taken two steps when she grabbed the back of my shirt and jerked me to a halt.

Fab cleared her throat. "Kevin, do you have any questions for us? If not, we're headed to The Cottages. Miss January's lost her cat again, and you know how upset she gets."

Spoon smirked at Fab. "I can't imagine you have any feline skills. Must be my step-daughter."

"Please don't say that in front of Brad," I said. Spoon and my brother were getting along these days; step-daddy talk would throw cold water on good relations.

Kevin's mouth dropped open and he turned to

Mother. "You married him?"

I glared at him. It irked me that Kevin never gave Spoon credit for turning his life around, especially when Mr. Straight and Narrow Cop had a fondness for strippers.

"I can handle things here," Spoon said, ignoring Kevin. "Pretty Boy's got an appointment in Miami." Spoon's eyes shot to the top of the stairs where Didier stood giving him the finger.

"We'll be finished up in a few," Kevin informed us. "If I have any more questions, I'll save them for the next family dinner," he said with a laugh. Everyone glared at him. Not long ago, I decided to play get-along and started including him in family get-togethers, which were never without a little drama.

"Madison," Mother started. "When we're done here, I'm going with Spoon. We're going out on the boat."

I walked over, leaned in, and gave her one of her patented stern looks. "Take your phone. And don't get in any trouble."

"What about him?" She nodded at Spoon.

"Don't get him in any trouble either." I hugged her and whispered in her ear, "Have fun."

Chapter Seven

Fab sat at the signal, revving the engine of the SUV, flirting with a young hottie who didn't want to race but wanted her to pull over. I clutched the arm rest and looked out the window. I wished she'd find another source of amusement. The light turned green. She took off and hung a hard right onto her favorite dead-end...or so the sign said. Only a handful of locals, and insomniacs with severe snooping skills, knew that the last driveway was a thru-way to the next street over.

As she blew through the wooded residential area, my phone rang. I looked down at the screen.

"When he calls me, it's some awful job he knows you'll say no to," I told Fab. I rejected the call and shut my phone off.

Instantly Fab's phone rang.

"Hi, Boss," she answered.

Finally, after incessant nagging and a few threats on my part, we now had a reciprocal listening agreement and put our phones on speaker. "She hung up on me again!" Brick started yelling.

"She answered, but the line was dead. Bad reception." Fab made a face.

"I want the two of you in my office five minutes ago," he said before he hung up.

"He and I need to go over the terms of my employment agreement," I grouched.

I had nothing in writing and insisted I would only take work on a case-by-case basis, but that was nothing more than big talk as we rarely said no.

In the contract Fab had with him, she never said "get screwed" to any of his jobs. In exchange, she drove the hottest cars in town until he wanted them back. I paid for my car, so I felt less inclined to be ordered around.

"What do you suppose he wants?" Fab asked.

"Think of all the jobs you wouldn't take and pick one of those. Are you keeping him as a client now that you've got your lighthouse?"

"I need him until I get other clients. Are you forgetting he pays cold hard cash?" Fab asked.

Of course Brick paid better than anyone in town. His jobs had a tendency to go sideways. Word had gotten around, and now he had a difficult time hiring freelance help.

I laughed at her. I knew this new idea of hers would eventually be a win-win. It was only a matter of time until she was back at Jake's, sharing office space with me at our private table out on the deck. I knew Fab better than she knew herself. It frustrated her not to be in the know, and she'd soon find her new location isolated and without the food service that Jake's provided.

"I'm a little jealous, but I'm thinking that with a little patience on my part, I might get your new offices for a tourist gift shop." I felt certain it would disappear in the night before I got any souvenir paraphernalia unloaded.

"You wouldn't, would you?" She looked wounded.

Fab's phone rang again and I sighed. It was probably Brick yelling at us to hurry up. She answered, but didn't say a word, putting it on speaker.

"Why in the hell can't you say hello? I know you're there, I can hear you breathing!" Mac yelled.

Mac Lane held the position of office manager of a ten-unit beachfront property that I inherited from my aunt. One day Mac showed up at the pool of The Cottages, demanding a job interview. Instead of conducting a professional question and answer, I hired her because she made me laugh and knew she could handle herself in a barroom brawl. Both highly sought-after skills.

"Hey, who works for whom here?" I yelled back, anticipating a highly entertaining conversation.

"Why is your phone off?" she continued, barely taking a breath. "You need to get over here."

I heard the thump in the background and knew it wasn't her foot stomping on the floor, but her tennis shoe kicking the desk in frustration. The lights that ran around the bottom of her shoes must have gone out again. Mac had regressed in her footwear choices. Every pair had to scream neon or have feathers or flowers. She wouldn't wear "boring" things.

"Brick first. Then you," Fab barked. "Hold the mayhem together until we get there. We've got to go." She disconnected, as she often did, without a friendly good-bye.

Chapter Eight

Fab pulled into Famosa Motors, a car dealership specializing in high-end sales and rentals. She screamed to a stop at the front of the showroom. Her driving must have started growing on me, because I hadn't complained once and I'd finally let go of the cheater bar.

Two salesmen leaned against a large column to the side, giving us a cursory glance before they went back to their conversation. They were new guys, which was no surprise as none of them stayed around long. These two reminded me of pimps: dark eyed with slicked-backed hair, dressed in their Florida uniform of shorts and tropical shirts that were unbuttoned to show off their bear-hairy chests, covered in gold chains.

"Hey, Bitsy," I yelled as we walked in and past her desk. "Your fake hair looks better than usual."

Bitsy was Brick's long time receptionist. Her biggest job qualification was a pair of double D's. Brick boasted that he promoted from within when he transferred Bitsy over from his strip club.

She also ran an unsavory side business of

selling information. I'd heard through gossip, which in our line of work frequently turned out to be the most reliable source, that Bitsy had screwed another customer, reselling the same information several times over.

Apparently, the victim showed up at Famosa Motors, making a huge stink until the security guards escorted him off the property. He left, shouting threats and obscenities. I wondered if Brick gave her the talk about the rules, when to and when not to screw people over. Long overdue, in my opinion.

Bitsy liked us even less than we liked her, which was saying something after she had screwed us over on a business deal last year. To show our displeasure, we tormented Bitsy as much as possible. On one visit, I pulled her hair and, to my surprise, it came completely off, revealing ugly, chopped-off, multi-colored hair. "I wish Brick would get rid of the two of you," Bitsy snapped. She gave us the finger.

"Oh, you're hurting our feelings." I wiped away a pretend tear, sniffing as though holding back the floodgates.

Fab and I looked at one another and giggled, gliding past her and up the stairs.

"I need a favor," Brick said as he flashed his loathsome smile. "I'd appreciate if the two of you would skip the drama and just do it. I'd hate to remind you that you both owe me."

I squinted at him. "You've got a lot of f'ing

nerve. If Mother were here, she'd beat the hell out of you."

Mother had met him a handful of times, and she'd never been impressed. *Smarmy* was the word she used when referring to him.

Fab laughed.

"How many times have the jobs you've given us exploded in a hot second?" I demanded.

"You could have just dumped this favor in my lap," Fab smirked. "But no. For whatever reason, you have to have Madison on the job. Does that sum it up?"

Brick sighed."You remember Carmine Ricci, Madison? He's got a job for you. I told him you already have a partner. He didn't like it, but accepted it. He's a preferred client, and I want you to take the job."

"Do you know any details?" Fab asked.

"He only said this job needs a woman's touch. I've got a number here and he's waiting for your call." Brick pushed a notepad across the desk.

I met Mr. Ricci on my first luxury car delivery. The experience was intense and a bit scary. He'd been a gentleman, but, then again, I'd never had the occasion to tell him, "No, I'm not interested." I was willing to bet that Mr. Ricci never heard those words from anyone.

"He's a mobster," I told Fab.

"There's no proof of that ugly accusation," Brick huffed. "Carmine's a retired businessman and any stories to the contrary are lies. I'll remind you, he's also a longtime friend of mine."

Brick was one of those people who expected other people to take his every word as gospel truth.

"Call him," Brick pointed to the paper in front of me. "He's waiting for your call."

Fab left her spot at the window that overlooked busy street below, surrounded by pricey commercial real estate. She made herself comfortable in the over-sized chair next to me, then dialed the number and put the call on speaker.

The phone rang twice and Carmine answered. "Madison?"

"Hello, Mr. Ricci. I'm here with my partner, Fabiana Merceau."

"Yes, partners. I don't approve, but Brick assures me that you only work in pairs. I have a matter of the utmost discretion that needs to be taken care of as soon as possible. Today, if at all possible. Are you available?"

I closed my eyes and shook my head.

"We can clear our schedule," I said, against my better judgment. I didn't think we had any plans, but with Fab you never knew. She had a tendency to spring jobs on me at the last minute.

"My mother is in a bit of legal difficulty. I believe she became overwhelmed by the legal system and has run away. She's in hiding. I don't think she'd leave the South Florida area, as she has no ties to anywhere else."

"She didn't kill anyone, did she?" I asked.

"Hardly," he sniffed. "She's eighty-five. I need her handled with care and brought back home without scaring her to death. I need someone to reassure her. My lawyers have made this misunderstanding a top priority, and I'm certain I can make the charges go away. She doesn't need to fear incarceration."

I shook my head at Fab and pinched the bridge of my nose. We looked at one another, both of us understanding that his story stunk.

"Do you have any idea of where we're supposed to look?" I asked.

"Brick has a photo and a list of addresses. He'll give it to you. I'm hoping to hear from you soon. Don't disappoint me." He hung up.

Brick reached into a side drawer and withdrew a folder, sliding it across the desk.

"She needs to be found and brought in nice and quiet."

"Did she commit a felony?" I scowled at him.

His slow response was noted.

"Carmine wants his mother back. If she's not found, I'll be out a lot of money, as I posted bail for Carlotta."

That was a nice non-answer.

"Cut the bull and spit out the truth," Fab said as she stood up. "Never mind. Let's go."

"Sit down," he half yelled. "She was charged with prostitution, pandering, and some other minor charges."

I looked at him with pure disgust, and looted the snack bowl on his desk, pouring the contents in my purse.

"That's the worst made-up story I've ever heard."

Fab and I had reached the top of the stairs when Brick yelled, "Wait! She runs a high-class prostitution ring, catering to the uber-rich out of South Beach. Other than this misunderstanding, she has a clean rap sheet."

"How are we supposed to find her?" Fab yelled back.

"Get back in here," he barked. "And no more yelling, unless it's me doing the yelling." He waited until we were seated.

"In addition to Carmine's list, I scribbled down a couple of possible hiding places. This requires discretion. She's not to know that her son's got his people combing the streets. She's not stupid; she turned selling sex into a multi-million dollar business. I suspect she's on alert."

"What happens to her when we return her to her gangster son?" I asked, taking Fab's former spot on the window ledge and watching the busy traffic below.

"He'll put a guard on her until the case is settled. He's got his lawyer hammering out a deal that doesn't include prison time, which will get blown to hell if she's running around making headlines. Or worse, speaks to the wrong person."

"We're not interested." Fab leaned against the door frame and turned on her heel. "You get another missing cat case, give us a call."

"Damn it. You're perfect for the job. Well, she is, anyway," he said, sitting straight up and pointing at me. "Which is why Carmine requested you."

I smirked and fluttered my eyelashes at Fab.

"A little old lady too much for you?" he asked me.

"Don't look at me," I told him. "Fab's got the gift with the older set. My expertise is crazy folks, the ones not quite ready for commitment."

I knew that Fab would agree that we didn't want anything to do with a case where a grandmother might end up in jail.

"I'll pay double if you bring Carlotta back to Ricci's house in one piece, with no drama." Brick's tone sounded a bit desperate, so my guess was he didn't have anyone else he trusted for the job.

"You'll pay quadruple if anything goes wrong, and I mean *anything*. We don't get so much as a scratch." I gave him an evil smile, remembering those were Creole's words.

"Done. Don't forget your folder." Brick picked it up and handed it to me. "Sooner is better than dragging your feet."

I scanned the list and followed Fab to the stairs, relieved to see all of the addresses were in good areas.

"Stay off the banister!" he yelled.

Fab ignored his rant and climbed on anyway, riding it to the bottom. "Let's make sure we get the quadruple pay without shots fired."

"Maybe she'll be like Miss January, drunk all the time. We should take Mother along."

"Your mother never listens to me," Fab huffed. I ignored her, flipping through the file's contents.

"This says the arrest took place in a high-end South Beach condo. I highly doubt she'd go back there anytime soon. We could snoop around to see if the yellow police tape has been removed."

"Let's not get arrested. How would we explain an association with Carmine Ricci to Didier and Creole?"

I handed Mrs. Ricci's picture to Fab. "To look at her, you'd never suspect she peddled sex for money."

Carlotta Ricci looked fit and trim, complete with character wrinkles. She looked like a woman of wealth, not prostitution.

"I should probably take a moment to mention that I had fliers distributed all over town. 'Need a pet finder? Give us a call.' Since you're always suggesting it." I bit my lower lip.

"You did what?" Fab yelled.

I covered my face and laughed.

Chapter Nine

Fab pulled into the parking lot of the Oceanfront Towers in Fort Lauderdale, where the Ricci family owned a penthouse.

"All of these addresses seem like a goose chase," I said as I scanned the list for the tenth time. "I thought this one looked like our best shot. The rest are large properties that must have full time staff, except one commercial property."

Fab had a great, albeit mysterious, connection that made us skeleton keycards. The building we were currently standing in front of needed real keys, though. I wasn't even mad, since this meant I got to use my handy lock pick and show off my breaking and entering skills. Mother would be so proud. I inserted the two pieces into the lock, turned them at opposite angles, and the lock clicked open. I wanted to kiss the doorknob, but didn't. I did a second door only a few feet later, with the same result.

Fab leaned against the wall, watching.

"My star pupil," she cheered as she clapped.

It surprised me that the only security in this high rise were the two doors. You'd think in a pricey waterfront building, the security would be more impressive. We rode the elevator as it shot to the penthouse, opening to a small lobby with one door.

"The television is on," I said, my ear pasted to the door.

"We'll surprise her." Fab smiled. "She's old; we each get one arm and haul her out."

"What are the chances she'll pull a gun out of her bathrobe?" I asked.

Fab pointed her finger at the lock.

"Here we go," I said, working my magic again. The door opened into a large living space with a high-end designer look; everything was in its place, but nothing was comfortable-looking.

Our little bail jumper lay on the couch fast asleep, in front of a large floor-to-ceiling window that overlooked a boat marina.

"Wake her up," Fab said and nudged me. "Offer her a ride to her son's mansion, so we can get back home."

"Why me?" I asked, reaching out and gently touching Mrs. Ricci's shoulder.

I looked down at her. Carlotta Ricci scored in the gene pool. An attractive, silver-haired woman, she looked a lot younger than her age and was in excellent shape. No ugly shift dresses for this woman, either. She had on jade-colored silk pants, and a very expensive pair of ivory satin pumps lay on the floor to match her top.

Startled, she clutched her chest.

"Who in the hell are you?" She sat up, flinging her legs onto the floor and blinking sleep from her eyes.

"I'm Madison and this is Fab. Carmine would like you to come back to his house and stay. He's working with his lawyers on a deal that doesn't include jail time. He's terribly worried about you." I didn't know that to be true, but it sounded good.

She retrieved a silver monogrammed cigarette case from the glass coffee table. She took one out and jammed it between her lips, biting down hard on the end.

"No, thanks. Now get out of here before I scream."

"And who do you think is going to show up?" Fab snorted. "Even if someone could hear you. Now you listen to me. This morning has sucked. I'm tired and cranky. Can't you just hop your bony ass in the car and go drive your son crazy?"

Mrs. Ricci put her glasses on and ran her eyes over Fab in a clinical way.

"You looking for a sugar daddy, Honey? I could get big money for you. Especially if you'll relocate to Europe."

"What about me?" I sulked.

She gave me a cursory glance.

"I could get you local work," she said, her dollar-sign eyes already back on Fab.

"Come on, Grandma," Fab said and motioned. "You're out of business for a while, and if you want to stay out of jail, you'd best stay out of trouble. Take it from me—you'll hate everything about jail. No silk anything on your skin and ugly, uncomfortable shoes. And the food is awful."

"Who in the hell do you think you are? Barging into my house doing the bidding of that snot-nosed son of mine." Carlotta cracked a smile and, in one swift move, slid a gun from under the sofa cushion. "Sit down, right over there." She pointed to two chairs in front of the window.

"Toss me your keys," she demanded and cocked the gun. "I'm leaving, all right—but not with either one of you."

I blew out a frustrated breath.

"Think this through. Once you flee, the authorities will track you down, bring you back, and perp-walk the runaway madam before the cameras. Then, no deal and no bail. You'll stay in jail until your sentence is served. I've been to your son's house; you can snap your fingers for whatever you desire. Are you ready for life on the run? Cheap motels and burger stands?"

"You sound like you speak from experience," she sneered. "Now shut up. Just be happy I don't want to shoot you unless you force me."

It made me squirm to watch her wave the gun around, knowing that with the slightest twitch of her finger, it could go off and there was no telling where the bullet would end up.

"You're stupid." Fab tossed her the keys.

"Take the SUV and go; we don't care. We'll find our way home and you'll never see our faces again."

"Do you have a valid license?" I asked. "More importantly, do you know how to drive? I got a really good deal on that auto and would like it back in one piece. No eating or sex, if you don't mind."

"You young people are revolting. I've never screwed in a car in my life," she sniffed.

"Can't we just take you home before you do something stupid?" I asked.

"Stand up, both of you. Hands in the air. Start walking toward the kitchen. Now!" she yelled.

I felt pretty confident she had no plans to shoot us. I looked at Fab and grimaced.

"Quadruple," she mouthed.

We walked through the dining hall into a kitchen that would rival most commercial kitchens, equipped with top-of-the-line appliances. The only thing missing was a private chef.

"Open the double pantry doors in the corner," she directed, still waving the gun. "Walk in face first, no turning around."

The pantry was much like a walk-in closet, but narrow, the shelves stocked with food and spices. Once the door closed, it would take some maneuvering to turn around with the two of us in the enclosed space.

She slammed the door closed behind us.

"Now be good girls. The first one who steps out gets the bullet."

We listened as she dragged a chair across the floor and blocked the door. I wasn't particularly worried. It would take a while, but we'd get out. If nothing else, we had enough bullets to blow the door off the hinges.

"Bye, girls!" Mrs. Ricci called out.

I smiled to myself. There were two things she had forgotten to ask for—our guns and phones. I leaned forward, head against the shelf, and texted Creole: *SUV stolen, being held in the kitchen pantry,* and then I input the address.

We listened for any signs that the banging of the front door was a trick.

Fab looked sideways.

"Two choices—kick or shoot our way out?"

"Since it's a shuttered door and not solid anywhere, I say we kick in the slats and crawl out." Flip-flops weren't ideal for bashing in the door, but at least I could put more power into my foot facing backward. I didn't want to boast, but I had previous experience with kicking a door open. The lower slats cracked with the first impact and then snapped in half with the second one.

"Lean into the wall," Fab instructed.

My movement gave her just enough room to turn so that she could use her tennis shoe, and she sent the rest of the slats flying across the floor. She got on her knees and pushed, sending the chair ricocheting off the stainless steel stove. She crawled out and opened the door; what was left hung on broken hinges.

My phone rang.

"What the hell is going on?" Creole yelled.

"I send you a text for help and you call instead?" I yelled back.

Fab laughed.

"Your phone went to voicemail. You know I hate that," Creole said.

"I guess I don't get great phone service while being locked in a crazy woman's pantry closet. Did you get the Hummer back?"

"Already called in. I'm a block away."

"Don't bother, we rescued ourselves." I hung up.

Fab, who was already halfway to the front door, motioned impatiently for me to follow.

"Mrs. Ricci is a sly one." Fab jammed the down button outside the elevator and nothing happened. The light above the door was dark. "She locked the elevator."

"We'll use the stairs," I said, and pointed down the hallway. "At least we'll be going down and not up. And stay off the hand railing"—I shook my finger at her—"or you'll end up black and blue if I have to drag you down the stairs."

"You first." She shoved me into the stairwell. "Who's going to tell Brick that another job went south?"

"I say we show up at his office, sweet smiles in

place. Actually, maybe not. He'll get suspicious. We'll gracefully accept cash and then scream obscenities in unison."

"Unison?" Fab asked, looking skeptical that we could pull it off. "We'd need to practice."

"I've got a few choice words all ready for us. Then, after we lock him in a closet at gunpoint, we'll see how long it takes him to get free. If we get bored, we'll leave him for the cleaning team."

We exited the building on the far side, and even though I knew the Hummer was gone, I hoped it would be there as I peered around the corner. Creole paced the driveway.

"Do you have a scarf I can use for a gag?" I asked Fab. "Creole's going to be testy because I hung up on him."

"Another lecture before sex?"

"Our boyfriends are a lot alike in some ways," I said.

"They also talk." Fab wiggled her nose.

Creole shoved his phone in his pocket and raced over to us, turning me around so that he could make sure I'd made it through my latest job in one piece.

He snapped his fingers at Fab. "Turn around," he growled at her. "It does give me some comfort when you two get into trouble together."

Fab gave him the finger and walked away.

"Local police just picked up the old lady and your SUV. Do you want her arrested?" Creole asked.

"Any chance that local law will give her a free ride to her criminal son's house? What about my Hummer?"

"We'll take Mrs. Ricci," Fab said, "when we pick up the SUV."

"She's a handful, full of colorful language," Creole said, and opened his truck door. He picked me up and kissed me. Hop in, ladies. You're going to lose your job with Brick Ass, because I'm going to beat the holy hell him out of him and let him know if I ever hear his name again, I'll give a fisherman a fifty to give him a one-way ride out into the Gulf."

"Did you forget about his brother, one of your co-workers? That will start a war."

"I'll give that bald bastard the same free ride as his brother. I could probably get a discount for two," he growled.

Creole wasn't completely wrong about that. There were certain parts of the docks where a person could hire most any job done for a few bucks.

Fab vaulted herself into the truck, making me look bad since I needed the foot rail. She stuck her head out the window and hollered at us.

"Kissy time is over. Let's get moving." She seated herself between me and Creole.

I tried to climb over her, but she crossed her arms and wouldn't budge.

"Do you tell Didier to hurry up?"

She returned my dirty look.

"Of course not. But do I need to point out that you're not him?"

I looked around Fab to see Creole.

"How did you find the SUV so fast?"

"Activated the GPS," he said matter-of-factly.

Uh-oh! Busted. Thank goodness I looked shocked, because Fab didn't need to know that I knew he'd replaced it after she rendered it useless once again.

"You planted another tracker without telling us?" Fab hissed at Creole as she looked at me, eyebrows arched.

I shrugged, wide-eyed. Let them do combat. I was fairly certain Creole would survive unscathed.

Creole slowed.

"Listen to me good. If you tamper with this unit in any fashion, I'll narc on you to Didier in a hot second. It's a small thing to ask and it's for your safety."

"Stop with the Didier threat. It's old and it doesn't work anymore." Fab sat rigid, eyes straight ahead.

"Ha! Didier looks like an easygoing pretty boy, but I know him; and if there's one man who can control your wild streak, it's him. In fact, let's test your theory. How about the three of us have a sit down, where I explain what I'm doing to keep you safe and how your response is to tell me to 'shove it'? See what he has to say?"

I knew Didier. He'd be livid if he were to find

out that she'd disconnected the GPS, especially when it had to do with her safety.

"You say one word and I'll maim you." She glared at him.

Creole chuckled.

Chapter Ten

A big neon arrow that Mac found at a yard sale hung on the office door at The Cottages. The sign pointed down the walkway, which meant she had escaped to the pool.

In addition to the property, I also inherited two half-dead tenants, both suffering from cancer: Miss January and Joseph. The doctors continued to insist that one day soon, my tenants would suck their last breath. Their response: the middle finger. Followed by a cigarette and vodka for Miss January and beer for Joseph, as they both insisted on maintaining their 'healthy' lifestyle.

Brad's girlfriend, Julie, and her teenage son hadn't moved out yet, much to her brother, Kevin's disgust, and lately he had begun to ratchet up the pressure. Kevin let me know that he thought my managerial skills sucked, as though I had personally invited the felons and other assorted riff-raff to occupy the units. The only normal tenant, besides Julie, was Shirl, a registered nurse at the local hospital, who came to stay for a few days and never left. The rest were tourists from the UK and Canada.

It was a quiet day in general. I cased the block, finding that no one lurked in the alley, and no one slept in the bushes. Everything looked peaceful, but anyone who knew The Cottages knew that could looks be deceiving.

Fab and I rounded the corner to the pool to find that best friends Shirl and Mac were in a heated game of ping pong, drinking beer between points. A sane property owner would ask where the worn, but still usable, table came from, but it looked fun, and I knew without a doubt it wasn't stolen.

"You can't drink on the job." I pushed open the gate.

"Then I quit!" Mac yelled and threw her middle-aged body in a chair, her ample chest bouncing around. She wore a pair of obscene short-shorts. I sighed, happy to see her skirt slung over a chaise. It only took me two days of sitting in the property office all day to know that I didn't want the job. I never regretted hiring the woman.

I gave Fab a nudge.

"It's your job to make sure she doesn't go anywhere. She leaves, and you can work in the office."

Shirl belly laughed, her body poured into an ill-fitting two-piece. "That would end any tenant problems. She'd whip her gun out and empty the place." She threw a raft into the pool and dove in after it.

Both women were curvy, fun, and always doing something outrageous. They didn't give a damn what people thought. It was an unwritten rule that Mac wasn't allowed to quit, and Shirl was the only tenant not allowed to move out. Shirl reminded me of the nurse in elementary school, a calming presence that always knew the right thing to say to convince you that you wouldn't die of a stomach ache.

I kicked off my shoes and sat on the edge of the pool, sliding my feet into the warm water.

Mac dove into the pool after Shirl and made herself comfortable, leaning back against the side, her head resting on the ledge.

"Let's get a few things straight," I said. "You go anywhere, and I'll send Fab to drag you back. And on the off chance you elude her, I'll send Creole after you."

"Creole!" Mac licked her lips, her brown eyes sparkling. "I won't ask for a raise if you arrange for a little game of hide and seek."

"He's mine, and I don't share." I glared at her. "Besides, what would your husband say?"

"Yeah, him," she laughed. "Your ex-husband broke into Cottage Seven and spent a couple of nights. Left it clean. He looked a little paranoid when I confronted him."

Last time Jax showed up in town, he moved into one of the units. He and his friends overstayed their welcome, ignoring threats of eviction. It surprised me that Jax moved out this time and so quickly, which had me worrying about him again.

"Did you talk to him?" I asked. He hadn't called me back, and now he'd shut his phone off.

"I blocked his path when he tried to sneak down the driveway." Mac played with the ties on her bathing suit top. I fully expected her friends to make an appearance any second. "He looked good, asked me not to tell anyone he'd been here. I told him I wouldn't say a word except to you, and he said you were cool."

"You couldn't call me so I could check the ex out?" Shirl huffed at Mac.

"Did he leave a forwarding address?" Fab asked.

Mac shook her head and launched into her version of the news.

"Miss January and Score were so drunk, they sat on the curb fighting. 'You're drunk. No, I'm not, you are.' I told them if they didn't take it inside, I would turn the hose on them. The sheriff hasn't been here in a while for nuisance calls, and I want to keep it that way."

Miss January looked eighty instead of the forty listed on her driver's license. It didn't help that she resembled the color of death, minus the blue tinge when your time is truly up. Good-natured, always smiling in an uncomprehending way, she wandered through her days in a liquored-up stupor.

"Did those two get into a brawl?" Fab's eyes

glittered with excitement.

"Miss January backhanded Score in the head, and he started whining. I guess she felt guilty, because she rolled over and crawled on his lap and kissed his hair a few times. Reminded me of two old cats: lick, lick, fight. I had Shirl check on them. We left him passed out on the bed and her on the couch, both snoring so loud made my ears ring, and I ran for the door." She imitated the noise interspersed with what sounded like choking noises.

Shirl nodded her head.

"Miss January shared with me that she and Score have regular sex, and then she gets out of bed and sleeps on the couch."

I burst out laughing at the look of absolute disgust on Fab's face. That was the kind of news I liked to spring on her.

"Sounds like business as usual. So far you don't have a single good reason for quitting." I flicked water on Mac.

Fab nudged Mac's shoulder.

"Don't spread it all over town, but I like you two. I'd hate to tie you to your office chair; it's not good for business."

Mac grinned at her.

"I forgot about the Earls—the Canadian tourists. They stayed for two weeks and then paid for an extra week, failing to mention they had a plane to catch and were leaving their grandson behind. He has a shifting story about vague job offers and moving out at the end of the week. Not going to happen; he's not qualified to do anything. I can smell it—he'll stay until we toss him."

"Whether Mr. Earl can come up with the money or not, he needs to get out. Give him one day to pack. If he avoids you or threatens you, call me and I'll send an evictor over. I'll call Spoon; he's got a guy who specializes in quiet relocation. I'm tired of being burned, and he's not staying for free," I said.

"That's not legal," Shirl sniffed.

"Who's he going to complain to? The sheriff? He'll be warned about the consequences of calling anyone. There's an organized group of low-lifes that move up and down the Keys, looking for some unsuspecting landlord to rent to them. They pay a month's rent and stay four more for free, while it winds its way through the court system," I said with disgust.

"Get your cheap shoes on," Fab pointed at me. "We've got stuff to do."

I held up one of my flip-flops.

"They're inexpensive, but aren't they cute?"

Fab turned up her nose.

"Couldn't you be a little nicer?" I made a sad face.

"No," she laughed at me.

I stood up.

"See you later, ladies. Remember the new rule: If you need bail money, it has to be during office hours. No more late night jail runs."

Mac walked up the steps of the pool and cannon-balled back in, sending water flying. Shirl screamed something about ruining her heavily-sprayed bouffant, and then started a water fight.

Chapter Eleven

I slid into a chair at our usual table at Jake's. Recently, the 'Reserved' sign I'd put on the corner table on the deck had been replaced with a tasteful 'Don't Sit Here' plaque. The ceiling fans whirred softly, and white Christmas lights hung from the railings and around the edge of the roof. Friends and family knew they could use our special table anytime they came into the bar.

Fab went to the kitchen and placed our order as I sat rifling through the mail. Phil came out and set down a pitcher of iced tea. Fab and I didn't drink in the middle of the day, unless we happened to be arrested or shot at on that particular day.

"Anyone got a lead on the rest of the body?" Phil asked.

"How did you find out?" I looked up at her in her usual uniform of butt-cheek shorts, showcasing her long legs to perfection. The dress code at Jake's was: wear what you want as long as you're appropriately covered.

"I told you once, what I don't know I can find out." Phil looked over her shoulder, surveying the bar to make sure her regulars were all happy.

Twelve stools sat at the bar, and she kept them filled with a disreputable mix of locals.

The enterprising law school student never failed to surprise me. She had informed me that she had a side business of selling information. Money back guarantee, she had boasted.

"Drug dealer. What do you suppose happened to the rest of him?" I looked at her as though expecting an answer.

Fab slid into the seat next to me. "I better not have missed anything," she poured herself a glass of tea.

"Grisly." Phil shook her head. "Anyone who would go to all that trouble would probably chop up the rest, sending anyone looking on a scavenger hunt for body parts."

My stomach flipped over at the thought that the killer or killers might come back to my house and dump said parts.

"Or," Fab spoke up, "if it's a message, the next drop might be the rest of the body. You know, in one whole piece, sort of."

I shook my head, trying to prevent the visual.

"We need to start locking the gate," I said to Fab.

"They'd just do a pitch and roll, and that can make quite a mess," Phil smiled. Fab and I exchanged looks. I could tell from Fab's expression that she thought Phil was crazy, too.

Phil positioned her chair so she could see into the bar.

"Who did you piss off lately?"

"Nobody!" I blew out a long breath. "Okay, Hot Shot. You want to be our main snitch? Find out everything you can about the dead guy and my ex-husband Jackson Devereaux, aka Jax, pronto. Jax has a business deal going on in the area; find out the particulars." I flipped through my phone and sent his picture to her phone.

Chapter Twelve

My backyard was one of my favorite places to read, nap, or just do nothing. I used it year-round as a large entertaining space for family and friends. I found a table to accommodate the entire family with comfortable seating, double chaises, and a pile of pillows.

It was another beautiful day, with the warmth from the sun on my skin and a slight breeze blowing in from the ocean, making everything smell fresh and clean.

"Did you talk to Brick?" Fab yawned.

"He called me, yelling about Mrs. Ricci and the abusive treatment she sustained at our hands." I pulled the back of the chaise upright. "She told 'Snot Nose' Carmine that we'd threatened her with the police and were adamant about taking her to jail. I knew we should've let the police deliver her to the mansion, but I wasn't in the mood to make Carmine mad."

"That's what we get for being nice and uncuffing her once we got to her son's front door. Good thing it was only the bodyguard waiting on her highness."

"I told Brick to calm his ass down and then relayed what really happened. She should consider herself lucky not to be charged with kidnapping, assault, and grand theft auto. I told Brick to messenger our quadruple fee right over."

Fab kicked my foot, holding up her glass for a refill. The pitcher of iced tea sat on the table closest to me. I'd made sun tea earlier, slicing up oranges that my neighbor had left on the doorstep.

"What did he say to that?" Fab asked.

"He started yelling all over again, saying he never agreed to anything other than the standard fee. I told him I didn't appreciate his attitude and that I wouldn't shoot him for non-payment, but I couldn't swear you wouldn't. He hung up on me." I stared at her. "It's time for you to get serious about finding new clients."

Fab hesitated, her expression serious. "I thought that could be your job. People like you, you have that annoying habit of talking to anyone."

"So you're saying I'm personable?" The groan she emitted made me laugh. "I'll think on it."

I knew the kind of jobs that she got on her own, and there was always an element that could be construed as illegal. She wouldn't be happy when I informed her I'd only agree to be backup on straight-up legal jobs.

Fab lay back and closed her eyes.

"If Creole kicks Brick's ass, that would solve the problem of whether I ever work for him again." I smiled at the idea. "You're his favorite anyway. He'll get over himself and call you."

"Are we going to have problems with Carmine Ricci?" she asked.

"The snot-nosed son?" I laughed. "I wonder if his mommy's ever said that to his face. She definitely has the nerve. I told Brick I'd be happy to meet with Mr. Ricci. I reminded him I still had the option of pressing charges against Carlotta, since my witnesses were some of Miami's finest."

"In our new business, you'll handle all customer service problems."

"That's probably a good idea." I flashed back to the only time she handled a client complaint. After five minutes, she'd threatened to shoot the guy.

"I told Didier about our misadventure before your blabbering boyfriend could say a word. We got into an argument about safety issues, and it was a good thing I didn't mention the GPS. We never stay mad at each other, which I like. We argue, I promise stuff, and then we have great sex."

"Creole got a work call, so all I got was a great kiss."

Chapter Thirteen

I slipped onto a stool at Jake's and banged my hand on the counter. "Bartender, margarita over here," I said loudly.

Two of Phil's regulars glared at me. Both were old men who drank from lunchtime to dinner, then stumbled home and showed up the next day. Rumor had it they both had wives.

"You drunk?" Phil laughed.

Mother roped me into helping her throw a surprise birthday party for Spoon. The deck was closed for the event, and she decided on a buffet, which made it easy for the kitchen. Then she ditched me, informing me she had to keep the birthday boy busy. She said that all I had to do was hang the bags of decorations she'd dropped off. She must have purchased a hundred balloons, but nothing to blow them up with. I called the party store and cut the entire order in half, including ones that didn't require any of my hot air, figuring everyone would be drowning in balloons. I also bribed the delivery boy to hang the banners.

Brad and Julie walked in holding the margarita birthday cake that Mother made them pick up from The Bakery Café. Another pink box held the cupcakes I'd ordered so that everyone could take one home. Brad and Julie both looked like they'd just walked off the beach. Julie had on a black crisscross cotton dress and sandals and Brad in shorts and flip flops.

I was about to ask where Liam was when he walked in holding hands with a teenage girl with long blonde hair and big blue eyes. He said something to her and she laughed.

I felt sad for a moment. He was growing up and, soon, wouldn't want Mother and me fawning over him. We'd only known him for a couple of years, which made me wish we'd been around from the beginning. Maybe when Brad and Julie got married, they'd have a baby.

It pleased me that Liam brought his friend right over to me. I wanted to like this girl.

Liam kissed my cheek.

"This is my girlfriend, Lindsey," he introduced. "My almost-Aunt Madison."

"Nice to meet you," I said. Lindsey smiled back and made eye contact. Before Lindsey could say anything, Fab appeared at my side and stared at the young couple holding hands.

"Who are you?" Fab asked.

"Ignore her," I said to Lindsey. "She can be abrupt."

Liam made the introduction.

Fab looked her over. "We'll take you out and grill you over lunch. I've got a connection for designer shoes for cheap."

Lindsey squealed, clearly not intimidated by her first meeting with yet another unofficial aunt. "I'd love that."

I refrained from an eye roll. I needed to remind Fab those shoes probably weren't legal. I'd been to the warehouse twice. It sat behind barbed wire, and you could only get in by invitation, which meant I had to be with Fab to go. The last time the guy looked insulted when I asked if he had any flip flops.

"Can we go in the game room?" Liam asked.

"Key's behind the bar," I said.

Jake's had a back room that sat empty when the previous owner used it as a junk room. After cleaning it out, my original plan had been to use it for private parties, but there had been zero interest. I'd turned it over to Mother to turn it into a game room. It had been open for a few months, but she still refused to allow anyone to use it, except for her poker cohorts. The bar got a cut, and her friends ran up the liquor bills, so my bottom line was happy.

Creole blew in the door, his shoulder-length black hair windblown. His blue eyes were drawn to pinpoints, and he looked angry. Why me? I hadn't kept anything from him lately. I stepped behind Fab as he stomped over.

He reached around her and grabbed my hand.

"You stay out of this," he said to Fab.

I shrugged at her, not sure what was up.

He pulled me along the hall to my office, which was the size of a broom closet and never used. All business dealings took place at my table on the deck. He opened the door and kicked it shut, pushing me up against it. Creole clenched the hair at the nape of my neck, and pulled my head back, his mouth slamming down on mine. The kiss deepened until I was faint from the effort, sensation tearing through me. His hands moved up and down my back, caressing and holding me close. He shifted down until he could lift me up, and my legs wrapped around his waist.

"I've missed you," he whispered.

"You're rotten," I said.

He let out a deep, rumbling laugh.

"I know. No would dare knock after seeing my entrance."

"When the birthday party is over, we're going back to my house. If you're done groping me, we should go back to the party before Mother gets here with the guest of honor."

* * *

Mother called Fab from a few blocks away. We herded the guests out to the deck and closed the doors. I couldn't wait to see Spoon's face when the balloons attacked. I set the juke box for continuous play so that our guests could dance after they'd had a few beers.

I was fairly certain no one had blabbed and ruined the surprise by telling Spoon. As long as I'd known him, he'd never celebrated his birthday, and this was probably not his first choice of a way to spend his day. Nothing that Mother did seemed to bother him, so I expected everything to go smoothly. He'd been told it was a Westin family get together.

Creole stood by my side just inside the deck doors as Mother and Spoon walked in.

"He doesn't know," Creole whispered. "Or he'd be casing the place, looking around to see who got invited. I don't want one of these. Promise me."

"I have something already planned for your birthday, and it's not a group affair. Although it *will* require a balloon and a party hat."

I walked over to hug Mother.

"Good luck," I whispered.

"He's going to love it," she whispered back.

I admired her confidence. Spoon was about to have his acting skills put to the test.

Spoon opened the door, balloons smacked him in the face, at the same time everyone yelled, "Surprise!" He froze, instinctively pushing Mother behind him. He recovered quickly, his body relaxing a beat, but the hard lines in his face remained. He'd been surprised alright, and not pleasantly so. He pulled Mother into his arms and gave her a big kiss.

He looked up at me and I winked, giving him

a thumbs-up for the quick recovery on a surprise he clearly didn't like.

Kevin wandered in with a different girl than the one from the last party we'd all attended. He certainly had a type: overly-large boobs. I wondered if this girl circled the pole for a living. She was almost a carbon copy of Kevin, actually: fresh off the beach look, sun-bleached brown hair, and sunburned face. In his sheriff uniform, you'd never guess he had a surfer boy persona.

An odd assortment of people milled around, all people who knew Spoon. It made me wonder how Mother knew to contact these people.

Brad showed up at my side, beer in one hand, his other arm around Julie.

"When did you get in?" I asked.

"Yesterday afternoon. We had to unload and get the boat cleaned up." He kissed my cheek. "Spent the night at The Cottages."

Brad worked the waters of the Gulf, his boat one of the larger commercial fishing vessels in the area. I suspected that, if he started a family, he'd retire. Now that he had a second career in construction, his retirement from fishing might be sooner than anyone thought. In my mind, I imagined a mock-up of the article to hit the stand stands in a couple of months, with Brad cited as having turned the Trailer Court into the new "it" place to stay on vacation.

"Let's do a family-only dinner. My house, you bring the fish...and cook it, of course." I chuckled. I once had a love of cooking, but since moving to Florida I turned that role over to my brother.

"Bike ride Sunday," Creole informed Brad. Recently, Creole and Didier had added Brad to their group. "The plan is to ride to Marathon and then have the girls pick us up. We can all have dinner and drive back."

Brad leaned in. "I know about the head."

Damn. I felt a twinge of guilt. I'd promised him that he wouldn't be the last to know about family drama.

"You talked to Mother already?"

"I talked to Kevin." He hugged me. "You okay?"

"You just got here. What did Kevin do, meet your boat on the dock?" I snorted.

"I told him," Julie explained. "Everyone in town knows, so I figured Brad should know. In case you forgot to tell him or someone said something."

"Don't confront Mother unless she's with Spoon. You can get the grisly details from Creole if Kevin hasn't given them to you. Better yet, Fab has pictures." I shuddered. "Feel free to come in through the French doors."

"I'm going to tell Mother that I know so she doesn't worry over telling me. I'll let her know I'm available if she needs to vent," Brad said.

I glanced over the deck, my gaze resting on Spoon and Mother. They were surrounded by his friends, relaxed and smiling.

"Have you met Liam's girlfriend, Lindsey?" I asked him.

"She's a classmate. They're not serious; they're too young," Julie cut in. I didn't argue with her. Brad winked at me.

Fab dragged Didier over.

"We're leaving," she announced.

"Do you approve?" I asked Didier. "The party just got started."

Fab answered for him. "All he said was to say good-bye to you and that I should let you know we're leaving."

"Fine," I grumbled at her. "But I'm not the hostess, Mother is. Go tell her you're leaving early. I'm sure that will hurt her feelings, but she won't say anything. She'll be nice, like she always is, because she loves you and wants you to be happy."

Fab and I engaged in a glare-off until she finally took Didier's hand and stomped across the room.

Brad clapped quietly.

"You're better at that guilt thing than Mother. The student has surpassed the teacher," he teased.

Creole nudged me and nodded to the jukebox. A bleach blonde woman with a wide blue streak down one side had started to gather attention. She turned and faced the room. In her cut-off shorts and an open-back top that tied in the back, she slithered her ample body up and down.

Spoon and Mother emerged from the deck. The blonde woman shrieked, "Spooner!" and barreled toward him, throwing herself in his arms. She then laid a big wet kiss on his lips.

He tried to pull away, but she wasn't cooperating and even looped one leg around his thigh.

"I need to be with Mother," I said to Creole. I flew to her side, catching up just as she tapped the woman on the shoulder.

The woman loosened her hold. Spoon stepped away and introduced her as Roxy.

"This is my girlfriend, Madeline." He pointed to Mother, who stood by his side.

Roxy looked Mother up and down and snickered.

"You're joking. She's old enough to be your mother."

The woman might be younger, but she'd lived a hard life that showed in every line in her overly-tanned face. The two couldn't have been more different. Mother was a blonde, too, but all one color. She also looked younger than her sixty years in her black silk capri pants and top. Roxy was in for a shock if she thought she'd walk on Mother.

"You look older than her!" I said, losing my temper.

Roxy scrunched her nose and mouth in disgust and balled her hands into fists.

If she took one more step, she'd find out that I didn't leave my Glock at home.

"Honey," Roxy said to Spoon. "We need to talk."

Spoon stood there like a lug and didn't say anything. The whole scene had started to garner attention; people stopped what they were doing to listen and stare.

If only Spoon would ask me, I'd tell him, "Push Roxy out the door and be done with this drama."

"Jake's is closed today for a private party," I told the woman. It wasn't, but she didn't need to know that. Spoon frowned at me and I frowned right back, letting him know he couldn't have it both ways.

"I'll walk her out. Be right back," Spoon said. He kissed Mother and whispered something in her ear.

Fab glared from across the room, arms across her chest. I nodded to the front door, her signal to go find out what was happening.

I put my arm around Mother. "Go check the buffet. You will not go to him; he'll come to you."

"What are you going to do?" She tugged on my arm.

"I'm going to make sure he knows where he can find you." I kissed her cheek. "Just be happy Fab didn't bring her gun. Roxy would dead and Spoon would have a hole in his ass."

I enjoyed the sound of Mother's laughter

ringing out.

I camped just inside the front door, waiting for the birthday boy to return. I saw Creole out of the corner of my eye and waved him away to go hang out with Didier.

Spoon came through the door. I stepped in his path, my hand in the middle of his chest forcing him to stop.

"Are you happy with the current location of your man parts?" I imitated Fab's creepy smile.

He growled at me, anger filling his face. Spoon wasn't used to being threatened by anyone, much less a woman.

I leaned forward and growled back. "Don't *fuck* with my mother."

"Roxy's just a friend. I'm not going to hurt either one of them," Spoon said lamely.

Men!

"You're going to have to; you don't get both." I turned and walked over to join Creole, putting my arms around him from behind. "I'm ready to blow this party. Go all cave man on me and drag me out of here. That way it's your fault in case something else goes wrong."

Fab reappeared and stood by Didier's side. "See you later." I winked at Fab.

"We're right behind you, except we're going out the back door."

"Like this!" Creole scooped me up into his arms. Holding me close to his chest, he kissed me, making a one-eyed escape out the front door.

Chapter Fourteen

One look at Fab's face, and I knew she had a scheme cooking under that long brown hair of hers. I needed coffee to ask what, and maybe I could control my curiosity and sneak out to the pool.

"I can't eavesdrop if you speak in French," I said to Fab and Didier. They were sitting at the kitchen island, indulging in their early morning sludge. Didier had found a new blend that was thick and smelly.

Didier tsked and shook his finger at me.

"That is a bad habit the two of you should break."

He leaned over and kissed Fab's head.

I reached in the cupboard and grabbed one of my favorite mugs, white ceramic with raised seashells. I turned and laughed at him.

"You need to change into something tasteful and black," Fab said.

I looked down at my white cotton skirt and sleeveless cobalt top and thought, *What's she talking about?* She had on her black ankle-length pants that I coveted and a spaghetti strap top that she usually wore under a jacket.

It clicked in that she must have a job that she'd failed to inform me about, and she needed my help. The microwave dinged. I poured hot water into my mug, stirring. I would go on whatever job she had, but not without a lot of drama.

"Okay," I gave her a straight-lipped smile. I grabbed my coffee and got three steps in the direction of the patio.

"Where are you going? We need to leave in an hour."

"How long have you known about today's job?"

"I forgot, okay! I wouldn't have remembered either if Raul hadn't called early this morning," Fab huffed.

"Why not just say so, instead of some sneaky con job?"

Didier laughed. "Madison does have a point."

Fab glared at him.

I never worried about these two as a couple. They fought passionately, and then the next time you saw them they were all lovey-dovey.

"Tell me this job has nothing to do with dead bodies." The thought had me nauseated. I still walked around the back way to get in the house.

"We're going to bodyguard for a funeral. The last time the Bonzai family had a final farewell, a fight broke out. So we're making sure everybody behaves."

I'd met a Bonzai once. He seemed fun. Translation: he drank too much and partied it up, had a couple of missing front teeth, if I had the right guy.

"Do we get to shoot them?" I asked.

"I promised we'd keep everything under control without shots being fired."

"My ass-kicking skills are not on par with yours, and you know that. What am I supposed to do besides stand there and look pretty?" I looked into my empty mug. "I'm going to need some serious caffeine."

They both laughed at me.

* * *

The doors of Tropical Slumber stood open, which seemed unusual. Then again, we never showed up for funerals. Not a single mourner milled around the main entrance area, and the few who arrived early were in the main viewing room. Mr. Bonzai was displayed at the front of the room, his profile poking out of the long wooden box. The entire room had been cleared of the usual church pews, replaced with long picnic tables.

Dickie came in through a side door and stood in the front next to the coffin. Well over six feet, painfully thin, and dressed all in black, Dickie's pale skin had the same pallor of the deceased. He had an unnerving persona, but once you got to know him, he had a huge heart, and he and I had become friends. I admired that he never judged anyone.

Dickie signaled to us and swept his arm out. "As you can see, this service will be a little unorthodox."

Dickie and Raul owned the funeral home. Dickie's talents lie in primping the deceased. He never cut a corner, striving for perfection and exacting on every detail. Raul handled the business side. Raul put his arm around Fab. They had cemented their friendship when, at her attorney's suggestion, she hid out at the funeral home to evade police questions.

"At least I put my foot down about the open bar," Raul said as he kissed her cheek. "I hope we don't get any more requests for a dinner-funeral. This is unseemly to me."

Dickie's sigh filled the room. He tapped the microphone at the podium.

"Service first, then food?" Fab asked.

"The older Mr. Bonzai seems to think if everyone is eating during the service, it will curtail any fighting. The last funeral we had for one of the Bonzai brothers, all nine put in an appearance. When the fight broke out, we were forced to call the sheriff, and three of them got arrested for drunk and disorderly. Dickie took a punch to the eye, bruised his eye socket," Raul related.

I winced.

"Funny thing about the Bonzai family, the old ones keep kicking along and the younger ones die off. Of course, it doesn't help they get drunk and do stupid stuff." Dickie looked disgusted. "Last one fell out of a tree, trying to jump in swamp water in the middle of the night. Probably better than getting eaten by an alligator."

"Sense apparently wasn't passed down in the genes," Raul half-laughed. "This one," he said, cocking his thumb at the deceased, "got drunk at a bar, decided to show off. He lifted a beer keg in the air, stumbled while holding it over his head, and fell. The keg landed on his head."

"The only way you can tell how he died is if you move his head off the pillow. The crown and back are completely bashed in." Dickie indicated that we were free to have a look.

* * *

The mourners filed in, some orderly, some pushing one another. They were exchanging insults, a few of them already drunk. The caterers arrived to set up the buffet, and most of the guests grabbed a plate before sitting down.

"What's the game plan?" I asked Fab.

She chewed on her lower lip. "We'll stand in the back like a couple of hall monitors and be on the lookout for trouble."

"And then what? We ask them to please

behave or go to the principal's office?" I shook my head at her.

Fab motioned Raul over. "Before the service starts, I'd like to say a few words."

I groaned, knowing she'd do or say something outrageous.

Raul winked at me, telling me everything would be okay.

"No you will not." I jerked on her arm. "Dickie can handle any announcements."

The female minister took her place behind the podium and rifled through her notes.

Dickie took the microphone, telling the assembled group that security had been hired and to please behave or he'd have no choice but to call in law enforcement.

The minister took over the microphone. "Please be seated." It took a full minute for everyone to stop talking and for the stragglers to find seats.

The minister tried her best to make an unremarkable man sound interesting. I suspected by the way everyone ate that the word had gone out: "free food." The minister was about to wind up her sermon when a man yelled some f-word-laced insults at the man sitting across from him. A couple of weather-worn women jumped in with their own colorful language. From the far end of the table, a launched biscuit hit one of the bickering women in the middle of her forehead. Someone snickered or laughed, and that apparently was the sign—fight on. Food flew in every direction.

Two older women, not completely devoid of sense, ducked under the table. At first it seemed as though they split up sides, picking a team. Soon, it rapidly degenerated into an everyone-for-themselves food melee. There wasn't a person that didn't have some particle of food stuck in their hair or hanging off their clothing. I freaked out when I saw that one man had blood dripping down his leg, but, on second glance, it was only ketchup.

Fab made her way to the front, pulled her Walther, and discharged the gun into the ceiling. The sound ricocheted against the walls and brought the room to a stupefied calm. None of them were making eye contact. The mourners all made themselves busy picking food off their clothing, flinging it in random directions, though some ended up with more food on them. An older man poured a glass of water down the front of his shirt, picking up another glassful to wash his hands.

"Every one of you, out," Fab ordered. The muzzle of her gun pointed to the door. "One row at a time. Don't even think about getting out of line."

"What the hell is wrong with this family?" one grizzled old woman asked, picking a string bean from her grey hair. "Can't they bury anyone without a circus ensuing?"

"You're all inbred!" a bottle blonde middle-aged woman retorted, her tone matter-of-fact.

"Oh shut up, Erma. At least my husband ain't my cousin," the woman shot back.

It didn't take long for the thirty or so people to file out, continuing to trade insults, threats, and angry gestures. The sound of engines starting could be heard through the doorway, followed by squealing tires.

Chapter Fifteen

I stopped speaking to Fab when I realized we were headed to Famosa Motors, and was more than a little annoyed when she pulled into the driveway. No wonder she'd been vague as to our destination, mumbling about a client. Wait until she found out that I had no plans to get out of the Hummer. I still hadn't recovered from the last Brick job.

Fab came around to the passenger side and unlocked the door. "Brick would like an audience. Get out or I'll drag you."

"Is there any chance this job is going to end in a hostage situation or shootout?" I stuck one leg out the door, against my better judgment.

"You're going to make me go out on a job by myself?" she frowned. "You know these jobs take two people — probably another car retrieval."

She really had no skill at making a person feel guilty. She needed to call Mother and go take a lesson or six.

I moved to get out and, instead, pulled my legs back in, slammed the door, and hit the locks. I made a face at Fab. It never got old to act like a grade-schooler. I wish we'd grown up together;

we'd have been best friends from the start and had fun times.

Fab threw her hands in the air and stalked back around to my side of the SUV. Withdrawing keys from her pocket, she hit the unlock button. "Get out. You're not funny."

"You know that's not true." I tousled her hair.

Fab linked her arm in mine and warned, "Just in case you think you're going to run off."

* * *

Bitsy, our favorite receptionist, had her ample behind parked in its usual spot behind her desk in the middle of the showroom. Her heavily made-up face etched into a scowl when we raced through the roll-up doors. She flipped us off and turned her back.

Fab moved her hand behind her back to where she kept her Walther. "You know, Bits-ass, there are other big-boobed, fake-blonde strippers that can do your job. Who'd ask questions if you didn't show up to work one day?"

I wanted to laugh but didn't, knowing Bitsy was stupid enough to try and outdraw Fab with the little pea-shooter gun she kept in her desk drawer. I tugged on Fab's arm.

"A dollar says I beat you up to the second floor."

Fab hesitated a second before she shot over to the stairs, leaving me standing there. I passed on demanding a "thank you" from Bitsy for distracting Fab from pulling her gun out.

"Hurry up!" Fab yelled from the top.

"You're such a show off." I ran up the stairs and hung on to the handrail just in case, not wanting to tumble backward.

Brick looked disgusted as we shoved each other to see who got in the door first.

"Are you two ever going to grow up? This is a place of business." He pointed to the leather chairs in front of his massive desk, which would dwarf anyone except him.

Fab and I had clearly changed roles, usually she manned the window and I sat in the chair. This visit she draped herself in the one of the chairs. After looting the candy bowl on the credenza, I went and stood by the window, enjoying the corner view of the palm-lined street. I scoped out the property to find the fastest way off the lot, for one of those just-in-case moments. I learned from the master. Fab was always on the lookout for the quickest escape route.

Brick shoved a picture across the desk.

"I've got a pickup for you two. This time it's a person, not a car."

Fab and I looked at one another. I noticed it was a booking photo of an older woman, though I found it hard to judge her age since jail wasn't a picnic and had an aging effect. She had pale, weathered skin, a hardened glint to her beady eyes, and grey stubbly hair. She didn't look like a grandmother who carried cookies in her pocket. Brick held up his hand.

"I don't want any excuses. It's an easy job. She's being released from Lowell in Ocala, wrongfully convicted, a little domestic dispute. She just wants to be reunited with her family and enjoy life."

Oh great, the middle of Florida.

We needed to start specifying that we were taking jobs in South Florida only. If I had my way, it would be only the Keys. In times like these, I was happy Fab wouldn't let me drive; a round trip would take twelve hours.

I flicked the photo back across the desk, scrunching my nose.

"Where did you get this case?" Not a stupid question for most people, but posing it to Brick would be a waste of breath. He had a low percentage rate with the truth, and getting all the information from him on anything was impossible.

"This woman can't possibly afford your helping-hand fees. Is she some criminal friend of yours, or perhaps their mother or sister?"

His clenched his jaw and glared at me.

"You two listen to me. I apologized for Carlotta Ricci and how the case didn't go according to plan. I also paid your screw-me rate."

"Thanks for reminding me." My mouth was drawn in a tight line. "A new stipulation to working for you is that if the job goes off the rails and over the cliff…in simple terms, if we get shot at, arrested, or kidnapped, the fee is quadruple. One more thing, too: you might want to think about Jimmy Spoon's reaction if anything serious were to happen to either one of us."

Brick's fist came down hard on the desk, his eyes growing dark and beady. "Are you threatening me?" he demanded.

"Just stating facts," I hissed back. "You know the man. Here's a big FYI: He's dating my mother."

I could see from the look on his face the last tidbit of information came as a surprise. For a man who did business in the Cove, it surprised me that he was ill-informed. It would behoove Brick to keep track of life there; his ignorance could end up biting him in the rear.

"Like-I-said," Brick stuttered, his anger abating a little. "Pick Mrs. Compton up. Take her home. How hard can that be?"

"You always say that," I reminded him. "Are we agreed on the new terms?"

"Yeah, yeah. But don't think you're going to screw me on every job. I should have a release date by tomorrow." He busied himself with the papers on his desk.

Fab stood up.

"Are you two done?" She didn't wait for an answer, having already cleared his office door.

I grabbed cold waters and two more bags of

Oreos from the snack bowl to calm my nerves from the stressful meeting and waved goodbye to Brick.

"Most people take one piece of candy, not the whole bowl," Brick snapped.

"Well I'm not most people. Besides, I share—one for her, the rest for me."

Fab waited at the bottom of the steps.

"Just know in the new business, you're handling all the billing issues."

"Have you thought about buying your own car and telling him to go to hell?"

"You sound like Didier. He wants me to find another line of work," Fab sighed.

Chapter Sixteen

I came through the side fence, returning from an early morning walk, a bucket of shells in my hand.

"About time you showed up." Fab smiled and shoved a glass of iced tea at me.

I squinted at her, and sat in a chair across from the lovebirds.

"Pardon me for being suspicious, but what do you want?"

"I'm just trying to be more gracious, show you I don't take you for granted."

"I suspect Didier's influence." I looked over at him, trying not to laugh. "Are you enjoying the one time you asked her to do something and she actually did it?"

"Cherie…" He shook his finger.

Every time I heard him say that French endearment as a two-syllable word, I felt chastised.

"Just spit it out. When do I ever say no? Well, sometimes, but just because it's so much fun."

"I got a new client and I need your help," Fab said.

"Aren't I an associate or some other such BS

title? How many people knew before me?"

Didier glared at me.

"It's not like I used the F word." I glared back. "What kind of case?"

"The client is Horton King, a yacht salesman up in Miami. He's out on bond for beating his girlfriend."

"Not interested. Have fun without me." I wasn't interested in helping a woman abuser.

"He says he never touched her," Fab said.

"That's what they all say. Or maybe she deserved it?" I arched a brow and smirked.

"Then why call us?" Fab asked. "I want you to go."

* * *

We parked in front of an all-glass building, which lay on Beach Boulevard in Fort Lauderdale. Inside the floor-to-ceiling sliding doors of the showroom, two-million dollar boats were on display. More than three dozen boats of various sizes were on exhibit around the lot. At least no oily salesman lurked nearby, waiting to pounce once we got out of the SUV.

"Miss Merceau." A man came around the corner of the building. Nice looking, fortyish, definitely worked out, with thick grey-silver hair that looked good on him. On a woman, that hair would make her look older than a stump.

He stuck out his hand, and he and Fab shook. I

refrained from licking my palm and sticking it out. Instead I put both hands in my pockets. I'd do anything to keep from shaking hands.

Fab said something I couldn't hear as Horton King invited us into his office.

Once seated, he opened a folder and shoved a picture across his desk. It was of a young blonde woman. She had thick black roots, a pair of blackened eyes, and a puffy mouth. 'Kelsey James' was scribbled on the bottom of the page.

He held out his hands, palms down, twisting them side to side. "Take a good look at my knuckles. Don't you think they'd be bruised?" He stood up and unbuttoned his dress shirt, taking it off and turning around for our inspection. "Not a mark on me."

"Tell us what happened," Fab asked, giving him a smile.

He seemed like a decent sort. Behind him on a table was a framed picture of himself with two teenagers, but I wasn't sold. I knew firsthand that the normal-looking ones turned out to be just as abusive as the ones who boasted of their talents. Scanning the office, I scowled; no snack bowl in sight. If he was about to launch into some long-winded explanation, I'd need a mini Snickers bar or something else with white sugar.

Lately Fab and I had reversed roles. She had swiped my patience gene, while I just wanted to go to the beach. Ever since we found the head, I felt unsure, even fearful at times, in my own home. I shook my head, refusing to allow the gruesome image to take hold again.

"We'd been dating about two months," Horton began. "Kelsey's high-strung, a bundle of energy. We got along great."

That was code for *'She's crazy but the sex was amazing'.*

Horton blew out a long sigh of frustration and ran his hands through his hair, settling back in his leather chair. Behind his glass desk, he had an amazing view of the dark blue waters of the Atlantic Ocean.

"We went down to Marathon for dinner," he said. "Kelsey was in a bad mood when I picked her up, a surly attitude from the start. I thought with a little food and drink we could salvage the evening."

He was hanging in for the jungle sex.

I tried to hold back a snort and instead it came out as a weird unidentifiable noise. Fab and King both stared at me. Fab toed my leg with her expensive pump. She had out-dressed me in a sexy black pencil skirt and a cream-colored, button-down silk blouse. I traded my tropical print skirt in for a black one and forced my feet into a pair of sliders.

"Can I get you something to drink?" he asked.

He turned and opened a small refrigerator, pulling out two bottles of water, as Fab requested. His back to us, I poked her arm and tapped my watch, fake yawning.

She shook her finger in a perfect imitation of her boyfriend.

"Before we got out of the car, Kelsey started a fight in the parking lot. She informed me that I was a snore-bore, that I didn't know how to have fun, and that she wanted to see other people." He paused. "Then she demanded money and said she'd get her own ride home. I told her I'd take her back. I stopped for a traffic light several blocks away. She jumped out of the car and took off."

"You just left her?" I scowled at him.

"The light turned green, horns began honking. By the time I circled the block, she was gone. I tried calling her, but she turned her phone off. A few hours later the cops beat on my door with an arrest warrant. They say she accused me of doing this," he pointed to the picture.

"Why do you think she fingered you?" Fab asked.

"No idea. I never hit a woman in my life; ask my ex-wife. We split because all I ever did was work, and she got tired of being ignored. I've never been arrested until now."

"How did you two meet?" I asked.

"At a grand opening party of a beachfront restaurant. She introduced herself, came on to me, and I went willingly. She's sexy as hell."

"Any ideas who did beat her up?" Fab asked.

He blew out a long breath. "I honestly don't know much about her, except that I really liked her and she brought fun into my life. In retrospect, I probably came on a little strong, wanted to move the relationship along, see each other more, and be exclusive. Why not tell me she wasn't interested? She wasn't shy. Instead, she just hits me with trumped up charges?"

"Have you been contacted by a lawyer representing her?" I asked.

He shook his head. "I can't contact her, either. She filed for a temporary restraining order, and it got served the next day. Frankly, I never want to see her again, but I need the truth to come out. This kind of a charge could ruin me and bring shame on my kids."

Fab took a worn black leather notebook out of her purse and asked him a few more questions, writing down all the information he had regarding Kelsey James, starting with how we could find her.

Norton handled himself well, answering all the questions in a straight-forward fashion. There was no hemming or staring around the office, and he came off as believable. I'd reserve judgment until I met Kelsey. Why file a police report against the wrong man?

While Fab assured him we'd be in touch, I scurried out the door and hustled back to the SUV.

"Couldn't you be nicer?" Fab glared at me.

"Now you know what it's like going places with you," I told her. "I warmed up a bit towards the end, considering I went in thinking he was an abusive pig."

"If everything he said is true, meeting Kelsey should be interesting," Fab said.

"Why couldn't you get us a nice lost dog case?"

Fab snorted. "FM Associates doesn't go out and locate lost dogs and cats. Those calls will be forwarded to you."

"As long as you come along and drive me."

"You're getting used to my driving!" She beamed.

"Yeah, it doesn't make me want to puke as much."

Chapter Seventeen

"Hungry?" Fab asked.

"I take it we're eating here." I stared out the window at The Hut. Fab had edged her way through the bumper-to-bumper beach traffic to slide into a parking space out front. It was a long square building, all open seating, and the roof was a series of tiki umbrellas.

"You have cash on you?" Fab asked. "We might need some bribe money."

"You do inform your clients that bribes are billed back to them and that they shouldn't expect a receipt?"

Fab ignored me and asked the hostess if we could sit in Kelsey's section, but the girl looked a little surprised and informed us that Kelsey no longer worked here.

"Let's go," I whispered.

She ignored me, headed to a table, and sat down. "Sit," she pointed to the chair. "We'll find out what the heck happened."

I opened the menu and perused the high prices. The restaurant was half-filled and, with the lunch rush long over, that meant that it was a popular place. "You know, I've never had a twelve-dollar hamburger that didn't taste like shoe leather."

"Get a salad," Fab said with no sympathy.

The waitress wore cutoff shorts and a t-shirt tied in a knot, showing off her toned and tan midriff. She came up to take our drink order.

"What happened to Kelsey James?" Fab asked her, ordering for me without asking what I wanted.

The girl's face changed instantly from a forced smile to one of suspicion. "She got fired. It's restaurant policy that we do not to speak about employees, past or present. If you'd like, I can call the manager." She turned and walked away.

"That went well." I reached in my purse, finding my wallet and took out several twenties.

She came back with our drinks. Her name tag read *Peggy*.

I held up a twenty. "Is this enough for you to tell us why she got fired?"

She eyed the money and looked between the two of us. "Who the hell are you two?"

Fab flipped open a badge and answered. "She got assaulted the other night, and we're here on behalf of the police department to investigate."

If you didn't stare too hard, Fab's badge looked like the real thing but, in fact, it was just a PI badge, easily purchased in a uniform store.

"She got caught stealing." Peggy jerked the money from my fingers. "Instead of ringing up cash sales, she pocketed the money and gave free drinks to her drunken friends. During liquor inventory, a few bottles turned up missing. They weren't directly connected to her, but who else could it have been? Gossip has it she had a habit of taking things out the back door at the end of a late shift."

Being a thief didn't answer who blacked her eyes and why.

"Do you know if she got a new job?" I asked.

"Your twenty ran out. You'll need to refill." Peggy held out her hand.

I handed over the money.

"Kelsey's working at a beach bar, The Whale. Only way you get a job there is if you blow the owner, Harold. Place does a kick-ass business." Peggy looked around. "I've got more information for sale. I get off in an hour; I can meet you somewhere."

"Bring us our check," Fab said.

"You'll need to hit the highlights of what I'll be paying for ahead of time to determine my willingness to pay," I told Peggy with a frown.

She put her hand on her hip, her lip curled up. "I can tell you all about her, right down to her shoe size. Is that enough of a preview?"

"Where do you want to meet?" Fab asked.

"There's a hot dog stand down the street. Looks like a hot pink wiener, can't miss it. Grab us a table and get me a coke, extra ice."

"She's so charming." I said, after Peggy set the

check down and wiggled over to a table of college boys.

* * *

"Two hundred." Peggy held out her hand.

The three of us had settled at an old, round metal table downwind from the fried food smell. I had to readjust my skirt, not wanting to get a rash from where the finish on the chairs had rusted.

The dog stand was located on prime real estate along the main highway that ran through town and up along the coast. If one leaned over and squinted between two neighboring buildings, they'd get the barest glimpse of the ocean.

Having been tricked on more than one occasion, I said, "I'll give you a hundred upfront, and if it's good information you'll get the rest. You waste our time, and she'll shoot you." I inclined my head in Fab's direction.

"Who are you two really?" Peggy looked wary, as if she was about to leave.

"Two women who bought you a soda," I said and pointed to it sitting on the table. "We're also willing to pay cash for what amounts to gossip. You deliver and you'll find we're good tippers."

Peggy stared out at the slowly passing traffic. "What do you want to know?" she finally asked. "Kelsey's a bitch, but I'm sure you know that already."

"Someone beat Kelsey up two nights ago, and she swore out a complaint against Horton King. You know him?" Fab asked.

"I met him. He came into The Hut all the time, picked up Kelsey sometimes when her shift ended. Seemed like a nice guy, not bad looking, reeked of money. Figured it would end badly. The poor guy was clearly in over his head; he was no match for Kelsey." Peggy half-laughed. "Did he do it?"

"He says not. There isn't a mark on him." Fab scrutinized her as she answered.

"More than likely it was the big gorilla she lives with, Gibbs."

"Man or an ape?" I asked.

Fab snorted at me.

"This is Florida; she could be shacked up with some hairy animal."

"Gibbs is her husband—or so they say; no one got invited to the wedding. A back to nature event on the Crystal River," Peggy said. "No one knows if they did it legally. More than likely he was the one to beat the crap out of her. It wouldn't be the first time. Probably found out that she was cheating on him—again. Here's what I do know: If Horton really did beat her up, look for him to turn up dead in a trashcan somewhere."

"If Gibbs beat her, then why finger Horton?" Fab asked.

"Because she's a vindictive bitch and has a

serious hatred for her ex-husband, who had her jailed regularly for sport. Since she can't get back at him directly, she vents her anger on every man she's been with since."

Peggy reached for my water bottle after downing her drink, unscrewed the top off and downed half, wiping her mouth on the back of her hand.

"Her first husband had her arrested several times; they'd get drunk, he'd mark himself up, and call the cops. She finally got a divorce when the judge told her if he ever saw her in his courtroom again she was going to big-girl prison. Now when she's done with a relationship, she has the man arrested—with the exception of Gibbs. Always trumped up charges. She seems satisfied with their mug shot and a day or two in jail. She never makes herself available to the prosecution, doesn't return the district attorney's phone calls. Even so, one man went to trial and got convicted, even though she never showed up and didn't testify against him."

"I'm surprised she's not dead," I raised my eyebrow at Fab. "How long has she been divorced?"

"Ten years. She's the gift that keeps giving." Peggy clearly had no love for Kelsey.

Fab shook her head in disbelief. "She keeps it up for the fun of it? What?"

"It's a game. It gives her control. Not to mention, under that sweet exterior of hers, she's mean and vindictive. She hunts for men on the beach, finds her prey, a few drinks later, and they're off for as much kinky sex as the guy's wang can handle. She's sexed-obsessed and not choosy," Peggy snorted.

She shook the empty water bottle.

"You going to finish yours?" she pointed to Fab's bottle.

Eww! Who drinks out of someone else's anything?

Fab pushed it across the table.

Peggy slurped the water.

"Kelsey lives to drive Gibbs crazy. She's an attention seeker—good or bad. Her and Gibbs will get along for a while, and then she'll disappear for days at a time. She'd take unscheduled days off work, so that when Gibbs came around, she was nowhere to be found. I know for a fact Gibbs has no idea she hangs out on the beach all day while he's at work and bangs whoever is available."

"Has she ever retracted one of her stories?" I asked.

"Nope. Evil bitch."

"Why don't you like her?" I asked.

"She slept with my husband." Peggy's mouth was a hard line. "I wanted to forgive him, but I couldn't. He was another one of her victims; she accused him of choking her during sex. Claims she blacked out, woke up with bruises around her neck. He didn't have a mark on him. Don't you think if you were being choked you would scratch, hit, do something? She had him arrested and wouldn't cooperate, so the case went nowhere, thank goodness. Except for the big-ass attorney bills."

We sat in a moment of awkward silence.

"I loved him. She wanted to bang him, another tic mark in her book. You know, she apologized, smirked that at least I knew he was a cheating dog. I really wanted to kick the crap out of her."

To my surprise, Fab patted her arm.

I felt bad for her, too. I'd been cheated on, but at least it wasn't with a good friend.

"Do you want my opinion?" Peggy continued on without waiting for an answer. "She pulled one of her infamous disappearing acts on Gibbs, and when she showed back up, he went crazy on her mangy ass."

"Do you know where she lives?" I asked. Fab had driven by the address Horton gave us, but it turned out to a deserted taco stand. We'd planned to call him later and verify the information he gave us.

Peggy chuckled.

"The address she usually gives out is a private mail box. If anyone shows up looking for her, she's nowhere to be found. A friend of hers owns the place and anyone who inquires, she sends away, informing them the box has been closed. Her phone number changes every couple of months. She calls it cleaning up her life." She picked up Fab's pen, wrote on a napkin, and handed it back. "Kelsey lives here."

There was an awkward silence. I wanted to ask another question to lighten the mood, but instead kept my mouth shut.

Peggy looked at her watch and stretched the band, letting it snap against her wrist.

"I've got to go. Tell Horton to hang in there. In a few months, the charges will probably be dropped."

Not in the mood to dicker, I felt we got more information than we hoped for and pushed money across the table.

She stood and counted it.

"You're right, you are a generous tipper. Thanks." She waved the money and walked to her Jeep.

We watched until she cleared the driveway, honking and hanging out the window, until someone let her cut in.

"Creole said that in some cases, the district attorney doesn't need a victim to pursue a case, depending on circumstantial evidence," I said. "I think a prosecution can be successful on pictures alone."

"What now?" Fab asked.

"Blackmail," we said in unison and laughed.

"First we need to meet Gibbs, see if he has marks on him," Fab said.

"'We' nothing," I shook my head. "You get gorilla duty."

"We'll stop by on the way home; daytime is

always good for checking out an unknown neighborhood. There's always a nosy neighbor that's up in everyone's business. Maybe one of them heard something. And that is your job."

"Knock… trumped up excuse… and I'll paste on my friendly smile and schmooze…" I thought out loud.

"You still have the religious pamphlets in that stupid box you insist we haul around." Fab looked pleased with her contribution.

"I also have a bogus petition that I printed off the internet and a clipboard, we could ask him/her to sign. Or, I overbought on some candy bars from a school fundraiser. They're in the box. We could sell those for our kid's school."

Fab turned her nose up, "I'd never allow my little Fabiana to sell anything door-to-door. She's way too cool."

I laughed until tears gathered in my eyes. "Think pretend. Besides, Fab Jr. isn't born yet."

Chapter Eighteen

The sign read Lazy Acres Mobile Home Park.

"This isn't so bad." Fab craned her neck out the window. "At least it's quiet."

The grounds were kept up, the grass mowed, but the buildings were tired and in need of another poor paint job.

"We both know the true test of a neighborhood is at night. That's when the fun people like to rock n' roll until the police show up."

"What are you doing?" Fab asked.

I crawled over the seat back and fished out the clipboard.

"Looking professional—grabbing a couple of cheap pens and a petition that asks people to sign to block a several lane extension that runs along the coast."

"Where?" Fab looked at me like I'd lost my mind.

"Daytona. No one is going to take the time to read every line. And if they do, I'll say, 'Oh damn, I grabbed the wrong one.' Flash the sad face, 'Not again,' and get the heck out."

We drove up and down the rows of mobile

homes, the directional signs turning us in circles until we found Gibbs's trailer parked on the last row in the far corner. The trailer was all locked up, with a single driveway under the awning, empty. A scrawny white cat was perched asleep on the patio ledge.

"Now what?" Fab asked, maneuvering a U-turn onto the narrow one lane road and pulling up in front of the trailer.

"I suggest we talk to the two women sitting on a porch across the way, staring at us. Your turn to make up a story."

She unleashed an exaggerated sigh.

"That's a terrible idea."

"Give me your badge," I told her, holding out my hand.

I hopped out of the SUV and crossed the street. I glanced over my shoulder, unhappy to see Fab still sitting in the SUV. So much for backup.

I smiled at the women, who eyed me curiously. I flashed the badge; their surprised looks vanished, replaced by an attack of nerves.

"I'm here to follow up on a domestic disturbance report. Could you ladies possibly help me out? This is our last stop for the day, and we'd like to fill out the report and go home."

One stood and ground out her cigarette in an ashtray that held the remnants of at least a pack.

"I'm Yoli," she introduced.

Both women were gray-haired and smokers,

long in the tooth, as my grandfather would say, but I sensed they could hold their own in a brawl.

"It was those two over there." Yoli pointed. They seemed surprised that someone called the cops. "Last time old man Barnes phoned in a report, Gibbs found out and threatened him, made him scared enough to pee himself."

"I'm Carnie," the other one spoke up, polishing off her cheap light beer. She smashed the can under her foot in one stomp.

"You don't want to mess with Gibbs," Carnie shivered. "That wife of his isn't the sharpest tool. She riles him up, he beats the snot out of her, and things stay calm for a while, until she gets it in her head to disappear. The last time it happened, she came walking up, looking like she'd been sleeping on the street. I hid in my trailer and turned up the sound on my afternoon stories."

"He's a prick," Yoli nodded.

"Why doesn't Kelsey just leave?" I asked.

"Gibbs would kill her," Carnie said with conviction.

"They're a weird couple." Yoli lit up another cigarette, took a long drag, and blew it in my direction.

I side-stepped and glared at her.

"Sorry," Yoli mumbled. "I've seen Gibbs parade her up and down the driveway on a leash. Then they jump in the truck and don't come back for hours. Nothing he does seems to bother her; she never fights back."

"It's easy to ignore Kelsey, since she never speaks to me. Wanted to borrow money once. I told her I didn't have any; she cussed me out and never even looked at me after that," Carnie said. "Gibbs knows he's unpopular around here. Any neighbor who has had a run-in with him fears him. I hightail it back in the house when I see them coming. Occasionally I force a pleasant smile, afraid not to say hello back or ignore him like I'd like to do."

"Have you seen Kelsey around?" I asked.

"Saw her limping and dragging out the trash can the day after the fight, sporting a couple of black eyes." Yoli's words dripped with sarcasm. "Don't like her. I'm not ashamed to admit I laughed when Gibbs screamed from the porch for her to hustle her ass and get back in the house. She turns up her nose, thinks she's better than everyone here, parading around half-naked in her skimpy outfits."

"I want to thank you both for your help." I smiled at them and rose. "There is nothing I can do unless she files a complaint."

They both smiled back and waved as I left.

"I want a raise," I huffed at Fab, crawling into the passenger seat. "You couldn't move your skinny ass and back me up?"

"You can't take two old women without using your gun?" Fab taunted.

"Ha! You should've looked a little closer. Ass

kickers, both of them. The only thing that scares them is Gibbs," I said. "Can't wait to meet him. Take me home. I need a swim and some take-out food, which is your treat."

"Why do I have to ask you what they said?" she sulked.

"That will teach you to sit in the car. Gibbs beat Kelsey that night. Apparently, there's no direct proof that your client didn't hit her or that Gibbs is the culprit. Kelsey is the only one that can clear your client."

My phone beeped, letting me know I had a text message. I groaned and read the message from Mac out loud.

"'*I have a surprise for you.*' Why does that scare me?"

Chapter Nineteen

"What in the hell?" I squeezed my eyes closed.

Nothing much shocked me, but the sight of two middle-aged women, Mac and Shirl, lying by the pool in bikinis and cowboy boots did just that. Fab made the drive back from Fort Lauderdale in record time. I'd just closed my eyes and shut my mouth as we rocketed down the highway.

"You need to tell them that that look doesn't work," Fab whispered.

I scowled at her.

"Hi ladies, what's up?"

"No, how are you? How's your day?" Mac said in a highly irritated tone.

"You both appear fine. And you have a job where you can sit out by the pool any time you want. Where's my surprise? If it explodes on my clothes, you're fired." I kicked off my shoes and walked down the steps to stand in the pool.

"Interesting outfit," Fab said to Shirl.

I looked down before rolling my eyes.

Shirl gave her a toothy smile. "Can I tell her the surprise?"

Mac grunted in affirmation, leaned back in her

chaise, and closed her eyes.

"Miss January got a kitten," Shirl announced.

"Another stuffed one?" I asked.

"Oh no, this one is alive and well. Named her Kitty Two." Shirl did a little dance move. Surprisingly, boots and boobs went in the same direction.

"Absolutely not!" I opened one eye. "She can't take care of the dead one she's already got."

Although Miss January had her cat stuffed, she didn't seem to remember that it had been dead for years. She had a tendency to carry it around and then misplace the damn thing, and I usually got the call to find it. Long ago, I got disgusted that the stuffing kept coming out, and had it restuffed. It looked like…well '*new*' wasn't the right word. Miss January didn't seem to notice, nor did it concern her that the cat didn't eat the kibble and drink the water she left on the floor every day.

"What will poor Kitty One think?" I asked. "Won't it be jealous?"

"You've lost your mind," Fab laughed.

I was afraid to ask, but forged ahead against my better judgment. "Where is she now?"

Mac snorted. "Drunk, passed out inside her cottage."

"Find Kitty Two a home, or make it an office cat," I said. "In case she asks during her non-drunk hour or so, make something up that won't hurt her feelings."

Mac burst out laughing. "The look on your face was priceless. I have Kitty Two in the office. I told Miss January I'd cat-sit while she slept off her drunk. Cute little thing. I can find it a home."

I stood up. "We're leaving. Try to refrain from hysterical texts unless it's actually an emergency."

"Not just yet." Mac pointed to a chair. "You might want to sit for this."

Fab started laughing.

"You're such a sympathetic friend." I glared at her. "What?" I threw up my hands.

"Joseph is depressed. He's having girlfriend problems." Mac looked toward his cottage.

"Svet is a life-size rubber doll. How much trouble can she be?" I asked.

One of Joseph's dead friends had bequeathed the attractive, voluptuous doll to him, complete with wigs and a closet full of impressive looking clothes, mostly lingerie. I liked Svetlana. So far she'd been the perfect tenant. Joseph would never get so lucky with a human woman.

"Poor Svet, she's all twisted up in the corner with a giant hole in her leg. Joseph thinks one of his drunk friends did it because they were jealous." Mac continued to laugh.

"Don't look at me. I use my surgery skills on real people," Shirl said.

"Call Spoon," I said. "He's got an auto repair shop. Surely he could patch her like a tire."

"You're awful," Mac declared. "That would

mar that creamy skin of hers."

"I have a headache," I whined. "There's a bonus coming to you if you get Svet fixed and blown up, and I never hear about this again."

The big smile on Mac's face told me that she had the problem already taken care of. I hated that all three of them were laughing at me.

"I do have some good news. Got rid of the poacher. I gave the key to Spoon's guy. Nothing friendly about him. Probably scares his own mother with those pin dot eyes…made the hair on my neck stand on end when he laughed. Few minutes later, Mr. Earl was throwing his stuff in his car."

I sighed. "Another happy ending."

Chapter Twenty

Fab made a face and answered her phone. She looked at me.

"Ellie Compton's being released in the morning." Noticing my confused look, she added, "Our prison job."

"What time?" I'd been on enough Brick jobs to know. The job sounded simple enough, but I wouldn't leave home without my Glock.

"Brick just informed me that she can get released any time after midnight, and normally the first one gets released in the early morning hours."

"I'm not going." I banged my glass on the countertop. "This means we could sit for hours in the parking lot. It's now a two-day trip."

I leaned over and looked out the kitchen window. I'd been doing that a lot lately, checking to make sure another dead body hadn't shown up. Blowing a sigh of relief, I turned to see Fab pull her phone away from her ear. Apparently, Brick heard me.

"Find someone else. I'm not going alone," Fab told him.

Whatever his response, she started yelling

back in French, which she reserved for when she was really mad.

"I quit. You can have your stinking Mercedes," were her last words before she hung up. A second later, her phone left her hand and slammed into the wall.

I sighed as I looked at the pieces. The last time I did that, the screen cracked and nothing worked quite right until finally, fed up, I traded it in. Now I felt bad. Fab and Brick had a long-standing relationship, going back before I met either one of them, and I wasn't going to be the cause of its demise.

I fished my phone out of my pocket. When Brick answered, he didn't say anything, just heavy breathing.

"This is my fault," I said. "Good excuse though—I've had a bad day. Let's forget the last five minutes, like it never happened. We'll pick up whatever her name is in the morning."

"Thanks, Madison. You need anything, call me."

I could hear the relief in his voice before he hung up.

Fab looked happy. "I don't have to give my car back?"

"Now would be the time to ask for a newer, shinier model. Brick wouldn't give you a hassle. You're his favorite. He wouldn't miss me, but I think he missed you already."

I slid off the stool. "Let's go. I need a nap if I'm

going to stay awake for this road trip."

* * *

We arrived at Lowell Correctional Institution and parked in front of the gate that prisoners walked through to their freedom. I called and confirmed that she was eligible for release at midnight, but more than likely we wouldn't see her until around six in the morning.

Creole and I had a system. When on a job, I texted the location. He confirmed back that Lowell, one of the state's largest prisons, handled all levels of custody and that it might be a long wait.

An hour later, a woman who vaguely matched the picture ambled out. She turned and gave the double finger to the back of the guard. Prison life had aged her, and she looked worn out.

"What did Brick say about her? You need to go get her so we can get the hell out of here." Fab looked skeptical.

I closed my eyes and took a breath. "Wrongful conviction."

"One hundred dollars says she drew the luckiest card of her life and got away with it." Fab continued to stare out the windshield.

"Bet with you?" I shook my head. "No way. You always win. We can't let her stand there. You owe me for being the welcome committee." I slid out of the car and called out.

Her once-blonde hair was now a dull grey. She slunk over and checked me out from head to toe.

"You my ride?" she asked, peering in the window as she hawked spit across the driveway.

I opened the back door.

"I'm Madison, and the driver is Fab." I pointed to the chest of snacks and drinks. "Help yourself."

"Can I use your phone? Let my son know that I'm out?" She slid her bony arm over the seat, damn near grazing my cheek. I jerked closer to the window.

I handed the woman my phone. I'd already forgotten her name. Grandma didn't seem appropriate, and my notes were in my bag on the back seat. Fab and I exchanged looks as if to say, *"Why are we picking her up if she has family?"* Both of us stayed silent so we could hear every word.

Nothing decipherable came out of her mouth, more like incoherent mumbling you'd hear out of a drunk. I looked over the seat back; she had lowered her voice and covered the phone.

Just out of prison — what does she have to hide?

When she handed me back the phone, I glanced back at her again.

"Happy to be out?" I asked.

Okay, a dumb question, but my attempt at friendly small talk and seemed better than, "How did you enjoy prison?"

Fab snickered and I shrugged.

"How long have you been in?" I asked.

She laughed, sounding like a rusty door screeching open.

"Twenty long-ass years. Good thing I escaped the death penalty, or I wouldn't have lived to see this day."

Lying-ass Brick! Twenty years. I should've had Mac run her prison record.

"What did you do?"

"Not a damn thing. Not my fault I was married to the dead guy. Doesn't mean I murdered him. The jury convicted me, because Artie's arm was found in a box in the attic. Someone set me up. If I were going to keep a souvenir, it would have been his dick."

"Where did they find the rest of the body?" I asked. Maybe her answer could help us in the quest to locate the rest of Jones' body.

"They didn't. The prosecutor decided that I put Artie through the wood chipper, only because it had some skin fragments. They weren't large enough to test and only my fingerprints were on the handle. On appeal, my conviction got overturned because they failed to maintain custody of the chipper. My lawyer proved that the DNA report had been altered."

"It's safe to say he was probably dead before stuffing him through the chipper, since he had to be chopped up. He'd be too big to go through whole," Fab said.

I thought for a moment. No chipper at the house or The Cottages, so pretty sure I wouldn't find Jones there.

"Artie was a bastard," she smiled. "Drop me off in Kenansville, my son's meeting us. It's a highway town just south of Orlando, slide right off the turnpike. It's next to the wildlife area." She cracked her knuckles, putting her hands behind her head.

Great-the middle of nowhere. If I weren't so unnerved, I might clap at getting rid of her sooner than expected. Her smile was creepier than Fab's.

I peered over my shoulder in time to see her put my purse back on the floor as she picked up Fab's leather tote. I motioned to Fab, pointing to the back seat. She looked in the rearview and jerked the wheel, pulling onto the shoulder.

I jumped out, shoving my Glock in the waist band of my jean skirt, and threw open the back door.

"Get in the front or get out. Your choice. It's rude to ransack our purses."

She gave me a hatred-filled look, which swiftly changed to a blank stare.

Before getting back in the passenger seat, she stood and scanned the highway. I hoped she'd take off—I wouldn't go after her.

I texted Brick the location where his client wanted to be dropped off and sent a message to Creole about the change of plans. I moved behind Fab in the back seat and didn't take my eyes off the woman. It was a long, silent ride; I hoped I wouldn't nod off. The good part about sitting behind Fab was that I couldn't see while she drove the turnpike like a racecar driver.

Kenansville appeared on my phone as a faint dot on the map. It boasted being an old ghost town. A small ad popped up for a café, guaranteeing down-home cooking.

"Next exit, there's a gas station. Drop me off." Ellie pointed up ahead.

Fab hadn't come to a complete stop when the older woman jumped out.

"Thanks for the ride," she yelled as she bounced across the street.

The truck stop, convenience store, and restaurant were located off the main two-lane highway with nothing but miles of trees in each direction.

"You better check your purse and see if anything is missing." I climbed over the seat. I breathed a happy sigh. We were rid of her and feeling no guilt about dumping her in the boonies, since she'd asked. "I already made sure she didn't lift our wallets or money. Let's get gas and get out of here."

"Should we really leave her here?" Fab asked looking up and down the highway.

An old beat-up pickup rolled noisily into the driveway, back fired, and came to a stop. Two scruffy-looking men wearing dirty t-shirts and shredded jeans, both seeming nervous, hung their heads out the window before jumping out of the truck. Ellie came out of the store and launched herself into one of their arms and then the other. She pointed to us and the trio came across the driveway.

"I wanted to say thank you and have you meet my sons." Ellie pointed the two in our direction and stood between the twins.

Neither of them appeared to be very high on the IQ scale, if they even scored at all. They both mumbled, "Hullo," in a sullen tone.

One stepped forward as if to shake hands with Fab, but instead brandished a gun, pointing it dead center to my chest.

"Get in," he said, motioning me into the back seat of the SUV. "You," he waved the gun at Fab, "get in the driver's seat. Don't do anything stupid, and I won't shoot you two and leave you both for the animals to eat." He grinned, a piece of tobacco stuck in his front tooth, obviously marking him as a chewer.

The other man took off in the truck, leaving a trail of black smoke in its wake.

With Fab forced behind the wheel and me in the back, Ellie slipped into the passenger seat with a smile. The gunman slid in next to me.

Chewer cocked his gun, tapping Fab on the shoulder, a reminder that he was ready to fire. "Drive out, nice and normal. No funny stuff."

"What do you want?" I asked. "Let's make a deal and part ways all friendly."

He ignored me.

"Turn right." He indicated a dirt road that weaved between a row of trees.

"Pull over." He threw open the door and reached across the seat to drag me by my hair, pitching me to the ground. "Get up and start running," he pointed deeper into the woods. "Report this to anyone, and you'll never see your friend again. Cops come after us and I'll shoot her. I have nothing to lose. I'm not going back to prison. Besides, a shootout will make me famous. I'll get my mug on the six o'clock news."

Fab stuck her head out the window and winked at me.

Just great, fun and games for her. I'm stuck in the wilderness.

He switched seats with his mother and climbed in next to Fab, with Ellie in the back. Fab pulled a U-turn and headed back to the main road in a cloud of dust. I covered my face until the dirt cleared, then turned and ran after them, although they'd already disappeared. I smiled as my fingers felt the cell phone in my back pocket, a smile that faded when I looked at the screen and couldn't get a signal. Too many trees.

Why couldn't Fab just shoot those two idiots dead?

I wouldn't be walking down the highway by myself, not a car or truck in sight. I headed back in the direction of the truck stop. It couldn't be more than a few miles. We hadn't gone far before Dimwit had us turn off the road. I had no doubt that Fab would be victorious, but how long would it take? I couldn't stand on the side of the road.

Once I got a hold of Creole, he could activate the GPS tracker. Hopefully Fab hadn't dismantled this one. She did a good job making every unit looked like it malfunctioned.

I didn't so much worry about Fab being with Dimwit and his mother. It worried me more that the son would do something stupid. When Fab got tired of the game, she'd figure a way to get them out of the SUV, and she'd be back to get me.

Halfway between me and the truck stop sign up ahead, I reached an emergency road side box. I sent a silent thank you for the signal on my cell. Creole's phone went to voicemail. I sent a 9-1-1 text to Creole and the same to Brick.

I tapped my foot impatiently. I hated waiting, but there was no way of knowing how far I would get up the road before I'd lose service again. I smiled at the sweet sound of my cell ringing.

"You okay?" Creole demanded.

I cut the retelling short, started with the meet and greet of the twins.

"I'm happy you're okay," he sighed. "Don't worry about Fab; she'll be back in one piece. They deserve whatever she dishes out."

"I'm thinking I followed all of your rules today. There should be a reward or something." I blushed, even though there was no one around.

He laughed, a deep rumble. "Go back to the truck stop. I'll send someone for you. I've got a friend who lives out there, beard down to his belt buckle. Ask him what his favorite beverage is, and if he doesn't say 'moonshine', don't go anywhere with him. I'll call you back."

The phone rang again and this time it was Brick. It surprised me, as he usually went AWOL in these situations. I told him what happened, and he let loose an impressive string of profanity. This time, he didn't disguise them by saying them in Spanish.

"I'm calling the cops and reporting the carjacking," I told him. He didn't need to know I'd done the next best thing—I called Creole. I waited for Brick's reaction.

"No!" he barked. "I'll get my brother on this and get her back in one piece."

The elusive brother, who I'd met a time or two, was a commendation-winning detective for the Miami Police Department. To hear Brick tell it, his resume was impeccable.

"Be quick about it. I'll do what I have to do to support Fab's claim of self-defense when she shows back up with two dead bodies. Those two imbeciles aren't going to get out alive. Did you know your client probably wood chipped her husband?"

"They never proved that," Brick said.

"If Fab comes back with so much as a scratch on her, I'm going to shoot you." I hung up on him. I did briefly wonder what one did with wood chipped remains, but put it out of my mind.

I called Creole back, and he answered on the first ring.

"Hang in there; I'm sending someone to pick you up," he said.

"Cancel that call. I'm not leaving the gas station until Fab shows up. Brick's calling in the big guns, his brother Casio." The sign was so close it spurred me to walk faster.

"Spoke with the boss; he put a call out to the local police. He asked that they be careful when pulling over the Hummer. The woman behind the wheel was more than capable of returning the duo in body bags with no harm to the public," he joked.

I finally arrived at the truck stop and took a seat on a bus bench.

"Your bearded friend just rode up on his bicycle." It was hard to tell his age with all the facial growth. He had a waist-length beard, a cigar hanging out of his mouth, and his silver hair pulled into a ponytail.

Now that's a trick — smoking while riding a bicycle.

"Put him on," Creole said.

He slammed on his brakes, resting the front tire of the bike against the bench in front of me.

"Hey, Red," his lips quirked into a smirk.

I put my foot against his tire.

"Don't bother getting off until you tell me

your favorite beverage." I lifted my skirt, showing my Glock.

He threw his head back and laughed.

"Are you threatening me?"

"Not if you stay where you are and answer the question."

"If I were younger, I'd drag your ass home and keep you naked for a week," he winked.

"Stop stalling," I fingered the handle of my gun.

"Moonshine." He jumped off his bike and set the kick stand. "Happy now?"

"Here." I held out my phone. "You've got a call."

Judging by the one-sided conversation, I was certain Creole was extracting a promise to stay by my side. The man frowned briefly at the phone. Plans to go fishing were made, and they hung up.

"Name's Pinter. Family name, before you ask. Me and your boyfriend cooked up a plan. If your friend hasn't shown up by dark, I'm taking you home."

"On that?" I eyed his bicycle. No extra seat, not even a basket.

He sat down next to me and we stared down the highway, the occasional car going by.

"I've got a sweet 1960 Rambler at home, waiting for a road trip." He patted my knee. "Don't worry about your friend. Creole says she's as tough as they come."

How is it that Pinter and Creole were good enough friends that the man would stage a bike rescue?

"You're telling me your car still runs? I'm impressed."

"Found it at a wrecking yard, one back in line from getting squashed. I got it for a song and restored it myself."

"I have an appreciation for old cars. My father restored old Mustangs as a hobby," I said.

Oh look, another car just went by. That made two in the last twenty minutes.

"How about I treat you to a meal?" Pinter offered. "They usually have a couple of hot dogs leftover that have been sitting in the warmer unit all day."

"Share a bag of potato chips?" I hadn't had a hot dog in a long time. I needed a sugary soda to keep from hand wringing over Fab.

We brought our gourmet meal back to the bench. I insisted on extra napkins, which had the clerk glaring at me. I covered the slats on the bench, throwing down the packets of condiments. I thought the clerk would be happy that someone bought the last two wrinkly dogs.

I poked the bun with my nail. Finding both ends hard, I tore them off, not wanting a chipped tooth.

Thank goodness Pinter was a man of few words; he kicked back and enjoyed his meal, forgoing small talk. We stared at the road in an easy silence.

"Thank you for the delicious meal," I told him. It wasn't, but at least it filled me up.

"That's a pretty lie," he laughed. "You're welcome."

An SUV came roaring up the highway, clearly over the speed limit, but a welcome sight as it got closer. I tried to gauge whether or not it would make the driveway. It blew by, missing the turn all together, followed by a screeching of the brakes and a squealing U-turn. Fab was back!

I held my breath and hoped she wouldn't smash the bicycle. I let out a whoosh when she missed the bike, leaving it intact.

Fab threw open the door and jumped out. "That was so much fun."

"Are they alive?" I asked, making her turn around, checking for blood. Creole always made me stand still for an inspection for blood and other assorted wounds after a narrow escape.

"You're getting too much like your boyfriend," she laughed. "Who are you?"

"Pinter, meet Fab." I pointed between the two. "Don't let her good looks fool you; she loves to kick ass."

"What the hell is that?" Fab pointed to the pieces of rejected hot dog bun and made a retching noise.

I laughed at her. "Give us the ten-word or less version of Fab's adventure."

She screwed up her nose. "They're alive." She gave an unladylike snort. "I broke the bastard's nose, but he'll survive. That old bag didn't get a scratch on her, but it will take a while to get her untied."

"Mother and son got into a fight. While they were distracted airing family dirt, I pulled my Walther. Sorry to tell you…" she frowned, "but you need a new passenger window. It cracked a little…well, a lot. I bashed bony-boy in the nose. The crunching noise was so satisfying. Sorry for the blood. With my gun in the old lady's face, I swerved over and gave them a three-count, and then kicked them out in the woods."

"Let's go home," I said. To Pinter, I said, "It's getting dark, we're giving you a ride."

"Not necessary." He had a smile on his face, hanging on Fab's every word, enjoying the retelling of her escapade.

I ignored him and pushed his bike to the back of the SUV. Fab had the door open, and we lifted it in. I held the passenger door open for him and hopped in the back. "Sit up front and give her directions."

"How did Creole end up with someone so pushy?" Pinter asked.

I laughed. "Creole's my cousin, sort of. Trust me, we're well matched."

Creole grew up as a neighbor to my Aunt Elizabeth, and she had unofficially adopted him. We joked about being cousins and anyone who didn't know us assumed that was why the Westins were so weird.

Fab turned down a narrow road, which started off paved but quickly became gravel.

"There's no lights out here," she said as she drove through the forest.

The farther she drove, the darker it got. She pulled up in front of a log cabin nestled between the trees, the porch overlooking an inlet of water that rustled by. Pinter's home looked modern and up-to-date, peaceful and quiet. Two Border Collies came of out of nowhere and stood in the middle of the driveway, their eyes glowing yellow as they waited. Pinter barely got a leg out when they ran to his side.

I held the back of my hand out to the dogs and let them sniff before I gave them a quick head rub.

"If you're ever in Tarpon Cove, stop in at Jake's bar. Tell the bartender 'Moonshine,' and get your meal on the house. That's going to be our new password," I said.

"Come back anytime. Go fishing," Pinter said. "You're both welcome. No need for an invite."

He stood and waved as Fab turned around. We drove back through the road nestled between the trees.

"What did Ellie and her sons want?" I asked.

"Gofer has a stolen car parts business. Not a lot of Hummers out here, so they saw a perfect opportunity. No overhead. When jailbird saw our ride, she called the twins. They flipped a coin to see who'd get to jack us."

Fab made zero effort to remember names.

"What's her connection to Brick?" I asked.

"I asked, and she grumbled she never heard of Brick Famosa."

This was another one of those times I was happy not to drive; the headlights illuminating the foggy road weren't enough for me. I wanted to go home and forget this day.

"I have to call Creole," I said.

"Did that already. I also talked to Brick. He sent his brother to collect the tied-up felons. Thank you for threatening him for me. Now that's a best friend."

Chapter Twenty-One

"Do you suppose it's safe to go in the house?" I asked.

Fab and I sat in the driveway, staring at Didier and Creole's autos parked in the front.

"I don't like it when they get together and one of us is not there to listen," Fab said.

"What about when they run around the state?"

Besides bicycling, the guys ran together and did push-ups. They didn't stop after one or two for a rest like I would.

"You can't talk and run. They're out of breath, so no chatting it up about what we might be doing," Fab said. "We know they talk, I just wonder what they share?"

"They know we're here," I said. I figured Creole didn't have to look out the window to know we were sitting outside. "Creole has a sixth sense. The longer we sit here, the guiltier we look, and we haven't done anything wrong today."

We jumped out of the SUV, and I followed Fab up to the door.

"What are we going to do about Kelsey?" Fab asked me, hand on the doorknob.

"Have we chosen a side?" I hesitated. "I'd like to meet the gorilla. But for now, no more work talk."

The guys must be mind readers. They were both in bathing suits. Didier wore an apron that made him look even sexier than usual, if that were possible. He moved to the kitchen sink as we walked in the door. Creole was putting together some fish kabobs at the island.

Fab slid over to Didier and they engaged in a long, smoochy kiss.

Creole wandered a leisurely eye over me, up and down. I blushed at the scrutiny.

He pointed upstairs.

"You're overdressed."

"Can you come upstairs and help me with my buttons?" I winked at him.

"Come over here." He crooked his finger at me. "I'll unbutton you."

I pouted and backed out of the kitchen, not wanting him to see that my outfit didn't have a single button.

"We slaved all day in this hot kitchen and we're eating in a half hour," Creole called, as I dashed up the stairs.

Fab ran up the stairs after me.

"Here's an incentive to hurry—there's a pitcher of margaritas in the refrigerator."

* * *

Fab beat me back downstairs, but she only had a couple of strings to tie on her hot pink bikini.

From the top of the staircase, I saw Creole, out of the corner of my eye, leaning over the barbeque. Wait until Brad found out that someone had figured out how to turn it on besides him. All I knew about it was that it looked pretty, all shiny stainless steel. The old one stopped working, which surprised me. I thought you just threw in charcoals and lit them on fire.

Opening the refrigerator, I smiled at the pitcher of my favorite drink. Creole had left a glass on the counter with salt around the rim.

* * *

I flipped on the lights that flooded the backyard; lights wrapped around the trunks of the palm trees, and every potted plant had a solar light stake.

Fab and I tossed inflatable rings in the pool. We swam around, splashing water everywhere. We squawked and yelled, then dissolved into laughter.

After the first few yelps of, "Help, she's drowning me!", the guys realized attempts at shushing us and evil glares had no effect, so they ignored us.

They both cooked us dinner — we didn't have to lift a finger — and they cleaned as they used the dishes. Creole barbequed the fish and vegetables on skewers and served them on a bed of risotto prepared by Didier. Too many vegetables in my opinion, but they looked pretty on the plate.

Didier was a health nut, and if he had his way we'd eat more of them, including drinking stinky green juice for breakfast. I didn't utter a word of complaint; I didn't want to hurt his feelings. Instead, I used my old trick from childhood and pushed everything I didn't like around my plate, hiding little pieces under big ones and making it look like I ate more than I did. Times like these called for a dog.

After I snuck up behind Fab and pushed her in the water, she grabbed my wrist and dragged me in along with her.

Creole towered over us at the side of the pool, glaring. "Could the two of you make any more noise?"

"Yes!!" we screamed in unison.

"You're cut off. No more wine." Creole pointed to Fab, then looked at me, "No more tequila."

He dove in and came up under me, lifting me in the air. Didier pulled off his shirt and threw it on the chaise.

"How are old you? You're acting like children—loud, noisy, pain-in-the ass children!" came a woman's high pitched voice.

"Where in the hell did you come from?" Fab snarled at her.

Mrs. Ricci stood in my backyard, looking down her nose. She was dressed in black knee-length shorts and a silk blouse, looking expensive. I spent a little extra time staring at her black leather slides. Her stance suggested it was her house, not acknowledging that it wasn't and she hadn't been invited.

How did she find us?

"You must be lost," I said through clenched teeth. "Let me give you directions and you can leave. Go back the way you came in."

Didier climbed out of the pool and, being a gentleman, offered her a chair. Apparently she asked for something to drink, because Didier went to the outside refrigerator and retrieved a bottle of water for her. She flashed her dollar sign smile and eyeballed him as though he were a banquet meal.

"Madison," Creole whispered. "She's uh…older."

Fab got out of the pool and stood in front of her. "Lift your top. Now," she barked.

Didier said something in French and Fab ignored him, but Mrs. Ricci laughed.

It surprised me when she reached inside her waist band and handed over her gun. "I want it back when I leave."

"Who is she?" Didier whispered.

"Take your eyes off my boyfriend before I kick the hell out of you," Fab sneered at her. "He's not for sale either."

I cleared my throat. "Let me make the introductions," I said, flashing a half-hearted smile. "Carlotta Ricci, Carmine's mother. You may remember her from the headlines; she just got arrested for being a pimp. We were hired to keep her out of jail, and she paid us back by threatening to shoot us and locking us in her pantry closet. You remember?" I asked Creole. "You didn't show up until after we escaped."

"The car thief?" Creole laughed.

"That pimp nonsense was made up by so-called journalists for headlines," Carlotta sniffed. "If I ever get to tell my story, you'll find out that I facilitated in making love connections between very wealthy discerning men and beautiful women."

"Does Snot Nose know you're out on the loose?" I asked. "That's her sweet nickname for her son," I explained to the boys.

"Oh shut up!" Carlotta yelled. "You owe me and I'm here to collect. I need to hire the two of you to hide me from Carmine."

Fab yelled back at her. "Have you lost your mind? Who has ever crossed Carmine and lived to tell about it? Besides, it's unanimous — we don't like you."

Carlotta, not to be intimidated, stood and got in Fab's face. "It's your fault I ended up caged in Carmine's house."

"Ten thousand square feet of waterfront property and plenty of household help to attend your every whim is hardly a cage," I said unsympathetically.

"What happened with your court case?" Fab asked.

"Carmine shelled out big. I got a fine and community service, and he took care of that already, but that doesn't mean I want to be locked up with a body guard watching my every move. When I mentioned re-opening my business and that I'd call it a matchmaking service if I had to, would even make it appear legit, he flipped out and locked me in a guest suite."

Fab fisted her hands at her side. "And when Carmine finds out we're harboring your old ass, what then?"

"Fabiana." Didier pulled her against his body.

The ringing of my phone was a welcome reprieve and, as I raced across the patio, I said to Fab, "Get rid of her."

I whooshed out a breath when I saw Brick's name. For once he might be the best one to help get rid of Carlotta, but I decided against it. He might call Carmine, to hell with Fab and me.

Rather than blow him off, I'd answer so he wouldn't burn up the phones.

"This isn't a good time," I said.

"Why the hell is her phone turned off," Brick yelled.

"Yell at me again and my phone is going off. By her, I assume you mean Fabiana. Does she know she's on call tonight?"

"Don't you dare hang up. I've got an emergency and I need you both. Now."

I never heard Brick sound frantic before. While I was inclined to be sympathetic, I had problems of my own. I looked over and saw that the madam had now made herself comfortable in a chaise lounge.

"Can't this wait until tomorrow?" I asked.

"Carlotta Ricci has run off and Carmine wants her found, pronto. Triple rate." Brick blurted.

"Quadruple! And that's not enough for that pain in the ass. She's here now," I whispered.

Dead silence.

"Are you still there?" I asked.

"Carlotta is at your house?" he whispered back.

I rolled my eyes. "You don't have to whisper. No one can hear you unless you yell. Yes, she's here, and she wants us to hide her. She wants to hobnob with the little people or get back to pimping or something, who knows."

Brick continued to whisper. "Keep her there and I'll call you back."

"You listen to me, I don't want you-know-who at my house or any of his goons. You promise me."

"Answer when I call back." Brick hung up.

I felt nauseated and hoped I wouldn't get sick. "We have a job tomorrow," I nodded at Fab.

Carlotta and Fab were in an animated conversation about Carlotta's demands and how we owed it to her to be helpful. Let them fight it out. I sat on the chaise next to Creole.

"I could put her in jail; let her sit there until Snot Nose picks her up." Creole and I laughed.

"I love that name. Wouldn't you love to see the big tough guy's face when she calls him that?" I continued to laugh.

I had turned the sound off on my phone, and it buzzed in my hand. I jumped and turned, walking to the other side of the pool. Creole followed me, and I leaned against his chest.

"What?" I snapped at Brick.

"Put her in one of those cottages of yours and let her mingle with the regular people. Let her enjoy a real life experience. She'll be running back to the mansion," Brick said. He was at ease now, his agitated tone gone.

"Are you out of your mind? She'll run off the guests with her sparkly personality. Does Carmine know and approve?"

"Keep me informed; let me know what she's up to."

"Don't you dare..." But it was too late, he'd hung up.

I knew just how to send Carlotta packing back to the mansion. I called the professor to find out if there was a vacant Air Stream.

"Do we have any vacancies?" I asked when he answered.

"We got two empty until the weekend. You need a place to hide out?" he asked in his crotchety style.

"I'm bringing over a woman to stay for a few days. I want you to lay on the charm and have her running for the road, the sooner the better."

"Speak the hell up. I'm not hard of hearing, because I could hear just fine before you called," his surly voice boomed through the phone. "A criminal friend of yours?"

"One more thing, you need to keep an eagle eye on the wily b...woman. She's slippery. Just consider it repayment for one of the many favors you owe me." Babysitting Carlotta would drive Fab and me nuts.

I stashed my phone in my pocket and went over to the battling duo. Interrupting them, I glared at Carlotta. "I've got a place for you to stay. One hint of trouble or anything illegal— you're out."

Fab looked at me like I'd lost my mind. Creole whispered to Didier, who relayed something to her, and she flashed her creepy smile.

"I thought I'd stay here," Carlotta said.

"You thought wrong. Now let's go." I leaned down and kissed Creole. "Be back in a half hour."

I didn't have to explain anything to him. I let him listen in to the calls so I didn't have to repeat anything.

"Fab can stay here. I'm coming with you. I don't trust Carlotta." Turning to the older woman, he lectured her. "I suggest you behave. I don't have any problem kicking your ass out of my truck and leaving you on the side of the road. No one has accused me of being a gentleman like Didier here."

"You have impeccable manners," I pressed my lips to his.

"I can't wait to see her face when she finds out her choices are a trailer or back to Snot Nose," he chuckled in my ear.

"Let's see how fast we can get there. Come along, Carlotta," I said, motioning with my hand. "You can have as much freedom from Carmine as you can stand."

Chapter Twenty-Two

"What the hell is this place?" Carlotta beat the back of the seat with her hand. "Answer me."

I was disappointed when she hadn't jumped out at one of the signals and run down the street. The scenario entertained me, until I thought of having to tell Carmine I'd lost his mother and I shuddered.

"You do have choices. You can stay here, return to the bosom of your son, or there's the Bluebird Motel, down the highway a few miles. Pay by the hour, cash only. They do a brisk all-night business, if you get what I mean. Decorated with mirrored ceilings, all night porn, and I hear the beds jiggle and shake in exchange for a fistful of quarters."

Carlotta had sucked every bit of sympathy from me after she pulled her gun on Fab and me. The only reason I relented and decided to be the slightest bit cooperative was for Fab. She wanted Brick as a client, and this would have the man owing her big. I smiled at the bill I would be sending him — to hell with quadruple rates.

Creole pursed his lips, but not before letting a snort escape.

I slid out of the truck and shut the door, effectively cutting off Carlotta's harangue. Just outside the picket fence, Crum leaned against his ratty red pickup in his tighty whities. He'd had exchanged his rubber boots for a worn down pair of flip flops. In his arms he held a gigantic ball of white fur.

"What is that?" I sputtered.

He looked at me as though I was one of those ignorant stoops he claimed to have taught at that top-rated college where he was granted tenure.

"This is Harlot," he introduced.

"Let me guess, you named her?" I snorted. "I assume that she's not grossly overweight, but pregnant?"

Why me?

"According to the vet, she'll be making me a papa in a couple of weeks," Crum beamed down at her.

"Are you competent enough to care for an animal?" I heard the truck doors slam twice behind me.

He sneered. "My IQ is far higher than yours."

"That doesn't mean you're capable of taking care of a cat." I stroked the fur around Harlot's head and ears. She purred in contentment. "There are cat rules. I will be back tomorrow with the list in writing. Which you will sign."

He straightened his spine more than usual. "Hello, Madame," he bowed to Carlotta, shoving Harlot in to my arms.

"Carlotta will be staying for a few days. If any thuggish-looking men show up, hand her over. No one is to get hurt." I pointed to Crum. "No complaining. Any problems, give me a call."

I felt momentarily sorry for Carlotta and then recovered my senses. "This place was completely renovated by my brother. He just got a favorable write-up in a big travel magazine. Whatever nefarious plans you're cooking up cannot be done from here."

"Come with me," Crum held out his arm. "I'll give you the grand tour. We have a hot tub," he winked at her.

"I didn't bring a bathing suit," she whined.

"Boss Lady here says no naked swimming. I'll give you one of my t-shirts." He smiled at her, eyeing her like a delectable morsel.

"Here." I gave Harlot back. "Cats aren't allowed outside. Nothing good comes from that. One more thing. Harlot gets fixed as soon as the vet says it can be done."

"We have to leave." Creole put his arm around me and steered me back to the truck. "Both of you stay out of trouble," he called back over his shoulder. "Bet you a dollar they do something horizontal."

I squeezed my eyes closed. "If they do, I hope one of them doesn't have a heart attack."

"Do you ever say, 'no' to these crazy-ass people?" Creole laughed.

"Not often enough. I used to be worse but I'm

getting better at it. I need a good twelve-step." I nuzzled my face in his neck. "Let's go to your house and have noisy sex."

Chapter Twenty-Three

The front door of Jake's was locked at this early hour. Though if it were open, I found myself thinking, I bet we'd draw the breakfast drinking crowd. I cut around the back through the kitchen. Creole dropped me off after I spent the night with him at his beach hideaway. Fab would be here any minute to pick me up. The coffee at Jake's wasn't bad, but it wasn't a caramel latte either.

I waved to the cook and made my way to the bar where I knew I'd find a bowl of snack mix. It surprised me to see Phil, who was hours early for her shift.

"Hey Boss, I got a surprise for you," she flashed a smirky smile.

I jumped at the banging on the front door.

"Stop that, Fabiana Merceau!" I yelled.

"What? You can see through solid doors now?" Phil chuckled.

I shook my head. "Who else? And she's so early." I jerked the keys off the top of the bar and unlocked the door.

"Took you long enough." Fab pushed her way past me.

I grabbed the back of her shirt. "Do you mind waiting outside? Phil has a surprise for me."

Phil laughed, leaning her elbows on the bar. She found the drama as amusing as I did.

Fab jerked away and slid onto a bar stool. "What surprise?" she growled. "Is the coffee made?" She slid over the top of the bar, trying to reach a mug.

Phil held her arms out as far as they would go. "So big, I couldn't wrap it."

"For all the hype, it better be good." I eyed her skeptically. Surprises had a tendency to be overrated.

She wiggled her fingers for Fab and I to follow her down the hall, back in the direction of the kitchen. She stopped in front of the little-used office door. It was a small, windowless, cramped space. Phil took a key out of her pocket and unlocked a padlock that the door never had before.

"Surprise," she said as she threw the door open.

I peered around and started to laugh when I saw my ex-husband stretched out on the couch.

"About time," he grumbled. "What a stink hole this is. Do you know anyone who's not crazy?" he asked me.

"This surprise sucks," Fab said.

I raised my eyebrows at Phil.

"You said you wanted to talk to him—here he is. That's another service I offer—dickhead locator." Phil grinned.

"Where did you find him?" Fab asked.

"Down on the docks, working on old man Grimes's boat. I told him he was wasting his time; the old goat didn't pay," Phil told us.

"I'm hungry," Jax said. "I can cook us up some breakfast."

Fab and Phil disappeared back to the bar.

I held out my hand. "This office is too small for one person. I thought you'd call me," I said to him. "Have you been okay?"

He hugged me. "Can we talk after food?"

"You cook, and I'll set a table out on the deck," I said. "The corner one is my office. Phil didn't hurt you, did she?"

"I came pretty willingly after she offered a blow job. The next thing I knew, she had me in handcuffs and pushed me into her SUV. Thought she was a cop, asked what's the crime? I didn't offer any money. Then she told me her real agenda. I was pissed, but I had no choice except to go along."

"Don't run out the back door, or I'll send Fab after you." I raised my eyebrows; he had no idea that that was her area of expertise, manhandling reluctant people to do as they were told.

I filled up a cart with dishes, orange juice, coffee, and bottled water and wheeled it to the deck. I loved setting a table. If this breakfast had been planned, I'd have come up with table decorations. I switched on the lights that framed the railing and the overhead ceiling fans. The skies had darkened, and thunder could be heard in the distance.

Phil carried out a platter of fruit. Jax followed behind her with a large frying pan. He'd made my favorite — a frittata, similar to a pancake, baked with vegetables and cheese. He cut it like a pizza and served us before he sat down.

Jax lost his grumpy attitude and turned on the charm, pouring juice and coffee.

"Why am I here?" Jax asked as he slid into the chair next to me.

"You won't answer your phone or return calls. How else were we supposed to chat?"

"Don't smile at me," Fab growled at Jax.

He laughed. "You're hot until you open your mouth."

Fab shoved her chair back.

"You sit down." I pointed at Fab. "Try not to provoke her into shooting you," I said to Jax. "Tell me why you really showed up in the Cove."

"Seemed innocent enough at the time. I got a one-time gig to drive a moving truck across the country. A longtime friend, Jones Graw, was relocating to Colorado."

Fab whipped out her phone. "Dickhead, tell us more about your friend, Jones Graw?" She waited until Jax took a bite of food before showing him the picture of the dead man.

Jax stared at the picture. It took a minute for

him to realize that he was only looking at his dearly departed friend's head. Jax's face drained of color and he looked away. "Who kills someone like that?"

"Any clue as to why Jones is missing his head. Or torso, however you want to look at it?" I asked.

"Turns out there was more than old furniture being transported. Once I got clued in, I upped my price. My sweet little money-making opportunity blew up in my face when Jones disappeared."

"I'm going to make a leap and assume you were moving something illegal," I said.

"Weed's legal now."

"Not in this state it isn't," I huffed in exasperation. "Any other players?" I asked.

He fidgeted in his seat, staring out at the water.

Fab, ready to beat him, stayed seated and glared.

"Rod Tanner. I haven't seen him since right after I heard about Jones being dead." Jax looked rattled. "Graw told me all arrangements were made through Rod."

Phil scribbled the man's name on the back of a napkin.

"Any idea of the current location for this other guy?" Fab asked.

"Aren't you the slightest bit worried that one of your business partners is dead? Is someone looking for you next? If so, hanging around here won't prolong your life."

"I'm not going back to South Carolina until this is over. I don't want to bring trouble home to my family," Jax said, lost in thought. "I need a new plan."

The questioning came to a halt as a relentless banging on the front door started. It could be heard even over the pouring rain that had just begun to beat on the roof. It wasn't Fab, as she sat across from me…so this couldn't be good.

"Open up!" a man's voice yelled.

Phil flew behind the bar, grabbing up the Mossberg shotgun. Fab and I drew our guns.

"Do you know how to use that?" Jax raised his eyebrows.

"We're closed," Phil called, racking the rifle.

"We don't want any trouble. We're looking for Jax Devereaux," the man said.

"No one here by that name," Phil yelled back.

I pulled Jax over to the stairs.

"At the bottom, make a right. It lets out on the beach. Keep in touch. You can send a message through Mac at The Cottages."

He kissed my cheek and murmured his thanks.

Half way down the stairs, he hurled himself over the banister, jumping to the deck before he took off running.

The banging stopped. Complete silence from the other side of the door. The three of us stared at one another.

"You two lay low." Phil picked up the phone and reported an attempted break-in.

"I'll sneak around the front, see what's going on," Fab said. "We could go out and hide in my office until it's all clear."

"Nice lighthouse," Phil nodded. "Stolen?"

"Why do people keep asking that?" Fab huffed. "It's not like you can stuff it in your pocket."

Phil and I laughed.

Chapter Twenty-Four

Fab and I tried to sneak across the parking lot. We had almost made it, when Crum and Carlotta came around the back of the lighthouse, arm in arm.

I did a double-take. Fab made a retching noise. Watching the two of them walk toward us sent a little shiver through me. They looked normal enough, but anyone who knew them would be scared. Crum had dressed up today in a pair of boxer shorts. Maybe Carlotta would be a good influence. If I had to put money on it, I would have bet heavily that she wouldn't be seen dead with him if she weren't desperate. Made me wonder what she was up to.

"Good morning," Crum said, looking rather pleased with himself.

"Do you suppose they're banging?" Fab whispered.

I tried to elbow her, but she saw it coming and moved away.

"How were your accommodations?" I asked Carlotta, knowing she'd never been in a trailer in her life before last night.

I also doubted that she'd appreciate the hard

work my brother had put into making the place into a happening tourist spot. Judging by the out of town license plates in the parking lot, the Trailer Court had been sold out again last night.

"The professor was positively delightful," she crooned up at him. "He made me feel quite welcome. He gives the best foot rubs."

Rendered speechless, I just stared.

Fab burst out laughing.

Crum cleared his throat. "I have two bedrooms, and I thought a woman of her stature shouldn't be by herself."

I wondered how much Carlotta had shared about herself, but I refrained from asking.

Carlotta giggled at him.

"Have you figured out your future plans after a good night's sleep?" I asked.

The two of them looked at one another and blushed, looking guilty. I sighed and hoped they wouldn't get caught horizontal by her son. I'd love to see the look on Carmine's face if Crum said, "You can call me Daddy."

"The professor and I are going to discuss my options. I'll let you know as soon as I've made my decision," she said haughtily.

One thing the two had in common — that same condescending personality.

At the top of my mental to-do list: call Brick and find out what was going on before this situation blew up in my face.

"Where's Harlot?" I asked.

"I found a…a friend gave me an old couch cushion, and I turned it into a bed for her. She's asleep in the sun on the enclosed porch."

I tried not to laugh at his BS story about his "friend". Wait until Carlotta found out that the esteemed professor dug around in the trash for that couch cushion.

Chapter Twenty-Five

"You know how you like surprises?" Fab asked.

Once I got in the SUV and the door locks clicked down, I knew we were headed somewhere I didn't want to go.

"I don't and you know that." I never seriously entertained jumping from a moving vehicle, and hoped I wouldn't regret not taking that foolhardy leap.

"I'm taking you to lunch — at The Whale."

Her toothy smile raised the hairs on the back of my neck.

I suddenly knew why. "We're confronting Kelsey James? Do you have your game day plan? Or is this why I'm being railroaded, to come up with something plausible before we get to Fort Lauderdale?"

"I thought we'd use a good cop/bad cop approach."

"You need me to be the nice person." I smirked.

I rolled down the window. The salty smell of the Atlantic blew across my face, another reminder of why I never regretted relocating to South Florida. The drive along Ocean Boulevard, although heavily trafficked in certain places, never got old. I craned my neck to watch the crystal blue waters crashing onto the white sand.

The restaurant was a nondescript building across the street from the ocean. It was a gorgeous day, baby blue skies, a few fluffy clouds, and there wasn't a vacant chair on the outside patio.

Fab pulled into a parking space next to a white jeep. She looked in the rearview mirror. Kelsey James was in the parking lot, a lucky blow for us.

"Right on time," she said. She jumped out and I followed.

Fab leaned against the driver's side door of the woman's car. "We have a few questions about Horton King."

The blonde woman wiggled her way across the driveway in barely-covering-butt-cheek jean shorts and a filmy hot pink top to match the ends of her hair. Kelsey didn't look happy. According to her driver's license, she'd just turned thirty.

I reached back into the Hummer and drew Fab's "police" badge out of my purse. Hopefully, Fab wouldn't ask how I came to be in possession of it, so I wouldn't have to admit to borrowing it and playing a little game with Creole. At first he wasn't amused, but he came around when he figured out what I had in mind. He did warn me against impersonating law enforcement, but there was no harm in letting people think what they want, even if it is incorrect.

Kelsey spotted us from a dozen paces away, a scowl lining her features.

"I don't know what you want, and I don't care. Now move." Kelsey tried to reach around Fab to get in the Jeep.

"We could go and wait at your trailer, ask Gibbs a few of our questions." Fab smiled, but it wasn't friendly.

"You're lame," she laughed. "My husband and I are simpatico. He knows everything there is to know about me. Tell him whatever you want. I'll call you out as the liar that you are, and he'll whoop your ass and toss you to the curb."

"He knows you've had a dozen men arrested on bogus charges?"

"That many? Men can't hit women and get away with it." She clucked her tongue. "As long as I don't press charges against him, he couldn't care less."

Kelsey turned to walk away and Fab grabbed her arm.

"Drop the charges."

She shrugged out of Fab's hold.

"Aww, is Mr. Good Guy afraid of a little jail time?" Kelsey wiped a non-existent tear from her eye. "A good lawyer will get the charges dismissed when I don't show up to testify. Out of my way, bitch."

"Do it now." I flashed the badge. "Or I'll drag every man you ever accused into court, and you'll be forced under court order to testify. Then you'll be on the receiving end of being charged with a felony or two and have a re-acquaintance with jail."

"You can't prove Horton didn't hit me."

A dark-haired man in dress pants and a dress shirt called, "Hey Kelsey," and waved.

I noticed his name badge, but his clothes were too expensive to be a waiter. The leather loafers cost more than a server would make in a month, so I took a leap.

"Your boss? Does he know you were fired from your last job for stealing? The job before that, you cleaned out the cash register on the way out the door?"

"Gibbs has a job, too. How about we show up there to ask a few questions about his wife and other men?" Fab asked.

"I'll give the prosecutor a call. Satisfied?" She walked around to the passenger's side, unlocking the door.

Fab, right behind her, handed her a business card.

"This is a lawyer who's expecting your call. No charge to you. If he doesn't hear from you in the next two days, we won't be back; we'll introduce ourselves to Gibbs instead."

Kelsey jerked the card from Fab's fingers and got in the car. After slamming the door and crawling into the driver's seat, she backed out of the parking lot, giving us the finger.

Fab and I pulled out behind her and went in

the opposite direction.

"You know what I noticed?" Not waiting for an answer, I continued. "She never said, 'but he beat me, bruised me', whatever. That's what I would've said. I probably would've thrown in some real tears, too. Getting worked over black and blue is a hideous experience."

"I felt guilty not believing Horton before I met her. But after reading the file Phil put together, I got over that." Fab's expression was grim. "Miss Hot Mess is reckless with other people's lives. It surprises me that she's still alive. Some people live under a shining star and get away with doing what they want, when they want. It's a bitch when it catches up."

Chapter Twenty-Six

Fab made faces and a couple of unintelligible noises at her cell phone, then ended the call with "text me." She threw the phone on the chaise next to her leg. I knew our short time lounging by the pool in the warm sun was about to come to an end. Hopefully, it wasn't something that would require guns.

"We've got a job," Fab announced.

"We? Funny thing, I never heard my name mentioned, and whoever was on the phone didn't ask for me."

Jazz looked up at me and meowed. Although he'd gone right to sleep like no human could ever do, he seemed to notice when I stopped petting him.

"Just once, can't you be agreeable?" Fab fumed.

"And miss out on an opportunity to irritate you? I don't think so." I pointed my finger at her, effectively cutting off her next words, and she glared instead. "I'm going to want something in return for all of my cooperation. Favors, IOU's, whatever you want to call them. You could replace your growl with... well... a smile would be too much to hope for, but something friendly. Say, when I click my flip flops, you do your cheery best. Are we agreed?"

"I don't like IOU's. We're like sisters."

"'Sisters'. That's so manipulative, but good. You only don't like them, because you didn't think there was a chance in some place excruciatingly warm that you'd ever owe me. Now that I have a drawer full, you're pouty. Deal or no?"

The ring of her phone broke the silence. She read the message. "Deal. Now let's go."

"Hold on, favorite sister. How about some details?"

"I'll tell you when we're on the road and you can't jump out." She laughed. "We need to change. Wear tennis shoes, and don't leave your damn gun on your bedside table."

I flinched at *tennis shoes.*

* * *

Fab blew down the Overseas Highway, past the shimmering turquoise and deep-green waters of the Atlantic and Gulf. The scenery never got old, rushing past swaying palms under blue skies with fluffy white clouds. Fab careened off the road at Islamorada, a city made up of small islands, halfway to Key West.

"It's a car retrieval job," she broke into my reverie. "There is a slight catch; this one doesn't have a GPS locator on it, so we have to find it first."

"It surprises me Brick would let a car off his lot without GPS, for as many that don't get returned. What are we looking for?"

"A 1960 cherry-red Corvette. White convertible top, in pristine condition."

"Nice! Do I get to drive it back?" I raised my eyebrows. "You can't drive both cars at once."

"You get to drive your car for a change. You have to admit, I'm a better driver."

I laughed at her. "You're delusional."

"We get one chance with this one, so we've got to be careful. I've only got a home address. It's on a one-way street. All the houses are jammed together, and the neighbors will notice a strange car. The woman has to know it's being looked for and isn't going to leave it sitting on the street."

"A woman! That's a first for Brick. He usually rents to dirtball men and criminal ones at that. What do you know about her?"

Fab was slow to answer. "Not a lot. She's easily excitable and doesn't want to give back the car."

"So she's crazy," I mumbled.

Nothing about this job added up, starting with Fab's evasive attitude. She'd been quieter than usual the entire drive. "Is this a routine retrieval? We find it, you jump out, get behind the wheel, and we drive away?"

Fab nodded.

"Do you have a description for her?"

"Precious Ivory is six feet tall, has waist-length black hair, and a big chest. She shouldn't be hard to spot."

"Wait. Who in the hell is the client?" I exploded.

In all the time I'd known Brick, he'd only had a soft spot for one stripper and that was Bitsy. I'd never seen her in one of his cars. He also didn't deal in classic automobiles. The only two I'd ever seen on the lot belonged to him, and they were brought in on a flatbed for service and went back to his house the same way.

"Okay, so it's not a Brick job," Fab said. "You'd never have agreed to help if I told you the client was Gunz. It's not like I lied. You assumed, and I didn't clear it up."

"Stop using that flimsy-ass excuse. Name one time I didn't help you. Just one." I poked my finger at her. "So, you're telling me that we're tracking down another whacked out, disgruntled stripper girlfriend of Gunz's. Are you forgetting the last one wanted to shoot you but decided I would make a fine substitute?"

"That's why you're my first choice to take to a shootout." Fab grinned. "You really are damn good, you know. Now if I could just get you past that shoot-to-maim thing."

"I'd better text Creole. If he gets mad about the short notice, be prepared. I'm blaming everything on you," I sniffed.

Fab pulled onto the quiet one-way residential street, a waterfront community that ran along a series of canals. The homes were built on stilts, each with its own individual dock to park a boat. She slowed for two herons jay-walking with no sense of hurry. Fab tolerated behavior in animals that she never would in humans. If these two laggards were human, the horn would be blaring.

She flashed up a picture on her phone. "It's the white house over there, the one with the hot pink trim." She pointed.

Two cars were parked in the driveway, neither of them the Corvette. There was no garage, eliminating that as a possible hiding place. From the roadway, each house had an open, paved space that ran to the waterfront. Most of the houses had it set up as outdoor living space, some with a small kitchen and barbeque area. This one had a large dining table with a raft of chairs to accommodate a crowd.

"Now what?" I asked.

"We can't be seen driving up and down the street. We lay low and out of sight. She's not going to hand over the car, and she knows Gunz won't call the police."

"Go back two houses and pull in the driveway," I instructed. "It's for sale and no one's home. Let me do the talking if we attract attention. You concentrate on not looking scary."

"I admire that about you. Your creative storytelling." Fab put the SUV in reverse and pulled into the empty driveway. "Great location."

I crawled over the seat and peered out the back window. It had a heavy tint, so no one would notice unless I pressed my face to the glass.

"What did Gunz do this time?" I asked.

"She caught him in bed with her best friend."

I groaned. "Some men are dogs. Horrible best friend, too."

Gunz had a kinky bent. He liked his sex delivered with pain, preferably from an amazon woman who had him trussed up. It excited him more if he thought there was a chance he wouldn't get out alive.

"Look." Fab nodded to the corner.

The Corvette pulled up to the stop sign and drove slowly down the street, turning into the driveway.

There was no doubt that the woman who climbed out of the car, one long leg after the other, was Precious Ivory. In short-shorts and stilettos, with butt-length dark hair hanging down her back, she stood by the door and scoped out the street. Her back to us, she bent slightly and paid an inordinate amount of attention to the driver's side door.

Fab crawled into the passenger seat. "What's she doing?"

"Has she ever seen you before?" I asked. "You need to jog by and check out every inch of the car. Too bad we can't borrow a dog."

Fab scooped her long hair into a ponytail, checking the street again before she got out.

Before the door closed, I told her, "Be careful."

Fab stayed on the opposite side as she walked up the street. Moving slowly past the Vette, she took a chance at loitering, knowing that the upstairs windows had a clear view of the driveway. A few houses past, she made a U-turn and doubled back.

I groaned, seeing a jean-clad pair of legs coming slowly down the stairs. I jumped out the side door and ran toward the house. Fab caught sight of me and took cover behind the neighbor's hedge. At the foot of Precious' driveway, I fell to the pavement. Sitting up, I grabbed my ankle and surreptitiously waved to Fab.

"Can you help me?" I called out.

"Someone's coming," I hissed to Fab, in case she was close by. "Don't take any chances. Just remember, Gunz has a track record of choosing unstable women." I massaged my lower leg and ankle.

Practically prone on the cement, I sat back up, not wanting an ambulance to get called. My only thought was to divert attention from Fab so that she could slip away unnoticed.

A tall, sixtyish man, with a hard glint to his eyes and shoulder-length grey hair tied in a ponytail, glared at me from the bottom of the steps, sending a chill up my spine.

His face showed years of a hard life. With one look, you knew this man wasn't to be crossed. He cleared the space between us in a few steps.

"No sleeping in the fucking driveway. Hit the road before I run over you." He spat, wiping his chin with the back of his hand, then wiping his hand on his torn jeans.

"Sorry, I tripped. Just catching my breath," I said. I grabbed the bumper on one of the pickup trucks to hoist myself up and earned a growl from the man. I made a show of standing up slowly, testing my foot before I limped back across the street.

I resisted the urge to look over my shoulder and ambled up the road. Fab had disappeared, but I knew she'd pop up in a minute or two. I needed to hone that talent. I stopped at the bumper of my SUV and bent over, hands on my knees. I didn't see anyone in the street, but I heard a car start.

An old restored pickup in immaculate condition pulled alongside me, and the man who'd just threatened me rolled down the window.

"Hey doll, want a ride?" he said.

This time I noticed his missing front teeth.

"Thanks, but I just live a few houses up."

"Whatever," he grumbled and then roared off down the street.

I watched Mr. Personality turn the corner before I ran around and jumped in the SUV. Even with my eyes glued to the rearview, I didn't see Fab coming before she appeared out of nowhere and threw open the driver's side door.

I arched my eyebrows at her. "Really, Fabiana. You have dirt on your clothes."

She made a face. "There's a wire stuck between the door and the jam that disappears inside. Most likely, she made it look like it was wired for some fireworks, but I heeded your advice and didn't touch it," she said, out of breath. "I was about to roll under the car when I heard you talking. See, I do listen sometimes."

"I hope you made it clear that the price goes up when there's a problem. My almost lying on the pavement qualifies as a problem."

"Did I forget to tell you it's a freebie?"

"Freebie," I said with disgust. "He knew where the car was parked. Why didn't he come get it himself? Why won't he file a police report? Because he stole the car from someone, or better yet, it has title problems, also code for stealing. A red Vette wouldn't be hard to find, especially since Precious is driving it around."

"Gunz is allergic to law enforcement. I need to go back over and see if she wired the passenger side."

"Forget it. You stick one leg outside this car, and I'll come around and drag you the rest of way out, toss you in the back, and drive us home."

Fab glared at me. "Don't threaten me with your driving. I need a moment to think how to get that car."

I bit back a laugh, but Fab looked ready to throw a full-blown fit. I liked when she yelled in French. Not understanding a word, I lacked the appropriate sympathy, prolonging her tirade. It could get pretty funny after a full minute or so of her screaming cuss words and me giggling at her.

"Threaten you with my driving? I haven't even pulled out my aces: Mother, Didier…and let's not forget Creole. He will actually strangle you, unlike the other two. You know how protective he is." I pulled my phone out of my pocket. "Which one to call first…" I tapped my cheek, giving her a pensive look.

Fab reached for my phone. Ready for her reaction, I jerked it out of her reach.

"Oh alright," she said.

"Would I give you lousy advice?" I asked her. "No!" I answered for her. "We're going to try something new for a change. We're going to walk away from a job."

"I'll need a good story," Fab frowned.

"Tell Gunz she had it rigged to explode. Dare him to open the door and play the odds. Maybe it's a car alarm, maybe not." I glared at her. "Why are you in business with him anyway?"

"He helped me get the cool office space. Who has a lighthouse? No one." She crossed her arms and scowled. "I didn't want some crappy trailer office."

"You wound me. You know I never do crappy. Old, maybe. I thought about getting an old house. Something with a porch so we could sit out front and watch traffic go by. I do like your choice, though. I wouldn't have thought of it. I didn't tell you, but Brad called and he loves it."

"Gunz is waiting for a call," Fab said.

Before she could get her phone out, a flatbed rolled around the corner and came to a stop in front of Precious's house and honked.

Precious bounced down the stairs barefoot, meeting the driver. They stood at the Corvette and talked. He handed her a clipboard, she signed something and ran around to the driver's side, dropping out of sight. A minute later, she jumped back up and nodded in the man's direction.

"This is an interesting turn of events," I said.

"What the hell is she up to?" Fab seethed.

The driver backed down the street, parking at the end. Precious jumped behind the wheel of the Corvette and pulled it up to the flatbed. She got out, patted the hood and blew it a kiss. It didn't take long for the car to be loaded and secured. As the flatbed rolled away, Precious waved and went back to her house.

"At least the truck won't be hard to follow," Fab said.

Chapter Twenty-Seven

Two hours later, after following the Corvette up the turnpike, the truck turned off on the causeway, north of Miami. Fab was in pure frustration mode, mostly because she had to follow the speed limit. At least I had something to look at as we drove over the flickering blue-green waters of Biscayne Bay.

"You'd better hope this guy turns off before we reach the ferry to Fisher Island, or this trip was for nothing," I said.

The island is private; the rich paid big money to mingle with those of their financial status. No one can step foot on the ferry without proper identification and a place to go. Uninvited lookers aren't allowed. Other private islands dot one side of the causeway, though most only have a sign as a deterrent.

Fab hit the steering wheel. "Now what?" The truck passed the last exit before the causeway ended at the open water. The choices were now down to the ferry or a U-turn.

I picked up my phone. "Is Brick in?" My tone was brusque, as I was not in the mood for polite chit-chat with Bitsy.

"He's out. I'll tell him your rude ass called." She hung up.

"She doesn't like me." I faked a sad face. "Brick can get us onto the island. We'll have to come back tomorrow."

"What are the chances we're going to find the 1960's Vette sitting in someone's driveway?"

"I'm telling you now, breaking into every garage is not on the list of options." I stared at her until she reluctantly nodded her head in agreement. "Why would someone let her hide what is basically a stolen car on their multi-million dollar property? What's in it for them?"

"This is a great story to get rid of Gunz. We won't mention that we have connections to get a pass for the island. Agreed?"

I flashed her a weak smile. The hairs on the back of my neck told me that getting rid of that bald bastard wouldn't be easy.

* * *

It surprised me when Fab pulled up to the docks and parked. I thought we were headed home until she passed the turn. She mentioned updating Gunz, but I thought she'd do it on her own in their new office. Some unfortunate fellow had taken the job of ridding the lighthouse of the noxious odor. To my surprise, he did a pretty good job.

"Are we hanging out in the parking lot, or

does Gunz have a boat slip here?" I asked.

Out of the corner of my eye, I saw Gunz lumbering down the sidewalk, and I pointed my chin in his direction. He glanced from side to side, as though expecting someone to jump out from behind the neatly stacked crates.

I silently chastised myself for not staying in the SUV and minding my own business. It was Fab's fault. I had to follow behind and stand close enough to hear every word, since she skimped on details in the retelling of anything.

Gunz scanned the parking lot. "Where the fuck is my car?" he yelled, throwing his hands in the air.

"Precious got rid of your car already. It's out on Fisher Island somewhere," Fab told him.

He continued to yell. "Why in the hell do you think I hired you? You get your skinny ass out there and get it back."

"Hey," I interrupted. "Lower your voice. Fab's not hard of hearing."

"Mind your own business, you scrawny bitch," he snarled in frustration.

Gunz isn't a man used to having anything he utters questioned. His menacing tone made me want to step back, but I forced myself to stand my ground and not puke.

He looked at Fab. "Why are you even seen with her? She's not in your league."

"Your girlfriend wired the door of your car to blow up. Before I could get to it, a flatbed transported it to the island. Go get it yourself. I'm not getting blown up for you," Fab said evenly.

Gunz's meaty hand shot out to grasp Fab's arm, digging his fingers into her skin.

"Step back or you're dead." I whipped out my Glock, aiming at the center of his chest, tempted to lower the aim to his minuscule friend.

Gunz turned at the sound of me cocking my weapon. "Nobody threatens me," he growled as he dropped his hands.

Fab jumped between him and me, hand on his chest. "Calm down and listen to me." She gave me a *'don't shoot'* look over her shoulder. "Put your gun away."

She was always grouching at me to shoot to kill. Now, when I was finally in the mood, she sucked the fun out of the show down. I compromised and lowered my gun to my side.

Fab explained to him everything she'd done.

I smiled my approval when she added a few details that she hadn't done, but it only made the re-telling of the story better. I'd have to tell Mother her tutoring was paying off.

Gunz shook his head back and forth like a bobble head doll the whole time she talked. His face was bright red. He didn't want to hear anything that stood between him and his auto.

"You know where it is, so go get the damn car. I know you can do it. Bring it back in one piece. She's a stripper; you can outsmart her," he said.

"Are you hard of hearing? She's not going!" I

yelled. I hadn't realized we had attracted attention; two fishermen leaned against the railing, watching the show. "You've got two choices, and neither one includes her services. Get it yourself or call the cops."

"If you know what's good for you, Bitch, you'll shut up." He took a step forward.

I raised my Glock. "I know. Call someone else and don't tell them it's wired to explode. While the sheriff is scooping up what's left with a teaspoon, I'll spread it all over town that you're the one to blame."

"Get her out of here," Gunz blasted at Fab.

Spoon materialized out of nowhere. "Is there a problem here?" He glared at Gunz. They nodded at one another.

Translation: They knew one another, but weren't friendly.

"Yes there is," I said, exchanging dirty looks with Gunz.

"Shut your mouth," Gunz roared.

Spoon slammed his hand into Gunz's chest, stopping his forward movement. "Apologize," he ordered. "Don't ever speak to her like that again. What's the problem here?"

Gunz mumbled something unintelligible.

Fab gave me the evil eye, and I ignored her and gave Spoon the details.

"Car's sweet. Always liked it. You want to sell?" Spoon asked Gunz.

"I want it back," Gunz grumbled.

"You find out who's harboring your car, and I'll retrieve it. Got a couple of flatbeds of my own. My boys will pick it up and dump it off anywhere you want. Use your manly prowess on Miss Ivory, and maybe she'll cooperate."

I laughed at the sex comment. All eyes turned and glared at me.

"Of course, you would owe me." Spoon grinned. "One more thing. These two are no longer available for the job. Are you listening, Fabiana?"

Fab ignored him.

"Did you hear me?" he asked.

I sighed in relief when she nodded.

"I can call you as soon as I get the address?" Gunz asked.

Spoon nodded his head in the affirmative, extracting a card out of his pocket and handing it over.

"One more thing. These two," he pointed to me and Fab, "they're both under my protection. Nothing better happen to either one of them—ever. Just to be clear, I'll kill you myself, and it won't be quick."

I'd seen his creepy smile before. Not only did it send shivers up my spine, it unnerved me and made me happy it wasn't directed at me.

Chapter Twenty-Eight

I stood at the kitchen sink watering the plants in the garden window, enjoying my ritual of morning coffee. It surprised me to see Fab pull into the driveway since, when I passed her bedroom door earlier, she had the Do Not Disturb ribbon tied around the handle. She thought she deserved privacy with Didier though, if the situation was reversed, she'd bang on my door and scream from the hallway. That's why Creole and I snuck off to his beachfront hideaway as much as we could.

I grabbed my ringing phone off the island counter. "You could just come in the house."

"Is Didier home?" Fab asked in an almost-whisper.

"Not unless he's sneaking around like apparently you are."

The line went dead at the same time that her driver's side door opened. Fab got out, coming around the front and dragging herself up the driveway. Fab was not looking her usual sexy self. She looked disheveled, her hair clumpy on one side. It had me wondering how the other person looked.

She peeked into the kitchen. "I need a favor."

"Is that grass in your hair?"

"You're not to say one word to Didier. Promise me."

"Not a word, unless asked by Creole. And on the condition that you give up every single juicy detail."

Fab let out a short breath. She labored under the misconception that she could best Creole at not getting caught sneaking around, and I hated to remind her in her weakened state that it hadn't happened yet.

"Didier's due home any minute. Stall him. I just need enough time to take a shower."

I watched her move slowly up the stairs. I could picture the reunion. Didier would take one look at her, frown, and they'd be arguing in French as he hustled her into their bedroom to wring the details out of her. I wondered if he ever got tired of squeezing the slow truth out of his girlfriend. I thought not, because Fab told me once he had creative ways of getting her to open up. She'd smiled as she said it, so his ways must be enjoyable.

Creole pulled up behind the Hummer, blocking it with his super-sized pickup truck. Good thing I didn't have a sneaky getaway scheduled for today. He put his face up to the heavily tinted windows of the SUV, first back, then front. Any coincidence that he showed up right behind Fab?

I eyed him suspiciously when he came through the door after picking the lock. I once offered him a key and he'd laughed. He was dressed for a day off. His hair was slightly damp, and he wore shorts and tennis shoes. I ogled his long, tan legs before making eye contact.

He lounged against the doorway, arms crossed, and a sinful glint in his eye. "What are you up to?"

I backed up behind the island. "I don't like your insinuation," I frowned.

He slid slowly toward me, knowing that whichever way he faked, I'd go that direction.

He crooked his finger. "Come over here, Babe."

"After you tell me why you were checking out the SUV."

"Your friend blew by me at a signal. I thought perhaps she might have a dead body to dump. You want to fill me in?"

"I'm going to catch you, you know," Creole teased as he went left.

I went right and laughed. "I don't know anything. You'll have to ask Fab."

I jumped when the front door opened.

"Why is this door unlocked?" came Mother's voice.

Creole's arm wrapped around me.

"Caught you," he whispered in my ear.

Mother entered the kitchen with an unhappy expression on her face, Spoon right behind her;

both had shopping bags loaded with food containers in their hands. Mother boasted of her home cooking, but in reality she was the connoisseur of to-go food. She served the food on pretty dishes and threw the containers in the trash.

"It's his fault." I looked up at Creole. "He was the last person in."

"Why do you look surprised to see us?" Spoon asked me, then peered at Mother. "Did someone forget to mention that she planned a party at your house?"

"Party?" I didn't bother to hide my confusion.

"You don't mind, do you?" Mother hugged me.

My family had an open invitation to flop at my house anytime they chose. "Of course not," I kissed her cheek.

The door opened again and Didier entered, travel bag in hand. He said an all-inclusive "Hello" and scanned the kitchen for Fab. Fab squealed from the staircase, and Didier tossed his bag aside and swung her around into a hug. I was the only one to notice her wince.

Brad and his family popped in through the front door. Liam brought up the rear with dessert boxes from the bakery, as always. Liam had long ago been assigned the job of getting dessert, and he did a good job always choosing both a long-time favorite and something new to try.

I turned in Creole's arms.

"You know, if you had gone all caveman after breaking and entering—thrown me over your shoulder and slipped out the back, we could be at your house doing naughty things."

Creole nudged me in the back and motioned in Fab's direction. She had left Didier upstairs and returned by herself, showing no signs of trauma. She looked her usual put-together self again, in black knee-length shorts and strappy sandals.

I intercepted her and linked my arm through hers. I nudged her through the French doors to a secluded spot on the far side of the pool. A favorite when you didn't want anyone overhearing. With an unimpeded view, you could see anyone approach and have time for a quick change of topic if needed.

"I need coffee," Fab whined.

"Then tell me what happened and make it quick." I gripped her arm and she winced. "You can't hide that you're injured from Didier. Look at me! Tell him yourself."

"I fell at the lighthouse." She looked away.

"What the hell did you do that you can't tell him the truth?" I shook my head. "And me. Your younger, more attractive sister."

It made me smile to see her smile. She had no come back, though. I wanted to hug her and reassure her that she'd be feeling better soon.

"Remember my corporate client? Turns out the information I gave him implicated the VP and his assistant. He wasn't satisfied with knowing who betrayed him to the competition and almost bankrupted his company. Now he wants to know why."

"Why don't you have him ask when he confronts the two of them? Or confront them separately and see which one decides to save their neck first."

Creole stood in the doorway, arms crossed like a bouncer. He kept a watchful eye on Fab and me as he monitored the activity going on inside the house.

"My client didn't confront either one. He must have a legal background, told me he doesn't want to ask any questions he doesn't know the answers to in advance. That's where I come in."

"You broke in again?" I yanked on the ends of her hair. "You snuck out in the middle of the night and didn't take me?"

"You made it clear you were averse to driving the getaway car for felonies. Before you go off on a tirade, you're right. It's my case; I should be the one to risk jail. Besides, I'd need you for bail and jail visits."

"Maybe I could have talked some sense into you."

"When do I ever listen?"

I hugged her gently.

"I hired Phil to dig around in the thieves' backgrounds. All she came up with were rumors of money problems and a gambling addiction regarding the VP. The assistant? Who knows, possibly love or money and she made a ton; her lover paid her well. My client wanted documented proof."

"Move along to the good part."

"You don't sound very sympathetic," she pouted.

I imitated Creole and growled at her.

"Last night I drove out to Plum Island and broke into his mansion. Unfortunately for me, he and the Mrs. came home early from a charity function, brawling. They were calling each other interesting names, back and forth, questioning about their parentage. I got caught off guard and had no time to make my getaway without being discovered. I wedged myself under a wooden ladder used for the top shelves of the bookcase."

"You should've called. What if something bad happened and no one knew where you were?"

"And get us both arrested? Believe me, I thought about it, but I couldn't come up with a Plan B," Fab said.

"How did you get out? Hurry up before we get interrupted."

Brad had taken control of the outdoor kitchen, setting up for all of us to eat and drink outside. The impromptu party had now been officially moved outside.

"Coffee," Fab groaned. "I can smell it, or I'm hallucinating." She noticed my irritation and continued, "I didn't think they'd ever stop fighting. I had to wait until they went upstairs and it took a damn long time before all was quiet. I hoisted myself out the window, lost my footing on the sill. I fell about five feet, landing on my back; the bushes broke my fall."

"Why not go out the same door you picked the lock on?"

"They brought the dogs in the house. Two big ones. They didn't seem to be particularly scary, but I was just afraid if they heard me or caught a glimpse, they'd start barking."

"I'm not giving you any more good advice, only to have you ignore it. Just so you know, Creole asked questions. It seems as though you blew by him on the highway."

"Can you keep him quiet?" she asked.

I shook my head. She always thought she could manipulate the alpha males in our lives, and I hadn't seen any evidence it had worked.

"I'm happy you're back, even in one slightly-blemished piece." I peeked over her shoulder. "Didier is headed this way. Good luck."

I kissed Didier's cheek and welcomed him home. Skirting around the pool, I headed straight for Creole's open arms. I congratulated myself for not running and drawing rude comments.

"You two looked intense," Creole commented, his blue eyes scanning my face.

I ignored his unasked questions. Since I hadn't been with Fab, I didn't feel compelled to share. I knew she'd see it as a betrayal. "What's the plan?"

"Early barbecue. Everyone has evening plans. Including us."

"You never said anything, so I made other plans." I smiled sweetly.

"A date or something?" His lips tightened.

"Not a date, more like something…" I said. I scooted out of his reach, turning my head to smile.

"You're not going," he yelled as I disappeared into the living room.

Chapter Twenty-Nine

I rolled to my side of the bed, enjoying the sight of Creole's bedhead and deep blue eyes devouring me in a wolfish way. We'd actually slept in—a rare occurrence, since we often woke up when the sunshine streamed in through the windows.

"What are you doing?" he asked.

"I'm checking out my legs. Do you think it's time for a pedicure?" I held my foot out for inspection.

"I like the hot pink toes." He ran his hand up and down my leg. "Why are your legs always so soft and smooth?"

"The hair doesn't grow back anymore— they're afraid. I used to wax, and I'd hear them scream, 'owie!' when I jerked them out by the roots."

Creole scrunched his nose. No waxing in his future.

"You haven't said a word about Fab's new business. Has she gotten a client yet?"

Uh-oh! Did he know something, or was this just casual conversation?

"You know, she stays busy," I said. That

sounded evasive, so I inwardly groaned and changed to a less dodgy response. "She did get a new account, a corporate account. She's keeping it separate from the legal car-boosting we do."

"Did you go along with her?" His tone was casual, but the detective didn't fool me. Right now he was in good-cop mode, but I knew he could hop back and forth between good and bad cop in a heartbeat.

He turned over on his back, pushing up against the headboard, tucking his hands behind his head.

"You know I like to hear about everything you do."

I made it a rule to never lie to him. Somehow he got me to include no vague story-telling in that promise. I rolled off the bed on the opposite side.

"I'll make coffee," I said as I scurried off in the direction of the kitchen.

"If you run out the door, don't forget your shoes. I'll track you down. You'll be the only naked woman running down the side of the road." He gave an evil little laugh.

I sighed, happy I had my back to him, because my cheeks blazed with heat. The thought of him in hot pursuit made my knees weak. I loved our little games of chase. He'd catch me and scoop me into his arms.

While waiting for the coffee to brew, I grabbed his t-shirt off the chair. Slipping it over my head,

I went out to the patio and cleaned off the table. The view over the Gulf of Mexico was spectacular any time of day, any kind of weather.

How Creole found this isolated piece of beachfront property amazed me. He had the last house on a dead-end that curved around the water. Only a handful of houses had been built here, the nearest one at least a quarter of a mile down the road. A real estate investor friend alerted him to the tear-down after the owner decided it would require too much cash for an investment property he wouldn't live in and couldn't unload on someone else at the profit margin he required.

Creole had stripped it down to the studs, keeping the original footprint. What had once been a small three bedroom home, he rebuilt into one large space with a separate bathroom that rivaled the kitchen in size.

Figuring his coffee was ready, I stopped my musings and went inside. My coffee only required a microwave and some mix. Creole preferred some sort of smelly dark roast. Not as bad as Fab, though, whose morning beverage brewed up into thick slime.

Creole ran his fingers up my back and pressed me up against the counter. "Hands over your head," he barked.

My hands shot up. He pulled his t-shirt over my head and wrapped his arms around me, nibbling my neck.

"You get the shirt back when you answer my questions." He pushed me down, kissing up my spine.

"You're so mean," I moaned.

"I see you're going to need a full interrogation." He left a trail of biting kisses across my shoulders. "Do you want me to stop?"

"Nooo," I whimpered.

"This time she didn't include me," I said breathlessly. "Not a word that she had a job or that she was leaving. Any particulars about the job, you'll have to ask her."

"Was that so hard?" He jerked me around and kissed me hard.

"If one of her jobs goes awry, you can't expect me to tell on her."

"Something did happen. Something she wasn't expecting."

He thought he had me caged, but I had a trick up my sleeve and changed the subject.

"What time do you have to leave?"

"Got the day off."

I unbuttoned his jeans and slowly unzipped them. I pushed them down his thighs. I tapped his leg and he stepped out one foot, then the other. I took his hand to drag him over to the bed, stopping short when he jerked me back against his chest.

"Here's fine," he whispered against my cheek as we slid to the floor.

* * *

Both of our phones started ringing at the same time. While Creole fished his phone out of his pocket, I went out to the deck to find out why Fab not only called, but texted 9-1-1. Since she was not given to theatrics, I had a bad feeling waiting for her to answer my return call.

"There's another dead body," Fab whispered.

"Where are you? Anyone else hurt?" I couldn't bring myself to say dead. "Tell me someone didn't dump another head."

"Everyone's fine," she reassured. "Take a breath. Calm down. Just get home and drag lover boy's ass along with you."

"I'll be right back," Creole yelled from inside the house.

"Got to go," I told her.

Creole was halfway out the door.

"You stop right there. I'm coming with you!" I screeched.

"You are staying here," he ordered. "It's not safe. I'll be back as soon as possible."

I raced into the kitchen and picked up his t-shirt, sliding it over my head. "If you leave this house without me, I'll walk to the main highway and hitchhike." I grabbed my purse off the counter and tried to push past him.

"Just please stay here."

"You listen to me. I'm going. It's my house, my family. How dare you make decisions for me!" I seethed in hot anger. "I can't believe that if my phone hadn't been turned on, you would have left me out here. By myself, with no transportation, in ignorance, while you figured out what to do."

He threw open the gate and opened the passenger door. "Get in."

Neither of us said a word the whole way back to my house.

He squealed around the corner of my street and parked across from the house. None of the neighbors were milling around, and there was no sign of a law enforcement vehicle.

The gate stood open, the body of a jean-clad male lying in the middle of the driveway. Creole reached for me and I sidestepped him.

"I might know him," I said.

At least this one had his head.

I paused when I heard my name being called. I turned and saw Fab run around the side of the house, Didier two steps behind her.

"Anyone we know?" I asked her.

"Never seen him before." Her eyes were huge; she looked unnerved. "Didier and I were going out for breakfast, and that's when we found him."

Creole was off to the side, his phone to his ear. The conversation was short. He stashed the phone in his pocket and motioned Didier over.

The guy confab irked me. I hoped Creole would share information.

"Did you get pictures?" I asked Fab.

When she nodded that she had, I said, "Let's go in the house." I looked over my shoulder and saw the guys still talking.

"Brace yourself; Creole's not going to want us to stay here. He made noises about us relocating when the head showed up. Maybe we should think about going to The Cottages."

"Don't take this personally, but there's no room service and way too many weird people," she said with a frown.

We avoided the front door, although the body was only a couple of feet away, and cut through the side path instead. Once inside, I headed straight for the kitchen window, where we had an unobstructed view of the driveway. Unfortunately, the body was in plain view, too.

"Creole and I are fighting," I declared to Fab. "He just tried to leave me behind with no intention of filling me in. He's not happy I made threats to get a ride, and the feeling's mutual."

Fab hugged me. "You'll make up. He's just trying to protect you."

"I could use some alcohol but, since it's not even noon, I guess I'll have water." I opened the refrigerator door. "Want to join me?"

"After the shock, Didier went ballistic. He's already agreed with Creole that we should stay somewhere else. He mentioned Miami Beach. When the two of them figure out they are on the same page, the pressure will ramp up."

"What in the hell is going on?" I whimpered, as I leaned over the sink, my head in my hands. Creole and Didier had moved to the end of the driveway. "Why has my house suddenly become a dumping ground for bodies? Bodies of men we don't know. I haven't made anyone mad lately. Have you?"

"It's a message to one of us or someone connected to us. It normally means stop whatever you're doing, or you'll end up in the same condition. We need to figure out the whatever."

Thankfully none of my family had stayed overnight after yesterday's get-together. Even though we were the only two in the house, I leaned into her ear and whispered, "Jax."

"Why are you whispering?" She peeked out the window. "They're still out there, haven't moved."

"Do you think this man is the other partner that Jax mentioned the other day?" I wrinkled my nose at her. "I've got Phil looking for him again so we can finish the conversation we started. She's good, better than any of the locals we've used in the past." I'd given Phil instructions to find him ASAP and to dig around for any information she deemed pertinent.

"I like that the ballsy blonde can back up her big talk with results." Fab continued to stare out the window. "Let's go to Miami."

"Too far for me. I'd be totally out of touch

with the Cove, and that's not a good idea. I'd rather hide in plain sight. You go and enjoy sitting on the powdery white sand, drinking your nauseating vodka drinks." I held out my pinky finger. "Swear you won't divulge our ultimate hideout. If we get separated, we meet up there."

Chapter Thirty

Kevin squealed his squad car up to the house with no lights on and triple-parked so that he was blocking one side of the street. He waved, catching me gawking out the window. At least it was a nice change from stomping over and threatening to arrest me on the off chance that I might have been the one to kill the guy.

It surprised me that the next car to block the street belonged to my brother. It also sucked. Ever since my brother and Kevin had become pals, all sheriff calls involving me got reported before I had a chance to make the call myself. On the upside, this meant that I could tell Brad that he'd be the one to call Mother with the grisly details.

"That makes me nauseous." Fab pointed to the four men standing off to the side. "When did they get so friendly?"

"Since they started hanging out together, challenging each other. Running, biking, always a competition to see whose is bigger." I smiled at her, knowing what she was thinking.

"Didier's."

I burst out laughing. "You're so juvenile."

"We have more company," she said, nodding to the driveway.

Two more sheriff cars drove up and, behind them, the coroner's van approached.

"I'm going out and sitting by the pool. If anyone asks, tell them I went to Key West," I said.

"Since your SUV is blocked in, that's not going to sell. Besides, you might want to hold off. The guys are headed our way."

The front door opened and Creole stomped in, Didier and Brad behind him. Whatever the bad news was, Creole had drawn the short straw.

"Pack lightly," he ordered, his lips in a hard line. "Leave your phones on the counter. I'll find someone to take care of Jazz."

I ground my teeth together and then pinched myself as a reminder to break that bad habit. "Where are we going?"

Didier moved to Fab's side and put his arm around her while she stared daggers up at him. Brad leaned against the kitchen door frame, a smirk on his face, knowing that ordering me around wasn't going to be well-received.

Arms across his chest, his best perp scowl on his face, Creole said, "I'm moving the two of you to a safe house until we figure out what's going on and get this case solved."

"I think asking would have been a better tactic. I'm not a criminal deserving of one of your tight-ass edicts. Fab and I can go to Mother's and take Jazz with us. No one's going to show up there."

Creole's hand slammed down on the island between us.

"You don't know that," he growled. "Don't you care if someone you know ends up dead?"

"We've proven we can take care of ourselves and be useful to law enforcement all at the same time!" Fab blasted him.

"I don't think Mother's house is a good idea," Brad spoke up. "What about black cat hair on her white furniture?"

She'd flip! I thought.

"Jazz does not get foisted off on someone just because it's convenient to you." I struggled to remain calm. "I approve wherever he goes, and that list is extremely short."

Jazz must have heard his name and sauntered into the kitchen. With all these people standing so close to the refrigerator, he probably thought he might get lucky. I picked him up and nuzzled his neck. Fab reached into the refrigerator, pulling out a butcher paper-wrapped treat. He meowed at the top of his lungs.

Didier hugged Fab. "You two need to listen. It is not acceptable if either of you ends up hurt or dead. This way, you'll both remain safe."

"We could call Mother and see how she votes," Brad said. "I can tell you, she hasn't wanted you to stay here since the head incident."

Fab walked into the living room, and threw

herself on the couch.

"Don't you think you could have consulted us and not just ordered us around?" I asked.

"Sorry I forgot my party manners, but your life is on the line!" Creole yelled.

Didier said something in French, and Creole calmed somewhat.

I set Jazz on the floor and flopped on the daybed.

"They do this all the time," I told Brad. "They're rude and never translate."

Brad kicked my foot and sat down next to me, leaving Creole to sit in a chair.

Didier said something to Fab in French. She erupted, and they started yelling at one another. Creole smirked, so I knew Didier was winning that argument.

Creole and Didier spoke three languages, Fab two, and I knew a handful of bad words in various languages.

"How many languages do you speak?" I asked Brad.

He smacked my leg.

"Five or six," he chuckled. "All dirty words, courtesy of the professor.

Fab took her phone over to the patio door. "Mac will take care of Jazz. I gave her instructions and told her if anything happened to him, I really will kill her. She's to spoil him and never ignore his meows."

My eyes teared up. Jazz would love lying in

Mac's big lap while she devoured one of her romance novels. "She's okay with cats?"

"Mac said not to worry, animals like her. She was honored to be asked. I told her she was our first choice."

"I don't want to go anywhere," I whined. "You go to Miami. I'll stay here and barricade myself in and shoot trespassers."

"There is a second option," Brad said. "I'm getting ready to pull out on a fishing trip."

The thought of being out on the open ocean, water churning around...or worse, getting caught in a storm, the sides of the boat battered from every direction, made me queasy.

I felt ganged up on. Fab's complacency and silence on the subject annoyed me. It was hard for me to believe she wanted to be locked up somewhere, being told what she could and couldn't do.

"Let's pack." I swept past her, picked up Jazz and kissed him until he meowed with annoyance.

"No electronics," Creole yelled after me.

I pulled out a black leather overnight backpack, a gift from Fab. The special part was that it had a false bottom. My aunt had installed a wall safe that I discovered when I removed a painting one day to hang one of my own. Luckily, she had used the same code on everything. The safe originally held a couple pieces of jewelry, which I gave to Mother, and some cash which I'd split with my brother. I refilled the safe with a stack of cash in different denominations, two guns, gifts from Brad, and several throwaway phones with minute cards.

I lifted the cover in the bottom of the bag, then took everything out of the safe and stashed it in the bag, along with a box of ammunition. No one knew I liked to hoard cash, but I had made a game of it since high school. Before replacing the lid, I put my notepad on top. I didn't worry about Fab because I knew she kept her bag pre-packed with pretty much the same things.

I threw in a couple of jean skirts with plenty of pockets, several t-shirts, underwear and a pair of tennis shoes in addition to another pair of flip-flops. It overwhelmed me looking in the bag, knowing I only had a change of clothing for a few days. And then what? How long would we be hidden away? I hated unanswered questions.

Looking down at my flirty skirt, I decided a change of wardrobe was in order. I peeled off the skirt and tossed it on the bed in exchange for my favorite comfort outfit, my crop sweats. I wasn't sure what to wear while hiding out, but these seemed like an easy choice, and I slipped into them with glee.

Creole opened the bedroom door as I was about to toss my bathing suit into my bag.

"You won't need that," he said. "You two won't be staying at the beach."

"Of course not," I mumbled. *Why should it be anywhere fun?*

I threw my toiletries in a separate bag, holding my breath as I glanced over my shoulder and saw Creole look in the bag. He didn't dig around inside, but he did check the side pockets.

I zipped the bag. "Where are we going?"

He didn't answer me.

I followed him downstairs and wondered if our relationship would survive. I checked the furniture. "Where's Jazz?"

"Didier is taking him to Mac."

Brad had also snuck out the door. No hug, no kiss, only a pat on the head when he sat next to me.

Men!

I hated all of the decision-making on my behalf. It would have been nice to know Jazz was leaving, since he'd been with me longer than anyone in the house. Creole glared at me in cop mode, and I had zero appreciation for his high-handed techniques.

I knew this was for my safety and Fab's. I just wanted to be consulted. Zapping away my decisions stung, and he looked too damn comfortable in this new role. This was my first taste of protective custody, where the agent in charge told you what to do and you just did it. I struggled to control my temper and drop the surliness.

Fab's continued lack of opinion astounded me.

It must be that Didier or Fab had another plan. As long as I'd known Fab, she didn't take direction at all.

"Before you ask," Creole said. "Didier took the Hummer. When he's done, he's dropping it off at Spoon's auto body shop, where it will be stored until you get back. It's not like its some old Buick; it sticks out and is well-known around town."

"Does Fab know we're taking the Mercedes?" I asked.

Fab stood at top of the stairs listening to the conversation, bag in hand. She had a pinched look on her face, as though struggling to control her irritation. So she wasn't just going along with the plan, not as much as I had thought.

Creole stood in the middle of the living room, his eyes shifting between the two of us. "I'll be driving you."

"Let me get this straight!" Fab yelled. "You're going to take us to some undisclosed location and leave us with no ride, no phones, and no electronics? For how damn long?" She stomped down the stairs, ending up in front of Creole, glaring.

At long last, there was the explosion. The angry words were sweetness to my ears, as I agreed with every one of them.

Creole pasted a patient look on his face, prepared for her tirade, probably wondering what took so long. He picked up two phones off the coffee table and handed one to me and the other to Fab, which she jerked out of his hand.

"My number is programmed in," he said.

"So if something goes wrong, we have to hope you answer your phone and that the call doesn't go to voicemail. Oh, and the big one, that you show up in time," Fab protested.

Fab stepped away from him and caught my raised eyebrow. She marched out of the house ahead of me and climbed into the back seat, which she never did, and I silently questioned her. She shrugged, saving her energy for a confrontation she could win.

"My house? My plants?" I asked.

"I've got it handled," Creole said. As he climbed behind the steering wheel, he handed me his phone. I looked at the screen, and it showed a picture of Mother.

"I guess you know," I said to her.

"I'm not happy either, but I love you and want you to be safe. Brad called and told me. We both want you safe." Mother made a kissy noise. "Don't be so hard on Creole; he's doing what he's trained to do."

"I love you back."

"You're a lot like me," she said with a laugh. "So try and behave for as long as you can. Hopefully it will be over soon. Pass the phone to Fab."

I handed it over the seat.

She covered the phone and kept her voice

down. I never heard the exotic Fabiana make a kissy noise before, and yet she did to Mother. It pleased me as much as I knew it would Mother. Fab handed the phone back. I looked at the screen and the call had been disconnected.

"No goodbye?" I looked at Fab.

"I'll tell you later what she said."

I wanted to put my head back against the seat and close my eyes, but I needed to pay attention so I knew exactly where we were going. I decided that for the moment I would change my attitude. I wanted to live, so I'd cooperate.

Chapter Thirty-One

Creole turned off at Conch Key. A few turns later, after passing a couple of drunks asleep on benches, he turned onto a side street across from a commercial section of the docks. Looking around the mostly vacant cul-de-sac, the ten foot high mountain of clam shells outside the fish businesses caught my eye. Two warehouses stood side by side. The next hurricane winds would blow the wooden one down.

Creole pulled up in front of a concrete building with an old weathered sign hung by a cord, boasting that it had once been a boat repair place. Withdrawing a remote from the console, Creole pressed a button and the barbed wire fencing parted to let us into the parking area. Another touch of the button, and a ground-to-roof steel door rolled up. Creole drove in, letting the door close automatically behind us.

Creole turned on his headlights. The two-story building appeared to be empty. The only other exits were a door at the back of the building and a small, grimy window that barely let any light in. A steep set of steps led up to the second level, a single metal door at the top.

"This is creepy," I said, not wanting to get out of the truck. In my new spirit of cooperation, I took Creole's hand as he helped me to the ground. He reached into the back and grabbed our bags.

Fab pushed me in front of her as I followed Creole reluctantly up the metal stairs. I hated stairs, especially steep ones. I gripped the skinny pole railing and started up, counting each step. Forty-four in all.

Creole surprised me by producing a key instead of a lock pick, and unlocked the red steel door. The door had a small square window, with a stained rag covering the glass. It opened into a huge concrete room. There was a strip kitchen along a side wall and a door in the corner that went, I assumed, to the bathroom. There was a pair of sliding glass doors that opened on to a chicken wire-enclosed deck. I could see an inlet of dirty water below, stagnant and murky.

I guessed that the place was once a business office. It was now partially furnished with the bare necessities, including two double beds on the far wall, a worn out couch, a couple of chairs, and an old maple table. The large space had tons of potential for a renovation, but that wasn't why we were here.

I eyed the dust balls and the dead roach on the floor and thought it could stand a good cleaning. I had all the fight sucked out of me. I turned away and sniffed back a tear and swiped at the corner of my eye.

"It's not even clean." I looked at Creole.

Fab looked ready to shoot him, which made me feel somewhat better. "This is the best you could do?" She looked around, hands on her hips.

Creole ignored us both. "Do I need to get someone to stay with you two, or can you be trusted on your own?"

"We'll be fine," Fab growled at him.

Creole blew out an angry breath and managed to bite back a retort. "There's food, television, and some playing cards and other stuff in the cabinet. I'll be back later."

"If you don't have an update for us, just call," Fab snapped.

"What don't you get? This is about saving your life!" He slammed the door.

I sunk down into an old kitchen chair with a worn out linoleum seat and covered my face with my hands.

"Don't get comfortable," Fab said sharply. "We're not staying long. He gets one day to solve the murder. Tomorrow we're breaking out of this jail." She slid open the patio doors and walked out to inspect the deck.

Thinking about a jail break sounded exciting, but in reality, I hoped it wouldn't include jumping from the second story. Fab inspected every inch of the wired-in enclosure, kicking it in a couple places. It only gave a few inches.

She pressed her face to look over the side and yelled over her shoulder. "There's a fire escape, if we could get to it."

I hated to ask, *Why can't we just go out the way we came in?* I didn't want to point out only one of us had cat burglar skills.

She came back inside, not happy to have to muscle the door closed. "We need to play this smart, not do anything rash. Let Creole come here tonight, see us calm and cooperative, ready to play ball." She turned around. "What are you pointing at?"

"There's a door. Let's try that first."

"You apparently missed Creole locking it behind him." She walked over to the door and tried the knob. When it didn't turn, she kicked it. "We'll be screwed if this place burns down."

"Where's your lock pick?"

"Your boyfriend forced me to turn it over, and he did it in front of Didier."

It would have been better to stand my ground and come up with a plan that we could all live with. One that didn't include an abandoned warehouse in a seedy neighborhood.

I looked at the lock. "We could shoot it off, but that would have to wait until tomorrow."

Fab flashed her sneaky smile and jerked her travel tote off the floor. She tossed out a change of clothing; clearly she had no intention of hiding out for long. Next she produced a cosmetic bag that she unzipped, removing a flat container. She unsnapped the lid and produced a tool kit, which contained a small flashlight that she shoved into her back pocket.

"Let's prop this open." Fab opened the door with one of her handy tools, and looked down the staircase, then motioned me to help her move the marred wooden table.

Wait until both Creole and Didier found out that we escaped from the warehouse under their radar...fully armed and ready for a getaway. I was not looking forward to the wrath.

Fab flipped the switch just outside the door, and only a single light bulb came on. For once, she didn't slide down the banister. She shined her flashlight on the lock of the small door next to the roll up, and expelled a long sigh.

"I guess we can forget this door." She poked it several times with another tool.

"This one has been screwed with, something's mucking up the key hole." She slowly flashed the light around the darkened garage and landed on a tarp covering something large. She ran over and whipped the cover off. The shell of a car sat on the ground.

That would have been too easy – a getaway car! I thought.

Clearly disappointed, she perked up and continued her search.

"Look at this."

I slid up in front of her to see that she'd not only found another small entry door, but had popped the lock.

"There's nothing down here to prop this one open," I pointed out. "Do you want me to stand guard?"

Fab bolted across the driveway as I stood in the doorway and scoped out the parking lot. It was empty now, but could hold a couple of dozen cars. Fab unlocked the entry gate and poked her head out. She surveyed the neighborhood from her vantage point.

I sighed with relief when the gate slammed behind her, glad that she hadn't taken off on a more personal inspection of the area.

Fab looped her arm in mine and we headed back inside. "We need a plan."

Chapter Thirty-Two

"We should take a vote," I said as I inspected the couch, sniffing the cushions before I sat down.

Fab hopped up on the table that we'd dragged back across the room after using it as a doorstop. We made sure to get it back in the exact spot, the only four clean circles on the floor making our job easy.

"About what?" she asked in exasperation. "In case you haven't noticed, there's only two of us. No tie-breaker."

"Focus," I said sternly. "Why are we doing this? To be obstinate? Because we think we have the edge to solve the case?"

"Brattiness aside, we're much more useful outside digging up our own clues. Who knows more lowlifes than the two of us? One of them might have the information to crack this case," Fab reasoned. "Besides, how long are we going to last in this rat hole?"

"It's not oceanfront along a white strip of sand, that's for sure." I looked around the room and shuddered. "Think about this for a minute. If we pull this off, we run the risk of looking for new boyfriends, unless we're dead because they killed us. We're going to get a taste of life on the run, which we always caution others is a bad idea. We'll also light up law enforcement radar."

She laughed, all smug. "I vote yes!" She accepted the challenge, and I knew she would enjoy every minute of it.

"That's two votes for going on the run." I used my fist as a gavel and hit the table. "Motion passed."

"We hide in plain sight, right in the Cove. We can't stay on top of anything if we hightail it out of town. We've got the upper hand, since the detective doesn't have a clue how prepared we are."

At the mention of Creole, I winced. Even though I was still irritated at the high-handed way he handled this situation, I had to be prepared that he'd leave me. Of course, if I had to stay here very long, that would also have a detrimental effect on our relationship.

Fab broke into my thoughts. "We need a car and a place to hide out."

"Brick owes us big time. But faced with police pressure, he'd turn on us and give us a flimsy excuse about it being for our own good."

We both stayed silent, lost in thought, scheming.

I spoke up. "We have Brick drop off a car, one that blends in, nothing fancy, maybe a low-key SUV or something. Give him a short window and a public place to drop. Don't contact him again until this is over. If Mother weren't *doing* Spoon, he'd be my first choice, but Creole has her wrapped around his finger. I can't trust that Spoon wouldn't give us up as a favor to her."

"Really, Madison." Fab channeled Mother's stern voice. "Such a vulgar term, 'doing'."

"You sound like a cross between Mother and Didier," I laughed.

Fab shook her head, but she smiled back. "We need a place to stay."

"Normally, we'd have our choice of hideouts. But in this case, there's only one."

"Tropical Slumber," we said in unison.

"It's perfect," I said. "No one knows how friendly we are with the boys." The friendship with Dickie and Raul had worked out well for all parties. I'd become friendly with Dickie after my aunt's funeral. Fab had won Raul over when she hid out there to evade law enforcement. They were both insomniacs, and she'd waxed him in board games. If anyone asked me if I'd have a couple of undertakers as friends—the boys would balk at the term, preferring Funeral Directors—I would've thought they'd lost their mind.

"If someone did decide to check out the funeral home, there's a ton of hiding places," Fab informed me. "No one would look in the crematorium. Fire that baby up and no would set foot inside."

I felt faint at the thought of hanging with dead people. I should have guessed that during her short stay, she would have politely tossed the place, checking out every corner.

Fab patted my shoulder.

"There's no contact with dead people," she said, guessing where my thoughts went. "Well unless...but they're very protective of their guests. There won't be any unexpected visitors. Raul once told me that it was hard for them to make friends."

I lifted the cover over the false bottom in my bag and pulled out a cheap burner phone, plugging in the charger cord.

"Is your cell charged?" I pushed mine into the wall socket and hid it under the mattress on the far side of the wall. "We need that car delivered tonight here in Conch."

Fab, the Girl Scout, had hers already charged and ready to use. She held it up and flashed it at me before she punched in a number and handed it to me. I rolled my eyes when Bitsy answered.

"This is Madison, I need to speak to Brick," I said, struggling to be polite.

"Hold on please," Bitsy said with more sweetness than usual.

I clicked my fingernail against the fake wood, after taking Fab's spot the second she vacated the table top. I sighed and handed Fab back the phone. "She hung up on me."

Fab punched the redial button. "Put him on," she said in a hair-raising voice. "Now."

A few seconds later, Fab mumbled into the phone and handed it to me.

Why me? I mouthed.

"Your idea," Fab replied quietly.

"Brick, we need a big favor." I decided to skip the pleasantries and get to the point of our call. "We need to borrow a small car that blends in, nothing flashy. Preferably with tinted windows. Deliver it to Conch Key. Leave it parked in the Shopping Bag grocery store parking lot. As soon as possible would be a good time."

"You two in trouble?" he groaned.

"Not yet. Can we count on you?" I asked. "One more thing. When the cops come calling, tell them you haven't heard from us."

"You need anything else, call me," Brick offered.

I tossed her phone back. "Surprised me. He didn't ask questions and went so far as to offer future help. He was too cooperative; I say we ditch his loaner as soon as possible."

Fab half-smiled. "When Creole shows up, you have to be nicer, no arguments. Don't be obvious, but try to weasel information out of him. Don't encourage him to stay the night."

She added, "Don't you be too nice. That will make him suspicious."

Fab turned on the television. It looked ancient; it wouldn't have surprised me if turned out to be black and white. Instead, it had grainy color with a handful of stations. Maybe the dog ears, or was it rabbit, would help with reception. Apparently, law enforcement didn't have a budget for cable in safe houses. Fab flipped through the channels twice and clicked it off, slamming down the remote. The cover fell off and one of the batteries rolled out on the floor.

A drab rug differentiated the kitchen from the rest of the room. I ransacked all the cupboards, finding nothing but mismatched dishes and a few cooking utensils. No coffee! We had to be out by morning. The cupboard in the corner held an old Clue game with most of the pieces missing, a pack of well-worn Bicycle cards, and a box of poker chips.

"The one who wins," I said as I shook the box, "Buys coffee when this is all over. I prefer The Bakery Café, as you know, and don't forget I like extra whipped cream."

"Don't make me hurt you. I'm out of patience," she groused.

We both jumped to attention at the same time, hearing the garage door rumble up.

"Hurry up, hand me five cards." Fab slipped into a chair across from me. "We should have waited downstairs and jumped him from behind. Tie him up, and steal his truck. Let one of his undercover cohorts come rescue his ass."

I shouldn't have, but I laughed. "If that scenario played out as you just outlined, he would kill us. No doubt." I tugged on a strand of her hair. "Remember, happy face or something close."

Chapter Thirty-Three

Creole unlocked the door and entered with a brown shopping bag in his hand. He held it up. "Dinner from Jake's."

I stood up and took the bag. "Thanks," I mumbled.

Damn… remember – happy face.

He eyed me cautiously. I smiled back at him, making an attempt to ease the tension from the room.

"What's the latest?" Fab asked. She picked a few cards out of the deck, then slapped them down on the table.

"I win," she lied.

I emptied the bag of food and passed on the chipped safe-house dishes, figuring we could eat out of Styrofoam containers with the plastic utensils provided. "I don't suppose you left the margaritas in your truck?"

He looked relieved that I appeared resigned. He dragged another chair out of the corner.

"The dead guy is Rod Tanner. I've got people running a background check on him. We'll find out who he works for, something that tells us why he ended up on your property," Creole told us.

Fab and I exchanged looks. That was Jax's other partner. Now that he was dead, would Jax be next?

"You've been vague as to how long you're going to keep us locked up 'for our own good'," Fab said, using air quotes. "Does this just go on and on and…"

"I can get a guard if I have to," he barked.

"Go ahead, see how that works out for you." Fab laid down the challenge.

"Stop it," I interjected. "We've agreed to play nice. Just know this situation can't go on indefinitely." I looked at Fab and gave her a demented smiley face. "Creole doesn't need to add on another layer of humiliation, does he?"

"Can you assure this case is top priority and that you're beating the streets?" Fab stood and leaned into his face. "That this isn't some side job you get to when you have nothing else better to do."

From his lack of an answer, I had a horrible feeling this might not be a short stay in this dump.

I interrupted their stare down and asked, "Where's Didier?"

"Almost forgot." Creole pulled his phone out and handed it to Fab. She disappeared out to the patio.

Creole easily lifted me on to his lap and into a

kiss. It saddened me to realize it was the first time his lips had failed to distract me from rational thought. I understood his need to protect me, but I felt emotionally pressured. I recognized that I still hadn't learned to put my foot down, say no, and make my point of view heard.

He pulled back. He wasn't stupid; he noticed the lackluster kiss. "Tell me you're not mad. Promise me you'll cooperate."

"My promise has an expiration date, so wind this up as soon as possible." I hated all this lying and sneaking around. But if I shared my feelings, we'd both have a guard assigned to us in a blink. "Are you staying tonight?"

"I've got some leads to run down. Besides," he half-smiled, "I'd be afraid to fall asleep with Fab here. I'll be back in the morning with breakfast."

"We both like pecan rolls," I reminded him. When he got here and found us gone…what then?

Fab came back in and handed him the phone. "Thanks for that. Didier's in Miami. Another consensus — no one is staying at the house."

I closed my eyes and thought about the warm pool water, but sneaking home to indulge in a long swim would be foolhardy. I knew we'd be caught. We'd have to be careful in choosing places to hide.

"I'd sit outside and give you some privacy," Fab sniffed. "But guess what? No furniture."

She flounced across the room and threw

herself on one of the beds, walking her feet up the wall like a kid who'd been sent to her room without any toys.

"Unless you want a mutiny on your hands tomorrow, have an update of some sort," I whispered in Creole's ear.

We both looked at Fab who had started to sing, la-la-la scales. I bit down on my lip, but burst out laughing anyway. Creole looked disgusted.

"Stop! You're hurting my ears." I shifted in my seat and winked at her. It felt good to laugh, and I planned to ask for more entertainment later.

Creole lifted me off his lap and quirked his brow at me, gathering up the pieces of the remote.

I shrugged.

He flipped through the six stations available and settled on a sitcom that had seen more time in reruns than it ever did in a regular season.

I nodded at the bed but Creole motioned me over to the sagging couch.

"She sniffed it earlier," Fab told Creole. "Said it didn't smell all that bad and didn't see any bugs. Although, I think some of the little ones are hard to locate."

I flinched but remained in his arms when I really wanted to jump up and brush off my clothes.

Fab finally stopped the noise making and, with a quick glance, it appeared she'd fallen asleep, but anyone who really knew her wasn't fooled. I put my head on Creole's shoulder and zoned out. I'd rather read than watch television, but I hadn't brought a book.

Mercifully the television show came to an end. Creole kissed me. I could tell that he was feeling guilty. Not as guilty as I was, though, knowing we were leaving after he did. I made up for my previous less-than-enthusiastic kiss.

"I've got to go," he said, looking relieved.

I walked with him to the door.

"Good night, Fab," he said. She snored in response and kept it up.

My chest shook with silent laughter.

"I don't think she's one bit funny," he whispered in my ear.

I leaned in and gave him a long, thorough kiss, knowing it would be the last for a while. We had our escape planned once he cleared the corner.

Opening the door, he gave me a quick peck. It surprised me that he didn't lock the door. He might trust me, but not Fab. I put my ear to the door, listening to his footsteps on the stairs.

Fab sniffed at the air and then laughed at her own antics. "I smell a set-up." She walked over to the door and jerked it open, standing in the doorway. She poked her head out and looked around. "No alarm bells." She ran her hand as far as she could reach around the door frame.

"Get your stuff together," Fab said.

We gathered up our hidden electronics, the

only things we'd unpacked. I wasn't sorry to be seeing the last of this place. Happy I wore sweats, I slipped into my tennis shoes, bending over to tie the laces. This wasn't the night for flip flops. I shoved cash and identification into my pockets and strapped my gun belt around my waist before pulling my t-shirt down.

Chapter Thirty-Four

The hitch in our getaway plan came as soon as we stepped outside and saw the unmarked police car parked at the front gate, blocking us in. So that must have been what the text was about that Creole got right before he left. He didn't trust us after all.

We had scoped out the property earlier and knew there wasn't another exit. Even if I could be convinced to scale the ten-foot chain link fence, the rolled barb wire along the top took that option off the table.

Fab pulled my arm and motioned me to follow. She paused to peek around the side of the building.

I kept one eye peeled to see if we had attracted the attention of our guard and followed her to the foot-wide seawall that ran along the back of the property. I peered over the side and gauged the distance to the deck below, which required an eight foot jump and enough thrust to miss falling in the two-foot strip of slimy water between the seawall and planked deck.

Fab considered this as just another challenge to overcome. She certainly didn't consider going back and coming up with another escape route.

She shoved her backpack at me and slithered around a tiny space at the far corner of the chain link fence, one leg at a time, butt hanging over the water. On her hands and knees, she crawled to a set of steps that had been anchored to the seawall.

"Watch what I do; you're going to copy me."

Why couldn't they go all the way down to the deck? I thought. At least they made the final jumping distance shorter.

Fab hoisted herself to a standing position, and scurried to the bottom step. She jumped! Landing in a crouch, she stood up.

My turn!

"Look only at me," Fab called. "Do not look down."

This wasn't fair. She wasn't afraid of heights; the higher it was, the more she could show off. She told me before we met that she'd learned to scale buildings. Fab felt comfortable jumping off roofs, always landing on her feet.

I tossed down both bags, rubbed my clammy hands on my pants and listened to her precise instructions. I crawled along the ragged cement, thankful I ditched my usual skirt. Before panic could set in, I made it to the steps.

Once I got to the bottom, there would be a five-foot jump. Another chance to fall into the water, hit my head, or break my leg. If I were really lucky — all three. I took a deep breath and forced my brain to go blank. I channeled my inner Fab which felt like a cheap copy at the moment. In place—now the jump.

"You can do this," Fab encouraged. "Don't close your eyes. Take a breath and land right here." She made an 'X' with her foot.

I stepped off and landed close to the spot, on my feet, then I fell on my butt.

Fab gave me a hand up. "Sometimes you surprise me," she laughed quietly. "Come on."

We ran along the deck, which ended at a vacant parking lot. Thankfully it had a full set of stairs to get us back to street level and completely out of sight of the warehouse. Once we made it out, there was no car lurking nearby to haul us back. We cut across an open field, running over a short bridge that would take us back to civilization.

"How far is that grocery store?" Fab asked, walking down the sidewalk, checking out the occasional car that went by.

"I'm guessing about a mile. Should we call a cab? What if someone sees us?"

"No one knows we've escaped yet. We can walk it in the time it would take to make the call, and get the car out here." She looped her arm through mine. "Watch where you're going and walk fast."

Turned out the grocery store was closer than I estimated. Upon entering the lot, I spotted the Famosa Motors vanity plate attached to a small

SUV that was parked off to the side.

Fab retrieved the keys from under the wheel well. I took my assigned seat on the passenger side.

"We barge in on Dickie and Raul and then dump this car at Spoon's with a return-to-owner note,'" I said.

Fab picked up her phone and punched in a number.

"It's me," she said.

No speaker phones on cheap throw-aways. Maybe if I scooted closer, I might catch a stray word or two.

"How soon can you get a plain-looking car with tinted windows, nothing illegal? And a box of phones. Soon means the next couple of hours." She paused, then continued, "Arrange a drop-off away from prying eyes. After tomorrow morning, this phone won't work anymore," she said with a laugh. "Later."

She threw the phone on the console.

"Gunz?" I asked. If he came through, I might actually have to be nice to him.

"He'll do it and keep his mouth shut. No one will be asking him any questions, because he's nowhere to be found unless he wants it that way."

"I've got some calls to make before Creole finds that out we blew the warehouse. I think I'll wait until early tomorrow morning."

Now that we were free to be killed by drug

dealers, or maybe by Creole, guilt set in. We should have made an effort to cooperate. I should have anyway. Damn, I disliked these nerve-wracking adventures. More guilt.

Fab snapped her fingers. "Where did you go?"

I shrugged and ignored her question. How would Didier react?

"Hopefully, we can score the guest apartment," Fab said. She tapped the steering wheel in annoyance but stuck to the speed limit, not wanting to attract attention. "They keep it rented to college exchange students. If you can overlook the fact that you're at a funeral home with an assortment of dead people, they give five-star service."

Poor thing, she's lost her mind.

Chapter Thirty-Five

Midnight loomed by the time we drove into the empty parking lot of Tropical Slumber Funeral Home. Through multiple remodels, all traces of its original incarnation as a drive-thru hot dog stand had disappeared. Fab drove around the back to where the living quarters had its own private entrance.

"The crematorium is over there." She pointed to a recently constructed large concrete building. "Over there is a six-car garage and workshop that Raul had built. They used to park the hearse and business car out front, but they kept getting vandalized, the hearse being the favorite target. Now everything gets parked in the garage. I had a friend who owed me a favor, came out to upgrade their security system."

"You softie." I smiled at her.

Not long after we triggered the outside flood lights, the inside lights went on as well.

Fab knocked on the door. "Raul, it's Fab."

Raul opened the door in just a pair of jeans. His jet black hair stuck up on end, his shirtlessness showing off six-pack abs.

He put a finger to his lips and waved us in.

"Dickie and the dogs are asleep. They're terrible guard dogs, but they make up for it with a mean game of Frisbee."

Raul ushered us into the entryway, decorated with ornate furniture, brocade fabrics, plastic slip covers, and gilded accessories.

"We need a place to stay." Fab hugged him. "But first I should tell you, although we didn't commit any crimes, the sheriff will probably be looking for us."

He raised the shutter and scanned the driveway.

"Do you have suitcases?" He opened the drawer of a small writing desk and extracted a pair of keys, handing them to Fab. "The apartment is empty. We haven't made arrangements to rent it anytime soon."

He stepped outside and unlocked a second door, which led to a hallway of stairs that went to the second floor.

"There's also a back exit. This key will work for both," he informed us.

I ran back to the SUV, grabbed our backpacks, and followed behind. The apartment turned out to be a nice open space, with a living room, a kitchen, and comfortable bamboo furniture in tropical colors. It had a bit of a Hawaiian feel. A short hallway led to several closed doors. Unlike our last hideout, this one was white-glove clean, not a speck of dust.

"You stay here," Fab said to me. "I'll dump the

SUV at Spoon's and be right back."

"You're not going anywhere by yourself," I scowled. "How are you going to get back? It's too far in the dark. You'll get mugged."

Raul spoke up. "Tell me where to pick you up and I'll be waiting."

Fab blew out the door, Raul hot on her heels, before I could come up with another objection. It surprised me that he took us in with no questions asked. I knew they were friends, but apparently Raul trusted Fab not to bring trouble down on his head. It would be hard to explain to most people that, although law enforcement would be looking for us, we hadn't committed a crime. Even I wouldn't believe that story.

Distracting myself, I explored the rest of the apartment. I discovered two large bedrooms, each with its own bathroom. Both had king-size beds piled with pillows, the rooms decorated like high-end hotel suites. I dumped our bags in the green bedroom. It had a natural feel, and I loved the chaise by the window. Each room had sliding doors shaded with shutters. I slid them open to find that they both had access to a shared deck. The view was not spectacular, but it would suit our purposes; we could observe the street and see the comings and goings from the parking lot.

My next stop was the kitchen. I took inventory of the cupboards, coming up with my favorite bottled water. No coffee for the morning, but we'd remedy that. Stopping at our favorite café for breakfast would be a bad idea, since any number of people would recognize us. I couldn't wait to suggest a gas station for our morning brew and a donut.

The leather couch looked comfortable, so I made myself at home, turning on the wide-screen television. I laughed at my choice of over two hundred channels. I stopped on the shopping channel and muted the sound, making a mental list of those I needed to call before sending the phone to a watery grave. We'd have to limit our calls and continuously change up the phones.

* * *

I began to get impatient, but I was too tired to pace the floor. I maintained a vigil staring at the door. Worry was a useless emotion, but I indulged anyway. If Fab got caught, she'd never let Creole take her alive. I wallowed in my melodramatic thoughts. He couldn't possibly have found us out yet. Could he?

Interestingly, I didn't hear the car pull in the driveway but heard the lock turn at the bottom of the stairs. Instead of a grand entrance—throwing open the door and shouting, "Ta-da!" Fab jumped her way up the steps. There would be no sliding down the banister here—too small.

"Gunz called," she said, closing the door and turning the deadbolt. "One auto returned, no drama, waved to the security camera. Gunz chose a late-model Chevy Malibu, gassed and awaiting my arrival in the visitors parking at the hospital." She tossed me a set of keys. "Just in case."

"Do we have a plan?" I asked.

"We will by morning. Let's get a couple hours of sleep."

"We're in the green bedroom," I told her, turning off the lights. "I'm not sleeping by myself. Think slumber party."

Chapter Thirty-Six

Fab got behind the wheel of the midnight blue sedan and scrunched down, her head just clearing the steering wheel.

"Call Creole," she advised. "Let him be mad. One less thing to have regrets about."

"After this call, I'll give you the pleasure of running this phone over." I winked at Fab, knowing her love of driving over irritating electronics.

"Voicemail," I whispered. I had to admit, I was happy for the reprieve. "It's me. I'm okay. Thinking about you."

Less than a minute later, I almost dropped the phone when it rang in my hand.

"Where in the hell are you?" Creole hissed.

"We haven't gone far. We're tracking down a lead."

"Tell me what it is and I'll do it," he demanded.

Judging by the noise in the background, he'd thrown something and it had shattered.

I winced and nibbled on my lower lip.

"I'll come back if you promise to let us stay and help with this investigation and not seclude us somewhere."

He was silent for so long that I knew he couldn't promise me anything. At least he didn't lie.

"Come back and we'll talk about it."

"I'll stay in touch."

"Don't hang up," he barked. "Tell me about this lead. Anything to do with your ex?"

"We know where Jax is. We're headed to have a talk with him."

"Leave the interrogation to me. I'll make sure he's snack food for the alligators."

"I don't know…"

He cut in. "I know for a fact he's involved with a big time drug dealer. My guess, that's where the bodies came from. They want him, and they will use you to make the exchange before they kill you both."

"I have to go. We're stopping for coffee."

"I brought coffee and rolls, which you'd have right now if you hadn't snuck off," he half-yelled, clearly trying hard not to unleash the full extent of his anger. "I'd like to know how you pulled that off. Are you at The Bakery Café?"

I heard the engine of his truck turn over. "That would be stupid."

"Can I reach you on this number?"

"I'll call you if we learn anything new."

"You think you can elude me?" Creole

snapped. "You think I'm not going to find your ass?"

Fab jerked the phone away. "You're making her cry, asshole."

"I'm worried about her."

"I suggest you call Didier. Listen to his advice and take it for once. We'll keep in touch."

"Put her back on."

"Sorry, she's looking out the window, trying to hide that she's sobbing her eyes out. Remember that the next time you yell so loud you can be heard in the next state. I'll tell her you're sorry." She hung up and pulled the back cover off, removing the battery and card.

"You laid that on a little thick." I looked at her.

"Sounded totally believable," she smirked.

Chapter Thirty-Seven

"It's a good thing we chose the delivery option," Fab pointed across the docks.

During the road trip, I called Phil and she filled me in on her plan. Once I recognized the address she gave me, we drove by and scoped out Brad's boat at the dock. It showed no signs of activity, meaning he had no plans of pulling out anytime soon. At least we didn't have to worry that any of his crew members would recognize us. That done, I called Phil back and asked for Jax to be escorted out to our car.

Fab parked at the other end of the lot and pulled in backwards.

"If Brad shows up and catches us, it will be one more person angry at us." I scanned the parking area, not recognizing any of the vehicles.

Fab perused the area.

"He just did," she pointed. "Well, he showed up anyway. There's Julie waving at Brad, and Liam lugging a big picnic basket. They must have plans." Liam's new girlfriend, Lindsey, was a few feet behind, also dragging a couple of bags. "I like the girlfriend. She's smart, told me she's taking French for her language requirement."

"Maybe I can get Lindsey to translate for me. I like her because her niceness doesn't seem like an act to impress adults. Liam likes her, and she doesn't look like she's thirty years old."

I held out my hand and pointed to Fab's phone.

"You couldn't just ask?" she sniffed.

"You broke mine." I grabbed it out of her hand and called Phil. "We're here. Where do we go?"

Fab snapped her fingers and motioned to the lone figure coming up the stairs; Jax looked healthy and tan. Another man met him at the top, flashing a badge as he slapped Jax in handcuffs.

"What the hell just went wrong? He got arrested," I said in confusion.

"Calm down, that's my guy," Phil said. "Follow him. When he pulls over, you'll get your man. There's an upcharge if you keep the cuffs."

"Cuffs or not?" I asked Fab.

"Oh yeah. It'll keep his ass from jumping out in traffic. I'm not in the mood for a foot chase."

I could hear Phil talking on another phone, letting her man know we were right behind him. The guy shoved Jax into the passenger side of his pickup truck, slammed the door, and turned onto a side street. He took care to avoid any main streets, instead turning right and left a dozen times before parking on a run-down patch of broken concrete at the end of a residential street.

Fab watched everything that went down, smiling at the use of cuffs; she nodded her approval at the circuitous route to the drop-off.

"We could do these jobs," she said. "Wonder what it pays?"

"Kidnapping people?" I looked at her like she'd grown another head. "What if one of them ends up murdered? Or dies of fright in *your* Mercedes?"

"Your ex doesn't look happy," Fab said, stating the obvious.

Jax's handler dragged him, kicking, out of the truck. Getting jerked around by his metal bracelets didn't improve his manners. He unleashed his temper on the man. Knowing Jax, it was probably creatively profanity-laced.

"I'll get him," I said, as I got out and opened the back door.

Jax saw me wave and exploded.

"What the hell? You can't call on the phone like a normal person?"

"Not when you keep it turned off. You and I both know you never listen to your messages!" I yelled back.

The other man had on the outfit of someone up to no good. Dark jeans, t-shirt, most of his face and hair covered with a baseball cap and large dark sunglasses to cover the rest. He shoved Jax in my direction.

"You need help?" he motioned to the car.

"Thanks, I can take it from here." I waved to

the man, who'd just made some sort of grunting noise and was now already halfway back to his truck.

"Hey Hon-knee," I mimicked his version of the endearment. "Need a ride?"

The truck pulled up alongside the driver's side of the car, tossing keys to Fab.

"Need the cuffs back. I've got some rope if you need it."

"You promise to be good?" I asked Jax.

"This…" Jax jerked on his cuffs, "was probably Fab's idea. Get them off."

"Add them to our tab," Fab yelled out the window and sped off. "I don't trust your ass."

She flipped Jax the finger.

"You hurt my feelings." I smiled at him. "I think you've been ignoring me."

He kicked the back of the seat.

"The cuffs were my idea," I said. Better for me to take the blame and avoid an unnecessary shooting.

"This is your fault." I wagged my finger. "I had no way of getting a hold of you."

"My fault? Of course, every damn thing is all my fault," he barked, his face red with rage. He continued to rant from the back seat. I lay my head against the headrest, finding it to be hard and uncomfortable. I'd wait him for him calm down.

Fab hit the steering wheel. "Shut up before I shoot you."

I wish I'd said that!

Jax had finally wound down. "Uncuff me," he snarled.

I looked at him over the seat. "Gee, Hon, no!"

Fab snickered.

"This isn't funny." He kicked the seat again.

"Ouch, stop it," I whined.

"My wrists hurt. Is this some kind of kinky foreplay?"

Despite myself, I laughed. "Yeah, I'm climbing over the seat back, and we're going to drive around town and do it." I collapsed into more laughter.

"You're not funny," he fumed. "What the hell do you want?"

"You know how many times you've told me I'm not funny? Hurts my feelings." I frowned. "You hate it when people repeat themselves. Well, so do I. So let's go through this one more time. I want information."

"Where are we going?" he asked. "The Cottages?"

He had calmed down somewhat, but I knew well enough to know he was still fuming inside. If he had the option, he'd take his chances and jump out of a moving car.

"Your days of sneaking into The Cottages are over. Where you end up depends on how useful you turn out to be. You've got choices here. A cushy stay somewhere, or I turn you over to undercover cops who will lose your ass in the system. You decide."

"There is one more option." Fab glared at him in the rearview. "I shoot you, which is what will happen if you don't answer every one of our questions. I'll have you cremated, no fuss, no muss. Ditch your ashes in the trash."

"Start at the beginning as to why you're here. Maybe you forgot something the last time I asked nicely," I told him.

"I partnered in a money-making opportunity, and it blew up in my face. My partners are dead. There were other silent partners, but I never met them and didn't get their names. Since I didn't have the money to ditch town, and because of my desire to not end up headless, I took fishing jobs. They're good paying, and I needed time to come up with a plan. Who's going to look for me out in the Gulf?"

"Skip to the good part," I shot at him. "What kind of deal? Who are the people you're running from? What do they want?"

"What happened to that uplifting story about getting your act together?" Fab asked, growling at the driver next to her.

A blue Mercedes stayed at her side as she blew up the interstate. Now that she'd grown bored and wanted him to go away, he wasn't taking the hint.

Jax mumbled something unintelligible.

"You already know we were transporting

product to another state. Jones and Rod got the bright idea of shorting it a little to make some money on the side. After Jones turned up dead, Rod told me they had sold every last ounce. This job was sold as a three-man partnership. Another thing Rod let me in on after the fact: we were nothing but delivery guys."

Fab looked over her shoulder and made eye contact with him.

"What was your part in this operation?"

"I'd help clean and pack for shipment, scrub the rental house, leaving no trace of a grow operation, and trek across the country to deliver it to the waiting buyer in Colorado." He maneuvered around on the back seat and stared out the window.

"How did you find out about your partners?" Fab asked.

"Rod called and told me we had to lay low when Jones turned up dead. He assured me that it wasn't related to the job, but once I heard that they stole the product, I knew that was a lie. His girlfriend broke the news, called all hysterical, saying he'd been murdered. She wanted names. I hung up and threw my phone in the ocean."

"Don't you think you should've left town?" I asked.

"Why? I never met the brains of this mess. Hopefully he doesn't know about me."

"Are you sure?" I asked.

"Yes!" Jax banged the table. "Besides, I didn't

have the money. I've had a handful of fishing jobs but, without references, I had to wait until the last minute to get hired on, just hoping that regular crew members were too drunk to show up."

"When are you leaving?" Fab asked.

"Why is this any of your business?" Jax leaned forward and yelled in her face.

"Hand me that bag," I pointed to Fab's backpack. "Oh, that's right, you're handcuffed."

Fab and I laughed as I leaned over the seat and grabbed it myself. I whipped out the picture of the dead guy who still had has head.

"Do you know him?"

"That's Rod. I hoped he'd just skipped town. He was tired of the whiny girlfriend and wanted to dump her."

"Can't you guys just say it's not working out instead of leaving the woman wondering what happened?"

"I'm going to be sick," he moaned.

Fab careened the car to the side of the roadway.

I threw the door open, jumped out, and jerked open the back door, clutching Jax's shirt and dragging him to the side of Highway One. None too soon, he barfed on the ground. I hopped back to make sure it missed my shoe.

"I want the name of the guy you screwed over," I said, kicking his foot.

He moaned.

"Name now. Or I'm going to relate the grisly details of the two murders. You know how I know?" I leaned down and yelled. "Your good friend, well his head landed on my doorstep, then his friend Rod. But they must have been in a hurry, because he still had all of his body parts. Let me connect the dots for you. They want you, and they know you and I are connected. They probably know that we were once married, so apparently I'll do until they can get their murderous fingers on you. By then we'll all be dead."

"Stop, you're killing me," he whined and moaned. "Gimme water."

Fab tossed me a bottle and I held it up to his mouth. "Take a sip or you'll just be sick again."

He rinsed his mouth out, letting it fly across the dirt.

"Bonnet," he squeaked.

Bonnet! Now I was the one who was going to be sick. I leaned back against the side of the car feeling faint. I looked in Fab's direction and she banged her head on the steering wheel.

The man had his hand in all things illegal. Rumor had it he was the king of drugs and gun running. Anyone who screwed Bonnet ended up dead. There was never a shred of evidence found that linked back to him. Bonnet's arrest would be a huge star on any police officer's career file, if only a case could be made that would lead to a long prison sentence.

"How much did you screw him for?" I asked weakly.

"I had zero to do with the money. I thought I was being smart, getting two thousand up front for what I thought was a simple moving job." He hung his head. "Rod told me after the fact that the shipment was worth a half-million, and that's not street value."

Fab leaned out the window.

"You done barfing yet? We need to dump your body and get a plan together to stay alive."

"This is worse than what I thought." I kicked Jax again. "Does Bonnet know the weed has been sold? I suppose he wants money. He knows you don't have it, so you and your friends are going to be made an example of, and then he's going to try to scare money out of me?"

I reached in the window.

"Give me the keys. I need to get his shirt off. He already smelled like sweat and fish and now…"

She ignored me and jumped out, clearing a wide berth around him.

"He'll run." She had the cuffs off in seconds.

He stared up at me, a silent question of, "What now?"

I reached down and pulled his t-shirt over his head. I wrinkled my nose at the smell; at least he didn't vomit on it.

"If you even think you're getting sick, use it," I said, throwing it at him.

He didn't wait to be asked and leapt into the back seat, probably afraid we'd change our minds and leave him behind on this less-populated section of highway.

I looked over the seat back. "Did you give one thought to how much jail time you'd get for transporting drugs?"

"Okay, I didn't ask enough questions. Jones was a friend. I took him at his word, believed him when he said he needed a furniture mover. Coming back here for a few days' vacation sealed the deal; you know I love the beach. If I get out of here alive, I'm going home and getting a regular job."

"Here's the deal," I began. I hoped I wouldn't regret this, but I needed to be able to find him; I didn't have the time or patience to run around South Florida looking for him. "You need a place to hide out. I've got a friend who needs work done on his boat, and you're going to do it. As long as you don't leave the boat, no one will find you. You'll run into Mother, and you better be nice to her or I'll call your mother and tell on you."

"You know I'm the favorite," he smirked.

"Not if she hears of your latest adventure," I threatened. "Listen up: you need to stay put until we can figure out what to do. You don't want Bonnet tracking you anywhere, much less back to South Carolina and hurting your family."

"I planned to tell you everything when I

showed up at your house. Then I met your two house apes, and we got interrupted at Jake's."

Fab growled.

"If you leave the boat, you're on your own." I dug through my bag, taking out a new phone and handing it to him.

"I don't want it. I'll get my own and give you the number," he said.

"Fab, will you tell him to start being cooperative?" I asked in a childish voice.

"Give it to me." He stuck his hand over the seat.

Fab rocketed back to the Cove and took the first exit. There was nothing but dirt lots on each side of the road and a short-cut down to the docks only known to locals. She slid into a parking space and scanned the boat marina. No lurkers. All appeared quiet, with most of the boats in their slips and covered.

"I'll be right back," Fab said. She slid the lock pick from her pocket. "I'll check it out."

"This boat is owned by a man named Jimmy Spoon," I told Jax. "You screw him and heaven help you. He's not going to like that I hid your ass here, but do a good job and he'll forget he's annoyed."

"You're the best ex-wife." He kissed my cheek.

"Yeah, well, I like you too. You tell anyone and I'll laugh. Our mutual goal is for both of us to get out alive. So please cooperate."

"I owe you."

"If you mean that, keep a low profile." I hugged him. "Let's go."

We passed Fab coming back from the boat; she stood guard at the entrance gate.

"Spoon will be showing up for introductions and bringing you food." I handed Jax a phone. "Don't make any stupid calls."

"There it is, 'Fantasy'," I pointed. "Fab and I are in hiding. You see anyone shifty hanging around, run. Send a postcard so I know you're alive."

I walked down the docks, calling Spoon. I wanted to curse when his phone went to voicemail.

"Found you a mechanic," I said, then hesitated. "He's on board now. Be nice. We need him alive for right now. Favor — he needs a bag of food and soda."

I would owe Spoon huge. Fab shook her head at me.

"What?" I said to Fab.

"Spoon's not going to be happy with you."

"Jax is not free-loading; he knows about boats and can fix anything. Mother will vouch for him." I dialed her number. "What's with people today? No one's answering their phone? Mother, we're fine and both love you."

"Could your dumb-ass ex screw a bigger dealer than Bonnet?" Fab asked in disgust. "We need a plan. And fast, so we can go home."

At least someone was answering their phone

today. Phil answered on the second ring.

"What do you need?" she asked.

"We're leaving this car, same place, need another one."

"Anything else?"

"You're amazing, by the way. Dig up all the dirt you can unearth on Bonnet. Weaknesses, skeletons, the more the merrier. We need leverage."

Fab held out her knuckles. "Good call on the car."

Chapter Thirty-Eight

We got back to the funeral home intact. I threw myself on the couch, stretching out, hogging the whole thing. Fab smiled wickedly and kicked my feet off, sitting down on the opposite end.

Raul returned the car to the grocery store, switching for our latest short-term rental. We heard a rumbling in the driveway and stared out the window, wondering what would make that noise. Raul informed us that we'd received a 1990's Buick sedan. Although noisy, it ran great, and despite the stained carpeting, there wasn't a lingering smell.

I settled back against the cushions. Fab kicked off her shoes and stretched her legs across the coffee table.

"You're always harping on a plan. So now what?" I asked.

"We package Jax up and deliver him to Bonnet." Fab brushed her hands together.

I shook my head, "You forget we like his family."

"I was only half-joking because when Bonnet finds out that the weed is gone and that there is no money for compensation, your ex will be dead and you'll be back on his radar."

"I don't think even the sale of Jake's would cover the cost of the weed, forget the interest those types add on daily. My guess, Bonnet's not stupid, just felonious. He's figured out by this time there's nothing to get back. How many dead bodies until he's satisfied?" I didn't have a good feeling about besting Bonnet.

"I want to go home." I made a half-ass attempt at not sounding whiney and failed. "Not that I don't like it here at Chez Funeral Home, but I don't."

Fab's phone materialized out of nowhere.

"What do you have for us?" she asked.

I knew by her tone and question she had our favorite snitch on the phone. Procurer of Information, as Phil labeled herself.

"Any weak spots?" Fab paused and listened intently. "Keep looking and do it fast."

She removed the battery and card and threw the pieces on the floor.

"Creole stopped by Jake's and left you a message just in case you called in. He'd like to chat," Fab told me. "Phil said he wasn't his usual sunny self, more like frustrated and angry. She called Mac and found out that he left the same message with her."

I grabbed a pillow from behind my head and curled up into it. "What's the latest?"

"Bonnet lives out on Bonnet Island. When you're rich, you can buy a private island and name it after yourself." She half-laughed, clearly not amused. "It's only accessible by boat, and it's purported to be well-guarded. Mr. B is well known to law enforcement. He keeps his hands clean by farming out the dirty work to his minions, who line up to commit a felony or two to stay in favor."

I sat up and scooted over, shoulder to shoulder with Fab.

"There's only one person who can help us and that's Mr. Bad Ass himself." I dialed and held the phone between our ears. Repeating everything was getting old.

After a pause and a cautious hello—no one liked blocked numbers—I said, "You remember when we first met and you told me you were a problem solver, big or small, didn't matter, and offered your services?"

"Where in the hell are you?" Spoon growled, his exasperation radiating through the phone.

"We need your help."

"Get your ass to the houseboat and plan on staying," he barked, hanging up.

It surprised me that Creole's phone went to voicemail after he'd left messages all over town.

"Meeting with Spoon at his houseboat within the hour," I told him.

I hugged Fab.

"I'm sorry," I whispered. "Bonnet's only interested in me because of Jax. You should go to Miami and stay with Didier.

"I'm not going anywhere," she sniffed. "Get off your ass and help me clean this place. We don't want to leave anything incriminating behind that will get the guys in trouble. Good time to be leaving, too. Several funerals are booked, so we'd have to stay up here or not return until after dark."

* * *

Spoon, in a fashionable pair of ragged jeans and a t-shirt showing off his biceps, leaned against the concrete wall on the side of the Dock Master's building. From his vantage point, he could keep an eye on the comings and goings or slip away unnoticed. I felt his eyes on us before we got out of the car.

I'd been under the impression he lived in the apartment over J S Auto Body, his primary business a couple of blocks away. It came as a surprise when Mother informed me he lived on the water. According to her, it had plenty of interior living space and an outdoor entertaining area, and she liked staying there. Any socializing he did was on his other boat, the one Jax was currently repairing. No one got an invitation to stop by here.

"You got any other bags?" he gruffed as he checked out our shoulder bags. "Promise me right now that you two won't be sneaking off anywhere, scaring the hell out of your mother."

DEBORAH BROWN

He held out his hand and helped us on board.

I climbed aboard and came face to face with Creole, who sat crunched down in a chair; he looked good, his long tan legs hanging out of a pair of shorts. I honestly didn't know what to say. "Sorry we jerked you around" seemed more like a fight starter.

It surprised me that he'd shown up, instead of writing me off and looking for a new girlfriend who'd graciously accept help in the life-saving department. The thought of him being with someone else pained me, but it would be my own damn fault. I also opted out of launching myself in his arms and begging for mercy, as it might fall on deaf ears. Instead, I offered up a weak smile.

He crossed his arms across his chest and didn't say a word. His body language read, 'Done with you.'

"Didn't know you'd be here," Fab flashed Creole a suspicious smile.

I could kick myself for not having the 'be nice' talk with her.

"Sit." Spoon indicated some deck chairs that were situated under cover. To be seen, a person would have to be standing at the back of the boat. He pointed to a bucket of beverages on the table. "Help yourself."

"Did you talk to Jax?" I asked, stalling the conversation to come.

"The only reason his ass is still on my boat is

280

because of your mother. She assured me that he knows boats and that I won't be disappointed. Besides, she still has some misplaced fondness for him, and it appears it's reciprocated."

Creole groaned and shook his head.

Spoon glared at him and continued. "As added incentive, I told him once he's done with the repairs, I'd get him a plane ticket to wherever he wants to go."

I relayed what Jax had told me and refrained from a single embellishment, telling them how the two dead men screwed Bonnet. I told them how Jax claimed a certain amount of ignorance in the beginning and that I believed him. The Devereaux and Westin families had history, and therefore I didn't want to see him sacrificed only to end up dead.

It hadn't escaped my notice that Creole hadn't said a word. Nor had Fab, who threw furtive glances in his direction.

"Leave Bonnet to me," Spoon said. "I'll arrange a sit down and come up with a truce. It might take a day or two; he'll want the meeting to take place out in the Gulf. You two stay here and out of sight. Under no condition do you leave this boat. Got it?"

We both nodded.

"Warning: All bets are off if Bonnet gets his hands on you first. Negotiations at that point might well prove useless."

Creole snorted. "You might want to issue a

warning of your own to Bonnet," his voice was calm and quiet, hard words spoken softly. "If anything happens to either of these women, retribution will be sought, and it won't be a quick bullet to the head."

Spoon held out his hand. "Give me the car keys. Where do you want it returned?"

Always faster than me, Fab said, "Leave it there. It will disappear in a couple of hours."

I hadn't realized I'd held my breath until I saw that the explanation went unchallenged. Fab covered for me. They thought the car came from one of her shifty connections. She must have come to the same conclusion as me, although we hadn't talked about it. We needed to keep the extent of Phil's abilities a secret. Spoon probably knew of her informational talents; he just hadn't connected her to us yet.

"Billy Keith is on the way over; he's sleeping on deck." Spoon wagged his finger, "Behave yourselves. I told him a well-placed bullet in one of your ass cheeks will stop the other one from escaping. I'll be stopping by tomorrow and expect to see the both of you." He climbed over the side and disappeared down the docks.

Fab jumped up, practically sending her deck chair into a spin. With a glance between Creole and me, she headed off in the opposite direction, looking eager to get away. I hoped this would be one time she wouldn't take cover close by and eavesdrop.

I gave myself a mental kick and moved to a small table in front of Creole, sitting down. "I'm sorry for the worry we caused."

"Are you really?" he spit out. "Sorry? You're damn lucky it's illegal to strangle you."

"I... uh... I'll make this up to you."

"Do you trust me?" He held up his hand. "Apparently not, with the duo Wonder Woman act you two pulled off." He stared at me and stood. "I have to get back to work."

"Don't leave like this. I really am..."

He cut me off. "I can't help with Bonnet. I'd like to put him in a prison cell where he belongs. Considering he manages to remain rather elusive when it comes to leaving his fingerprints on anything, I don't expect an arrest in time to help you."

I wanted to cry when he left without another word, a kiss, or a hug.

When Fab reappeared almost immediately, I wondered why I thought she'd go hide out in another room.

"I suppose you were listening?" I asked.

"That didn't go well." Fab hugged me.

"Is the beautiful Fabiana going all soft and sentimental?"

She snorted, a most unladylike sound. "His feelings are hurt. Hopefully he'll get over it and realize that except for the occasional quirk, you two are quite happy together."

I arched my brows. "Quirk?"

"Hey, can I get some help over here?" a male voice yelled.

Billy Keith stood dockside in knee-length bathing trunks, a t-shirt, and sun-bleached windblown hair. He had a couple of brown shopping bags in his hands.

"I ordered dinner," Fab announced, proud of herself.

"If one of those bags holds a pitcher of margaritas, I'm going to think you're the sweetest ever," I told Billy.

His laugh was a deep growl.

"I've never been sweet a day in my life. Don't let my boyish charm fool your ass."

That would be a big mistake.

I'd heard the rumors and personally witnessed his charm in a three-on-one fight in front of Jake's. Terrible odds. I'd been ready to call the sheriff, but Billy made short work of them, knocking them unconscious and dumping the bodies next to the trash for pick-up the next day.

Billy minded his own business and kept to himself. The only thing I knew for sure was that he worked for Spoon, doing something. One day at Jake's, I challenged him to play twenty questions. He didn't answer a single one. He just yawned and informed me, "You ask too many questions."

"Just give me a tidbit, free refill on your beer," I'd offered.

"I'm a NASCAR fan."

"Favorite driver?"

He stabbed his finger at me. "That's a second question."

My x-ray vision failed to see if there were margaritas in one of those bags. No matter. Soon I would stop feeling sorry for myself. I didn't take my eyes away as Fab helped to unload the dinner. No liquid refreshment.

Billy stretched up to his skinny six feet and cleared his throat.

"Listen up, ladies. I'm going to tell you the rules."

"Don't waste your breath," Fab hissed at him. "Here's the rule. You don't make us mad, and you won't find yourself gagged and bound to a chair."

I stepped between them and tried for a reassuring smile.

"Calm down, you two. We already promised Spoon. And besides, I like it here."

"If I can get the two of you to stay put and not have to hurt you, I get triple pay," he said.

"I like 'triple pay'," Fab told him. "We'll make sure you get your money."

Poor Billy. The fast acquiescence meant nothing, but why spoil his dreams of a big payday?

Chapter Thirty-Nine

We were on our second full day of lying around Spoon's boat. He had yet to show his face, nothing more than a phone call to say that he was working on negotiations and that we needed to be patient. Fab pulled a new phone from her bag and disappeared into one of the bedrooms. Turned out that Billy knew his way around a barbeque and the kitchen galley. He grilled us a perfect piece of white fish with vegetables. He fixed up a side dish of crispy fried potatoes, enough for ten people, which made me groan. Luckily, Billy had a healthy appetite, or a hidden third leg. I wasn't sure where all the food disappeared to on his thin frame.

After dinner I sacked out on some boat cushions and stared up at the stars in the darkened sky. The slight rolling of the boat made me drowsy. As I was dozing off, a hand clamped down hard on my mouth. My eyes flew open and I felt faint, realizing that I was staring up the muzzle of a gun. A pair of dark eyes that I'd never seen before stared down into mine. From the corner of my eye, I saw Billy lying motionless on the deck.

"Gotcha," the bright red-haired woman said, sticking a cloth over my nose.

* * *

The pain in my neck was excruciating. My head hung at an odd angle. I couldn't move my arms. I pulled, and something scratchy and unyielding bit into my wrists.

My eyes blinked open. Why was I tied up, slumped over in a leather chair? *Nice office*, I thought as my brain started to function. I skimmed over the lavishly decorated space to the chair next to me. Fab glared at me in pure frustration. She shook her head slightly, which I interpreted to mean, '*quiet*', since she hadn't said anything.

"We've been waiting for you to join us, Miss Madison," a male voice boomed from behind me. He moved past, his Top-Siders coming into view. He wore silk shorts and a tropical shirt. He was fiftyish, with a full head of grey hair. The man settled in a chair behind the massive burl wood desk. His gold Rolex caught the sunlight coming in through the large porthole window; he had the air of a wealthy boat captain.

"Let me guess: Mr. Bonnet?" I half-smiled, more of an exhale of breath.

The redhead in my vague dream draped herself across the corner of the desk, wearing a tight black pencil skirt and button-down shirt, the lace of her white bra peeking through. She wore stilettos that would make Fab seem graceful, but me, not so much. Would now be a good time to ask how many colors of dye she had to mix together to get that garish hair color? Had anyone ever told her that it wasn't a good look?

She caressed a silver finger nail file between her fingers, a look of excitement in her eyes that unnerved me. Whatever dirty work that needed doing, Bonnet chose her.

"Good, introductions are over. I have a few questions for you ladies. If I deem you fully cooperative, you'll be leaving here fully intact. If not…" He smiled and managed to maintain a mean glint to his dark eyes.

Fab cut him off. "Skip the detailed threats and get to the questions. We get that you're a bad ass."

"Where's Jackson Devereaux?" he boomed.

I fought to suppress a gulp. *Here we go!* "I saw him a few days ago, on the docks in Lauderdale. Said he was leaving the area."

Bonnet clinched his fist several times. "Where's he going?"

"Normally, I'd say he'd go home, but I suspect he'll show up on some friend's doorstep. He's lived several places around the country."

"Does he have my money?" Bonnet cracked his knuckles.

In the silence of the office, it was an unnerving sound; even Fab had a slight reaction.

"He had nothing to do with the sale of your product. It was sold by the time he hit town, and he never took a cut. That scheme was the brainchild of the two entrepreneurs that have already turned up dead." I made a split second decision to stick to the facts as closely as possible. I had no idea what he did and didn't already know. Getting caught in a lie could be detrimental to my health.

Bonnet never took his eyes off me as I answered his questions. "How do you know Devereaux's telling the truth?"

"Jax isn't a particularly good liar. He has no reason to lie to me, anyway."

Fab shifted in her chair. She too was trussed up. "You murdered the two that ripped you off. What do you want from us?"

"I want Devereaux and my money !" The big man pounded his fist on the desk.

He already had his answer. So now what? The 'what' made me inwardly shudder.

Fab and I jerked at the fierce pounding on his office door. The redhead slithered off the desk. Well over six feet tall, she walked with an exaggerated wiggle. She cracked open the door and stuck her head out. She exchanged words in an excited voice. It was hard to distinguish if she was speaking to a male or female. Once concluded, she slammed the door, motioning to Bonnet to join her in the corner for a private chat.

I winked at Fab, happy we were both alive

and not fish food. She had a look of concentration, doing what she did best, trying to eavesdrop. I listened, but couldn't make out one word of their whispering.

The door closed behind us, the footsteps unhurried as Bonnet made himself comfortable behind his desk, smiling at the two of us in a way that made the hairs on my neck tingle.

The redhead slinked up behind me and leaned over. "Get up," she barked in my ear. She gave me a helping hand by twisting her fingers in my hair and propelling me out of the chair with a none-too-gentle shove. I sailed across the room, banging my head on a second door that I'd missed from my previous vantage point. Fab, with her killer muscles, managed to lift herself from her chair to a standing position. Fab got the same manhandling shove, but she didn't stumble.

Red unlocked the door, held it open, and swept out her hand. "Move," she ordered.

We brushed by her and entered a long, narrow hallway, then down a short flight of steps with only the dimmest light bulb overhead.

"Stop at the open door." The redhead snapped her fingers. Raising her skirt, she withdrew a knife from her garter belt, the blade springing up. I stood still and tried not to squirm, certain that she'd leave us bleeding. "You can thank Boss-man for this. I wanted you hog-tied and gagged." She pushed me inside.

The blood came rushing back into my arms, and my fingers tingled when I flexed them.

"Go ahead, girlie," she told Fab. "Try and get away." She sliced the rope away.

"Get comfy," she laughed. "Make all the noise you want; no one will hear you. I'm going back to lobby to give you guys a little one-on-one time."

The door slammed behind her, followed by a key turning in the lock. The room was smaller than a jail cell, with a stained concrete floor, an old rusted out toilet in the corner, and small sink. The only light source came from a small window that held no chance for escape.

"Don't you dare faint," Fab grouched. "You're pale even with your tan. Sit. I'll help you; you're not as coordinated as I am."

I squeezed my eyes closed, trying not to succumb to fear. Despite the guilt and feeling selfish, it calmed me somewhat when she sank down next to me.

"Now you listen to me," she said. "We're going to get out of this hell hole."

I put my head on her shoulder. "You always say that. How are you going to get us out of this one?"

"Have I ever been wrong? No!" She leaned her head against mine. "I'm not sure, but I promise you this. I'll be around to give the redhead the attitude adjustment she so richly deserves."

"That amazon scares me. Way worse than you ever did."

Fab sniffed. "When were you ever afraid of me? You need a little refresher to your memory. You targeted me, then stalked me until I agreed to be your friend."

"Not exactly, but it's a damn good thing I was persistent." I laughed softly. "What do you suppose is happening upstairs?"

"I think someone with large muscles made contact, possibly showing up looking for us. Let's hope," she sighed. "If that's the case, Bonnet might think twice about hurting us before setting off a war. Spoon will never let our disappearance or deaths go unpunished. Those stoops upstairs know we had nothing to do with ripping him off, no matter how simple-minded he wants to play this game."

"Why would someone have a room like this?" I couldn't think of a single reason that had anything to do with something normal. "Do you suppose we're out on Narcissistic Island?"

"I shudder to think. This room has such a creepy vibe. Nothing good happens here, you can be sure." Fab eyed the window; without a ladder, there would be no looking out. "We're out on his island. I came to on the boat ride over here, but Amazon caught me and chloroformed me again. I don't think we get out of this without Bonnet's benevolence."

Bonnet would want a trade. What would he accept?

Fab and I leaned together and used each other as pillows. The room was eerily quiet, not a sound could be heard from anywhere in the house.

"Do you suppose we missed the button for room service?" Fab broke the silence.

"How come you're so calm?" I laughed.

"I'm hungry."

Chapter Forty

At the sound of a key in the lock, I jolted forward. Fab's arm across my chest held me in place.

"I guess they didn't forget us. My butt is numb and my back aches," I mumbled.

"Shh..." she said. Amazon stood in the doorway. She had reapplied her bright red lipstick to match her dagger-like fingernails. Against her pale white skin the red made her look like a vampire. Make that a vampire holding a .357 Magnum in her hand.

At this close range, someone would be a long time cleaning up blood splatter and remains off the walls.

"No one said you could sit." She laughed, a high pitched deranged sound. "Hurry your asses up. I'm out of patience."

Fab grabbed my arm and headed to the door as we were once again herded down the hallway and up the stairs.

Fab, always the gutsy one, asked her, "How long have we been here?"

She eyed Fab, assessing her as a worthy opponent perhaps. "It's the morning of your second day. Enjoying yourself?"

Fab stared back and never flinched. "What do you want?"

"I'm authorized to negotiate your release within the hour. Mr. Bonnet is owed five hundred thousand plus interest and penalties, but you can't put a price on the inconvenience. So, rounded out, he'll settle for one million."

"Dollars?" I shook my head in disbelief, waiting for her to say, "Cash only." Bonnet had to know we couldn't come up with that kind of money. What game was he playing now?

"What do you really want?" Fab asked. "Bonnet has to have accepted by this time that the money's gone, and he's not getting it back. Another thing, the longer you keep us here, the higher the chances that law enforcement will motor over with a warrant that allows them to sniff in every nook and cranny. I know if we're not returned in one piece, Bonnet's days of sliding under the radar are over."

"Shut up and sit," Amazon ordered.

I must be the weak link; she stood behind my chair and fingered my hair, pointing the Magnum at my temple.

Minutes later, Bonnet burst through the door. "It was nice to meet you ladies." He laughed, enjoying some private joke.

We both must have looked confused.

"You're free to leave," he added, waving his arm. He settled himself behind his desk and turned his attention to a pile of paperwork.

Amazon waved her gun at us, holding the main door open. "Let me show you out." Her laugh tinkled like an annoying wind chime.

Fab and I exchanged the "this is too easy" look.

Red motioned us forward. The office opened into the living room on the second floor, with one hundred and eighty degrees to enjoy the views of the Gulf. It wouldn't surprise me if Amazon threw us out of one of the floor to ceiling sliding doors, which I noticed opened onto a wrap terrace that overlooked overgrown mangroves and a private lagoon.

The house was breathtaking; it was too bad we weren't here for a girl lunch. The floors were highly polished wooden planks, the furniture one of a kind pieces built for the room, and the walls were filled with personal photos of laughing, smiling people and paintings of Key West. A spiral staircase led the way to the upper floor. On one side there was a solid wall of books, and the ceiling was painted with an underwater scene.

Amazon leaned against the open door. Fab put her hand in the middle, preventing her from shutting it once we crossed the threshold.

Before she could utter a word, the redhead purred. "Did you need directions?" Her 3-inch long fingernail pointed across the Gulf of Mexico to the northeast. "The Keys. Twenty minutes by boat, ten minutes by helicopter. I'm not sure how long it takes to swim eight miles. Maybe you can hitch a ride from a passing boat." Her eyes swept the water as she pushed Fab aside. She laughed heartily and slammed the door.

We raced down the stairs and sunk our toes into the sandy beach, sucking in the fresh air for the first time in days. Judging by its rotted condition, the old shipwrecked boat next to us had been resting on its side for quite a long time. Mangroves and palm trees surrounded the island, all seemingly growing out of the clear, blue-green waters. From here they looked like an impenetrable forest, surrounding the three-story main house, guest house, and several buildings.

Fab hustled me through the trees, making sure we weren't visible to anyone looking out the windows of the house.

"Would you think out loud, please?" I demanded. I breathed a long sigh that we were free at last of creepy Bonnet and his scary sidekick, but until we got off this island, they were still in control.

"I don't know about you, but I'm tired, hungry, and thirsty; not ideal conditions for a swim. I figure eight miles for two average swimmers such as ourselves would take us six to seven hours of continuous swimming." Fab scanned the Gulf. "There's not a boat in sight."

"Fair warning: I'd probably drown first. I'd rather Bonnet shoot me, but he'd delegate to

Amazon, and I wouldn't get lucky enough for a clean shot. She'd make sure it was a hideous death. Why does the choice have to be Bonnet or an appetizer for sharks and alligators?"

"You have a third choice," Fab cuffed me. "Me. Now stay here and out of sight."

"Where in the hell do you think you're going?" I almost shrieked, grabbing at her shirt, but she twisted away. "Don't leave me here by myself."

"I'm going to sneak around, see what I can find to aid us in our swim to shore."

"They'll come looking for us when they don't see us bobbing around in the water," I argued.

"Listen up, I'm in charge." She shook her finger. "Neither one of them are going to get their expensive shoes dirty coming out here, slogging around in swamp water.

"If you don't let me come with you, when you get us out of here, I'll complain to Didier that you were mean and made me cry."

"You're not crying." She looked suspicious.

"My stories are far superior to yours. I'm ready to play follow the leader."

"You are a pain in my—"

"Aah!" I cut her off. "'And then, Didier, she cursed at me'."

She snorted and shook her head. "Hang on to the back of my shirt if you need to."

"If you tell me we're going to get out of this alive, I'll believe you and not worry so much."

"Forget about dying," Fab reassured. "Bonnet's rich and flaunts it. He has to have some excellent toys around here somewhere. When it gets dark, we'll help ourselves and get off this island. We can ditch them on the other side."

I bent down and rolled up my pants. I was tired of them after three days, but I knew it was not a good time to complain about wanting a change of clothes.

"Where's Creole?" I wanted to scream. "I wish he'd kissed me one last time. But no, he had to stomp away mad." I felt more guilt whining about kisses. "Spoon going to show up anytime soon? He has to know by now that we didn't leave under our own free will. We wouldn't have knocked out Billy. Oh, Billy... I hope he's not dead."

"Bonnet's dumber than he acts if he thinks he's going to cross Spoon. He's got himself a dangerous enemy. If he did any checking at all, he knows there will be a heavy price for kidnapping, murder, or anything else. Payback is going to be ugly. I just hope Spoon doesn't let the redhead run loose. That vacant stare of hers gave me the chills."

Coming around the far side of the island, peering through the trees, we spotted the helipad. There was also a large storage building, doors closed, that I presumed held the helicopter when not in use. A large yacht was anchored a few yards out and under cover.

"All big yachts have water toys; we'll check the storage area underneath. Maybe we'll get lucky and find a wave runner or a speed boat." Fab reached in her back pocket and withdrew a lock pick and waved it at me.

"What do you do, sew them in your clothes?"

"Here's the plan. We lounge out here in the brush until dark and hope Bonnet doesn't have dogs that he plans to unleash. He thinks we're going to die on this stinkin' island and gloat over our remains. That's what he thinks. Later I'll swim out and check out the yacht."

"Whatever we steal, he'll come after," I warned. "There's an old rowboat over there along with some other dry-rotted items. I don't see any oars."

We sloshed through the water and found places to sit on one of the hundreds of old tree roots growing above ground. At least we found a spot where we weren't sitting in water.

"Those two are probably having a good laugh. They know we haven't gotten off this island and could care less. They're waiting for us to come knocking, beg for help rather than starve to death."

I smiled at her. "If I had to choose one person to be stranded on an island with, it would be you."

Chapter Forty-One

I had already figured out that I'd never survive this without Fab, who never gave up and had a spine of steel. Soon the skies would be dark, the only light a half-moon and a few stars. As much as I wanted to be home, I dreaded the escape plan. Still, I pushed all my what-if thoughts from my mind.

"No splashing," Fab hissed.

We crept along the shore, ankle deep in water, though our clothes had just dried from the previous splashing around. That was about to change when we dove in, fully dressed. Thank goodness we were in South Florida. If it weren't for the warm night air, we'd freeze to death.

"Doesn't it worry you that we haven't seen Bonnet or his sidekick?" I asked.

"The upside is that we haven't had to dodge automatic gunfire. He didn't let us walk out the front door because he's such a nice guy; we have to get out of here before we find out firsthand what his plans are."

"Are you sure about this? Please be careful," I squeaked. "Can you see where you're going?"

Fab turned and grabbed my shoulders. "Take

a breath. We're going for a little swim, around the far side of the yacht to the back. If Bonnet's got one thing with an engine, we're out of here."

"You're driving, right?"

"I'm going to remind you that you said that." Fab's laugh floated on the water.

It felt weird to swim in sweat pants and a t-shirt. Probably easier than Fab's blue jeans and ruined silk top. The late night swim felt good, made me less grimy, but I'd have enjoyed it more if I were at home in my pool. There was a certain comfort swimming in the shadow of the large yacht.

"Hang on." Fab clamped my hand on a railing that ran from the bottom deck down to the water. "I'm going on board to see if I can find a flashlight or something so I can figure out how this door opens."

Slowly treading water, I kept a watchful eye on the out buildings, not sure what I'd do if I saw someone. A loud bang broke the silence of the night and scared me witless, and a few more I identified as coming from inside the boat—and silence. I shivered that Fab had been surprised by something unexpected, possibly the redhead. I couldn't do this by myself. Even though the helicopter hangar blocked the view from the house to the boat, Bonnet would surely have security that kept tabs on us as we sneaked around. I'd never believe he was as disinterested as he'd like us to think.

The garage door made a whirring noise and slowly opened straight up. Fab stood in the opening.

"Don't go anywhere," she said as she disappeared into the space.

The inside compartment was full of the coolest water toys ever, a perk of being very rich. Jet skis, slides, canoes—the climbing wall made me laugh—and a wide assortment of inflatables. Fab would laugh at my choice of transportation—the water bike. I'd have to pedal my butt off, but I'd only ever been a passenger on a jet ski. Not to mention, I forgot to sign up for a hotwiring class.

Fab reappeared and side stepped the ledge. She held out her hand and I climbed up the stairs.

"You're going to need these," she said as she tossed me a pair of men's flip flops. I looked at her feet and she had slipped on a pair, I almost laughed knowing that she hated cheap shoes.

"Help me pull this out." She had singled out a wave runner that conveniently had the key in the ignition. "We're not starting it until we're ready to leave. According to Randy, the start of the engine will carry over the water and Bonnet will investigate."

"Stupid question, but who in the hell is Randy?"

"Full-time deckhand. His job is to make sure everything is clean and in working order. Nice guy," she sighed. "I felt bad giving him a black eye and tying him up. I told him not to be stupid and show his face before we left. Sent a message through Randy for Bonnet—we're filing a kidnapping report."

Poor Randy, getting his ass kicked by a girl. I hoped for his sake that Bonnet didn't kill him.

"Put this on." Fab retrieved a life jacket off the floor.

"Do you know where you're going?" I asked.

The shrug of her shoulders wasn't reassuring.

"I felt your scowl in the dark," I said as we climbed onto the wave runner.

"Hold on tight." She fired up the engine, jammed her foot on the gas pedal, and we flew across the water.

Chapter Forty-Two

When we realized that no lights were behind us and that there were no engine noises of someone rapidly approaching, Fab slowed to a less hair-raising speed. I relaxed enough to lift my head, where previously it had been scrunched in the middle of her back. I looked at the rapidly-approaching coastline over her shoulder as the ocean spray beat us in the face, completely saturating our already-wet clothes. Fab made a straight line to where the brightest concentration of lights dotted the shoreline.

As we approached the shore, she cut the engine and we coasted in, not wanting to attract attention. We ditched the wave runner, tying it alongside rental water equipment for a five-star resort down on the docks at the end of Duval Street. We were free of Bonnet for the moment, but not ready to savor the victory, since we were still one hundred miles from home.

Wandering the streets of Key West in the middle of the night, hungry, thirsty, no cell phone, no money—it blew big time. I didn't want to complain out loud, but this place was definitely more fun with a credit card and some cash. Neither one of us had a local connection we could roust from bed.

Fab spotted the water fountain and, with so little water pressure, she had to shove her face down as close to the bubbler as she could get. When finished, she wiped her face with her stained and torn top and made a sweeping gesture.

"Drink slowly." She patted my back. "I don't want you to stand up and barf."

When I finished, I grabbed the back of her shirt and wiped my face.

"You're not funny," she growled. She picked a long piece of seaweed off her pant leg and flung it in the gutter.

"You know that's not true. What's next, oh fearless leader?"

We headed down Duval Street in the direction of the Overseas; we had a couple of miles to figure out what was next. Walking home seemed improbable, since it would take days, not to mention it was illegal. The two-lane highway in each direction, stretching from the southernmost point of the US to Tarpon Cove, banned pedestrians.

Fab steered me to a clean and bird poop-free metal bench across from Hemingway's bar. The bar boasted standing room only every night for live music, dancing, and drinking. Tonight's crowd had dispersed, leaving behind the diehard drinkers. With so few people, we assumed that it must be nearly closing time. It shut its doors at four in the morning for a few hours, long enough to clean and re-open for the breakfast drinkers.

Fab, arms crossed, kicked her foot until I put my hand on her leg, which was more polite than kicking her to stop. At the sight of rapidly-approaching headlights, she jumped into the street and flagged down the lone cab. It barely slowed when she had the door open and slid into the front seat.

It was a brief conversation, and then the driver yelled, "Get out, or I'm calling the cops!"

Angry, she got out, turning to yell her regards to his ancestors as she flounced out of the street, throwing herself down next to me.

"That went well," I said.

"I tried to convince him we were stranded and would pay triple if he'd drive us to Tarpon Cove. Do you know that he had the nerve to ask, 'Where are a couple of homeless chicks going to get that kind of money?'"

"Let me guess, in response you tried to carjack him, and that's when he wanted you out?"

"That bastard wanted a blow job in exchange for one hamburger. Said I'd have to share it with you. I unleashed a string of profanity. I may have mentioned his minuscule manhood, and that's when he got mad."

I bent over, putting my face on my knees, and started laughing. "Did you even try to negotiate for two hamburgers?"

She frowned, looking shocked, and we both started laughing.

I shook my finger at her. "So, your beautiful, sexy self is a bit scruffed up. Worn-looking or not, get up off this bench and use your man skills."

"Look at me!" she shrieked.

A young drunk couple staggered by, took one look at us, and hustled down the street.

I pulled on a strand of her slightly matted hair and made a sad face. "If it makes you feel better, I bet I look worse."

"Plan C, or is it D now? After giving a brief thought to boosting a car, I remembered how much I hate jail. Besides, it's been a while since of either of us has been arrested, locked up, or contemplated a jail break, and it needs to stay that way."

Fab's whining comforted me in an odd way.

"We could go to the police station and tell them we know the chief in Miami, but I doubt they'd believe us. What are the chances they'd call and get him out of bed?"

"Big zero." Fab scanned the street; with the exception of the occasional drunk straggler, the famous street was deserted.

"Maybe there's a pay phone around." Although I knew that, in this cell phone age, finding a pay phone might be like an archaeological mission.

"No money," Fab reminded. "Hitching a ride

at night is a terrible idea, and not even a good one during the day. We could sleep on the beach and wait until morning."

"We could call collect," I said.

"You can't do that anymore. As soon as the person on the other end of the line hears collect call, they'll hang up."

"Jail calls are collect," I said excitedly. "You can hear the person's voice on the other end, so you know who it is, and you're under no obligation unless you press 'one.' If you took a jail call once in a while, you'd know these things. We would have to choose someone with a landline."

A police cruiser came around the corner and cruised slowly down the street. The back seat empty, he pulled alongside the curb.

Before he got the passenger side window down, Fab whispered. "I don't think telling him our sad story is a good idea."

"You can't loiter on the bench all night," he eyed us evenly. "Against the law."

I looked to see where he pointed and figured it was the street sign I couldn't read. With only the street lights for illumination, I could barely make out what the officer looked like inside the darkened car. My guess, if we were dressed up, we could sit on this bench as long as we wanted to, but you can't upset the tourists with homeless milling around. I knew they had a large population living somewhere. I guessed the Main

Street was off limits.

Since I did friendly better than Fab with the legal types, I asked, "Could you direct us to a pay phone?"

I wanted to beg him to call Mother, but that didn't seem like a good idea. He might ask questions I couldn't answer truthfully.

He looked surprised. "About a mile up, in front of the Conch Motel." He must have noticed our look of surprise that there were none closer. "There are only two on the entire island; the other is under the bridge at the beginning of the Overseas, in front of Kay's Cafe."

I thanked him. Fab poked me and motioned me to get a move on. The officer waited while we shuffled off in the direction he suggested. A patient man, he continued his vigil until we were two blocks up the street.

I glanced over my shoulder. "I guess he wants to make sure we don't double back and warm that bench. How long is this walk going to take?" I groaned. "My feet are falling off."

"A long damn time if you don't speed it up." She tugged on my arm. "We've got another problem—who are we going to call at this hour?"

"Since I don't know what time it is, Jake's is probably closed and no one will answer again until mid-morning. Mac keeps bankers' hours."

Fab snapped her fingers. "The funeral home answers 24/7. You know Dickie and Raul would pick us up, dead or alive."

"Since we're alive, hopefully they won't bring the hearse," I said. "Does it feel like no one is looking for us? What about Bonnet? He's a vindictive bastard. Why didn't he follow us? We didn't get this far to end up dead."

"I figured Spoon or Creole or someone would have kept a watchful eye on that island, and might intercept us once they saw the Jet Ski blasting across the waves in the dark. Would it be too much to ask that someone meet us at the docks where we tied up? It's a no-brainer, since it's the most logical place to come ashore, and the closest."

"What plan letter are you on? Got one for when we get back to the Cove? I vote we sneak into the house, take turns standing guard, take showers, get clean clothes, and shoot uninvited guests."

The Conch Motel sign flashed in the distance. We finally trudged up to the white run-down motel. It hadn't seen any TLC in a long time, and the sign boasted No Vacancy. Exhausted and with our adrenaline rushes running low, we glared at the damaged concrete where the phone stand had been, the pole sheared off.

"Now what?" Fab scuffed the sidewalk with her flip flop. "My feet ache from these crappy rubber things. How do you do it?"

"My feet don't know any better. The few times they've graced a pair of designer heels, they stung all night. I will admit, flops weren't made for hiking across town. But thank you for snatching them up, or we'd be barefoot and our feet would be beyond thrashed."

A flatbed rumbled down the street, back firing, brakes screeching as the driver came to a stop.

"Hey girlies, you want a ride?" An old man, what little hair he had sticking straight up, shouted out his window. He leered, running his eyes up and down our bodies, starting with Fab.

"He likes you," I whispered. "Step up and work your magic." I nudged her. "Maybe he's got a phone and we can decline the ride."

Fab had a high success rate with men in general, old men in particular. The chat seemed to go well, no shouting or threats of law enforcement. I don't know what she told him, but she turned and gestured me over and gave me a hand up onto the back of the truck. We settled with our backs against the cab. When he put it into gear and lurched forward, I clutched Fab's leg.

"Too tired to lie. I told him the truth. He uttered a curse word, mumbled something about hoping to get his whistle cleaned by the two of us. Blowjob, I presume."

"He must be old," I laughed. "I eavesdropped on my grandfather once and heard him say that. It was the same trip when I brought home the condoms and put them on my fingers to show Mother. She gave a flimsy explanation that they were balloons and not to waste them. I assured her that Grandfather had a giant box of them. It wasn't often I rendered her speechless, but I was too young to savor the moment properly."

"I never knew mine. He's a face in a family photo on the fireplace mantel."

Fab rarely spoke about her family. They didn't approve of their free-spirited daughter, and they expressed their displeasure at her not meeting their expectations. They had cut ties long before I met her. Mother embraced her as a second daughter, and I knew they both enjoyed the relationship.

"Herb doesn't have a cell," she said. "He's giving us a ride to Kay's; turns out she's an ex-hooker with a big heart."

With no traffic and only the occasional car passing by and a few red lights to contend with, I guessed at ten minutes to get to our destination. I was happy to get the ride; the walk would've been painful and long. Herb pulled up in front of an old blue square building. I jumped off the side and waved, while Fab went over to the driver's side to thank him.

It was a quiet waterside area, no signs that it attracted the late night illegal trade. The sign across the street said Mobile Home Community. It took up at least one block, and it was in decent condition. Besides Kay's, there were a couple of nondescript commercial warehouses.

"I told him free meal at Jake's anytime he was

passing through," Fab said. "He apologized for misjudging us as down-on-our-luck hookers. Said he couldn't remember the last time he did a good deed, and that it felt good." She headed straight for the phone, walking around it before lifting the receiver. "Now what do I do?"

"Wait for the annoying woman and her recorded message. If you're impatient, press '0' and see if that gets you an operator."

"No answer." Fab slammed the receiver down.

"Nooo," I stamped my foot. "Did you have the right number? You promised the guys would answer."

"We'll have to wait until daylight and hitch a ride."

"Mother will kill us when you tell her it was your idea to hitch rides." I scooted around her and grabbed the phone off the hook, this time no dial tone. I beat the phone against the pole and listened again.

"What in the hell are you two bitches doing?" a bleach blonde, wrinkled up woman yelled. "Breaking the only pay phone in town. I make good money off that phone."

"It doesn't even work," I yelled back.

"It takes a while to start working again after someone makes a call. Like your friend just did. Get moving, and if you come back, I'll fill you full of bird seed," she threatened and raised the rifle from her side.

"Birdseed?" I sneered.

"You spend a few hours picking it out of your ass, and you won't come back here!" She racked it, the sound unmistakable.

Fab cut me off in my foolhardy attempt to confront the old woman and pushed me behind her back.

"I'm Fab Merceau," she stuck out her hand. "You must be Kay. I think we can come to a mutually beneficial deal that doesn't have us touching your money maker over there." Fab tossed a glance over her shoulder.

Kay ignored her hand. "You don't have anything I want, so go, or I'll call the police."

"Look we've had the worst day ever," I yelled as I tried to get around Fab, who blocked me with her arm. "Old Herb brought us here to use the phone. He said you had a big heart, where the hell is it?"

"Ignore her." Fab waved her arm behind her back. "Listen to my deal. You say no and we'll leave; you'll never see us again. I can promise you that."

"You got one minute, and then I'm calling the cops," she pulled her cell phone from her pocket.

"We live in Tarpon Cove and got stranded here. As you can see, we have nothing. Make a call for us, and when our ride gets here he'll pay you a hundred dollars — throw in a sandwich and water for each of us, and you'll make double the money."

"Where am I calling?" she asked.

"A funeral home. They're good friends and will come pick us up."

"Three hundred," she countered.

"Larcenous heart more like it," I said loudly. "We want chips."

"Deal." Fab held out her hand.

"Keep your hands to yourself. I'm making the call. Not saying I don't believe you, but I don't."

Fab gave her the number.

"Do you know someone named Fan?" Kay asked whoever answered the phone.

"Fab," I hissed.

"What's she look like?" She asked next. After a pause, "Does she have a friend?"

"This guy says you're the calm one." She looked at me and belly laughed. She held out the phone after hitting the speaker phone. "Some guy named Richard Vanderbilt."

Fab reached for the phone and Kay jerked it back, putting it on speaker. "Dickie, this is Fab. We're stranded in Key West; we need a ride and three hundred dollars."

"Are you two okay? I'll have Raul drive; he ignores speed limit signs. It will take us an hour and half, maybe sooner since he's driving."

Kay told him the address and easy directions off the highway.

"Do you like peanut butter and jelly?" Kay asked Fab.

If I hadn't been so hungry, I would have been tempted to launch myself on her and beat the hell out of her.

"How much extra for a decent sandwich?" Fab growled.

Chapter Forty-Three

We took our sandwiches, pretzels, and nuts outside and ate them on a tired old bench. We sat in full view of Kay, who worked behind the bar and kept one eye on us with a threat that if we moved, she'd shoot us.

It seemed like forever, but as it turned out, only an hour later, Raul and Dickie rolled up before us in their Navigator. They both did a double-take, not concealing their shock at our shabby appearance.

I looked down and got a whiff of salty fish stink from my clothes. A thin layer of gritty sand covered my arms and lower legs, and my cheeks flushed red in embarrassment. I hoped I didn't stain their leather seats.

Fab got cash from Raul and took care of Kay. The two of them had called a silent truce, but she and I continued to trade glares.

Kay followed Fab out the door and checked out the SUV. "I honestly thought you two were full of it. When your ride didn't show, I planned to offer more peanut butter in exchange for you washing the dishes and cleaning during lunch rush."

I turned away, clasping my hands together, so I wouldn't be tempted to give her the finger. Her high-pitched giggles followed me to the passenger door. I climbed in.

"If I said thank you five hundred times it wouldn't be enough," I said to Dickie and Raul. "I'll pay you back tomorrow. Anytime you need anything, you call one of us."

Fab gave me a butt shove and slid in next to me. They stared, horrified at our condition.

Raul looked in the rearview and backed out. Fab and I smiled. At long last, we were on our way home. He smiled at both of us. "We are honored that you called us. You're our best friends in the Cove. The only two people who don't think we're weird."

Dickie nodded his head in agreement. "Don't worry about us ever telling anyone anything."

"I feel bad if we took you away from your work. You were the only ones we knew that would answer the phone in the middle of the night," Fab said.

"We don't have a funeral until tomorrow. I have Martha Livingston to dress, but she's not going anywhere," Dickie said and they both laughed.

Fab and I smirked at one another. We were finally getting used to funeral humor.

"Dickie and I want to hear every word about what happened. We made a bet the story would be great. We worried after you left, tried to keep up through town gossip, but no one was talking. We even called Jake's several times and we got the same response every time: 'Not here'."

Happy to be alive and headed up the Overseas Highway, I let Fab fill them in as I leaned against her shoulder and closed my eyes.

"Have them drop us off at the main beach parking lot, and we'll sneak in the back way," I whispered.

It seemed fair that they got all the details, since we used their business as a hide out. Fab got into her role as storyteller before her rapt audience of two. She made our escapade sound exciting and more in control than it really was. Several times she threw in details that never happened, making the story sound like an exciting adventure.

"Come back and stay with us," Raul offered, and Dickie seconded. "Anyone shows up asking questions, we'll hide you in the crematorium."

"It just got a good cleaning," Dickie said.

"No!" I screamed inwardly, shuddering at the thought, and kept my eyes closed.

"We'll be fine," Fab reassured him. "We need clean clothes. And frankly, I'd rather shoot Bonnet than stay on the run the rest of our lives."

* * *

Dickie and Raul threw out good reasons as to why we should remain their house guests. Much to their dismay, and under protest, they dropped us off at the beach. We reassured them and promised to stay in touch on a daily basis until we could come out of hiding.

We went down to the water and walked along the shore. When we were opposite the stairway by my house, we raced across the sand and snuck up the back steps. We stuck our heads around the fence. Nothing in the backyard had changed, not a single item out of place. We cut across to the French doors, which hadn't been tampered with.

"There's a key under the flower pot." I nudged Fab.

She rolled her eyes at me and inserted her trusty pick into the lock. Everything in the darkened living room was in the same place we left it. I had a sixth sense for knowing if something had been touched, and nothing stood out.

Fab skirted over to the drawer in the kitchen island, taking out a loaded Beretta and checking the chamber. You never knew when you'd be enjoying morning coffee, and someone unwanted would show up.

Fab headed up the stairs, gun cocked, to check out each room. "You stay at Creole's hideout, and I'll go to Miami until we get this figured out."

The plan sounded good, except that I didn't think I'd be welcome at Creole's. Fab wouldn't be happy that I failed to mention my change of plans. And if she found out, she wouldn't leave me to fend for myself. She deserved a happy reunion with Didier, though. One of us should be happy, and my vote went to her.

"All clear up here," Fab called down from the top of the stairs. "Everything in its place. I'm going to shower and pack a bag. I'll sneak out the back again. Gunz is picking me up. And you?"

"I'll give you a head start and follow."

"Cheer up. We're alive."

It didn't take long for Fab to come back downstairs carrying a small leather duffel bag. She flopped onto the couch while I went upstairs to shower.

The warm water from the rainfall shower head sprayed down over me. I retrieved a sea sponge and my mango apricot body wash and went over my body three times, making sure not a speck of ick was left attached to my skin before I gave the same thorough treatment to my hair. I had to force myself to get out, the hot water turning lukewarm.

I bundled up in a white cotton robe, comfort clothing, and had to remind myself I had to be prepared to run. I changed into a running skort, followed by a lightweight sweatshirt. My feet were so sore I couldn't bear the thought of stuffing them inside a pair of tennis shoes. That would have to wait. First things first, I put my lock pick in my back pocket. Never again would I leave the house without one. I followed that with cash and identification and then my final accessory. I grabbed my gun holster from the drawer.

I came back downstairs feeling a tiny bit better. "I don't like leaving you," Fab said. She put a phone on the counter and a Sig Sauer. "We stay in touch and call each other every day." I reassured her I would be locking up and leaving right behind her.

I threw my arms around her and hugged her. "Thank you," I whispered.

"Don't go thinking you were all slouchy in a crisis. You forget, I've seen you in action. Don't get used to being solo for long."

"We'll talk later," I said. "Watch your back." Fab waved, and once the door closed, I stared at the clock on the stove and waited, counting down the minutes.

I went into the kitchen to savor a cup of my favorite coffee that I hadn't had in days and enact my hastily put-together plan.

I found my electronics, my laptop and phone, on the granite island where I had left them. Creole didn't trust us from the beginning, and as it turned out, he had good reason. I scanned the internet, checking for news stories on Bonnet and was disappointed. No dead bodies had shown up anywhere.

I pushed small discs under the legs of a large, solid-wood buffet that housed holiday dishware and was impossible to move anywhere, but with this little invention it made it easier to relocate a heavy piece of furniture and this one was headed in front of the French doors. Anyone trying to enter would find that the door would open only a crack, giving me time to be cocked and ready; my Beretta and Glock were fully loaded. Moving to the front door, I shoved a chair under the knob.

I dashed upstairs and snatched up my favorite pillow and then returned to the main level, double-checked the door locks, and added another chair to the front door. It might not keep someone out, but it would make a ton of noise. I grabbed a cold bottle of water from the refrigerator and my phone and then stretched out on the daybed. It was perfectly placed for a view of the patio and front doors.

Chapter Forty-Four

I woke up in the near-dawn hours feeling disoriented, unsure as to why I lay fully dressed on the daybed. The unwanted memories came rushing back. I grabbed the Beretta and listened to the sounds of the night, hearing crickets and cats howling in the distance, letting everyone they woke up know they were having sex. The seashell nightlight from the kitchen illuminated the foyer, letting me see that the chair and chest were still in place.

The last thing I remembered was putting my head on the pillow. I felt guilty for not calling Mother to let her know I was back in town and okay. Instead of dragging her out of her sleep, I'd wait until the sun came up to call her. I reached for a baseball cap that Brad left behind on his last visit, and stuffed my red hair neatly underneath. I guzzled a cup of coffee along with two aspirin. I waited for the pain to ease in my feet before shoving them into a pair of confining tennis shoes, wincing as my swollen toes came into contact with the unforgiving leather. I tweaked my undercover look, pulling my hat down and donning a pair of large, dark sunglasses.

I rolled my bicycle down to the beach. I knew my SUV was at Spoon's garage behind barbed wire and locked, with electric fencing and no chance of getting it out without Spoon giving the okay. I rode along the hard sand down by the shoreline as far as I could go before pushing it across the beach to the main road. The streets were deserted. I pedaled to Jake's faster than I thought I could, noticing that even the drunks had gone home to get some sleep before resuming their drinking. I picked the back door lock and parked the bike in the far corner of the kitchen. Phil would see it and come up with a cover story. I headed for the Trailer Court.

Much to my surprise, the Trailer Court had become so popular that the parking lot was full every night, the Vacancy sign off. Tonight was no exception. It drew a quiet crowd that wanted to spend a few days with their feet kicked up before they moved along. No one milled around, all seemed quiet. I heard a crunch on the gravel behind me, so I pulled the Beretta and twirled around.

"Hold on, Sister, don't shoot." Crum put his hands in the air. "I'm not armed."

It was too early in the morning to be staring at the irate professor in his jockey shorts. Instead of his signature rubber boots, he was adorned in flip flops. It made me never want to wear the shoes again. They probably looked better on me, because I always had clothes on. I needed to prank Fab with wandering around the house in my underwear and boots. It would have to be when Didier was out of town.

"Just the man I want to see," I sighed and reholstered my gun. "I need to borrow one of your crappy trucks. Preferably one that runs. Set a fair rental rate and I'll pay you when I return." I wanted to mention he should wear shorts, pants, something, but it would be a waste of breath.

"You insult my vehicles and then want to *borrow* one. Your negotiation skills suck."

I should pull my gun again; he'd lose the snooty look.

"How many times have you told me you hate it when people can't get to the point? Are you or aren't you? I don't have time to waste. I want the red one if it runs."

He disappeared inside his trailer and came back out with a set of keys in his hand. "Are you in trouble?"

I ignored his question. "Has anyone been around looking for me? Any gossip?"

He shook his head in the negative. "I noticed you haven't been around. Normally I see you every day. I didn't ask any questions. Your name hasn't been mentioned once. I assumed you went on vacation."

"Anyone murdered? Found dead?"

He sucked in his breath. "No, that I would have heard."

"You're not to tell anyone you saw me, unless I turn up dead. Understand?"

He reached out and patted my shoulder. "The dead part would be distressing. I'm not sure your brother would let me live here without you around. You tolerate people's idiosyncrasies more than anyone I've ever met."

"That's so sweet." I wasn't sure what else to say to what I felt sure was a compliment.

"There is one thing. Not sure if this is a good time," he said, not making eye contact, just staring down and wiggling his toes.

I blurted out, "Carlotta? Where is she?" I'd forgotten about the troublesome felon. I perked at the thought. Carmine owed me big; maybe he was the solution to the Bonnet problem.

"Well... uh... hmm..." He shuffled from one foot to another.

"You promise me right now," I hissed at him, "that she's alive and well."

"She was the last time I saw her. You know the woman's crazy."

I rolled my eyes in his face. "That's rich, coming from you."

Damn it, I didn't escape Bonnet to now be on the run from a retired mobster.

"You need to breathe," he said. "Come over here and sit down so I can explain."

I threw myself in the rickety webbed chair, defying it to collapse under me. I'd beat Crum over the head with what was left of the aluminum frame. He dragged a bench over and plopped down.

"I had to get rid of her," he started.

I groaned, wrapping my arms around my middle.

"No wait." He held up his hand. "Listen to me. I had to call Carmine and have him come fetch her when she had contacted some of her old clients and planned on resuming the flesh trade."

"Call Carmine?" I thought I'd be sick.

"Did you know she procured women for sex?" he grunted. "Why don't I jump into the middle of the story, you know the part about how I got rid of her."

About out of patience, I clenched my fists, restraining myself from a good scream. Brad would be pissed if he had to issue refunds to our overnight guests.

"Carlotta told her son that we were engaged. She had me play along, convincing me it was the only way she could get out from under his control. I did like her."

"Would you have married her?" I asked.

"I never experienced the feelings like I did with her, but I'm too old to think with my member."

I ducked from the dramatic pose of his arms, one hand now on his brow. If I didn't know better, I would have thought he taught drama instead of engineering at that overpriced college.

"After you left, Carmine showed up in a

stretch limo. Carlotta introduced me as his new step-daddy, and that caught him off guard. I thought he'd strangle her on the spot, but instead he handed me his business card and told me I'd need it when I couldn't stand her bullshit anymore."

"I sniffed it in the air; she was up to something, sneaking around, all cagey-like. Well, my intuition was spot on, and no one creeps around in the middle of the night better than me. I tailed her. She had no idea I spent nights spying on her. She scoffed at my high IQ."

"Yes, I know, it's off the charts." I closed my eyes for a moment, willing my headache not to come back.

"The other night I eavesdropped on Carlotta's phone call, procuring girls for a big party on some rich guy's yacht cruising the Caribbean." Crum stood and started to pace. "The client requested specific girls, and when informed a couple of them wouldn't go for the rough stuff, he got mad. After an exchange of threats, she upped her fee and told him it would be up to him to tell the girls what was expected."

"Sit down. You're making me queasy. The next you thing you know, I'll barf."

His brows knit together; he looked appalled and quickly sat back down.

"She caught me listening, and the murderous glare she tossed my way, I knew she wouldn't tolerate being crossed. I'm not very good at playing ignorant, so I pretended that what she had just done didn't revolt me, pretended excitement. I did ask, 'What if one of them dies?' and tried to talk her into dumping the client. Or just tell him she'd find women who were willing."

Poor Crum looked exhausted.

"That morning she demanded to rent her own trailer—long term. Even a stupid person would figure out she wanted it for an office. I lied and told her we were booked, said that I had no control over the reservations. I went to bed early that night. I woke up and she stood over me staring, scared the crap out of me. I swear she had something in her hand, but I didn't get a good look at whatever it was. She didn't say a word, just turned and left the room. The look on her face..." Crum shuddered. "I think she planned to kill me. Harlot hated her and hid from her."

"Is the cat okay?" I had a soft spot for animals and abhorred animal abuse.

He nodded. "I waited until she went for a walk and called Carmine, told him the entire story. He thanked me and hung up, leaving me to wonder if he planned on doing anything. I didn't have to wait long. Around midnight, voices woke me up. Three men stood over the bed, two in black suits and one with a doctor bag. One put a finger to his lips and motioned me out of bed. I slid out and grabbed my shorts. That's when Carlotta woke up and she recognized them.

Crum wrung his hands as he continued. "The spitfire came out of the bed swinging; she put up a fight, swearing like a longshoreman. She got in a couple of well-placed kicks before the Doc jammed a needle in her arm, and that was the end of the show. The suited ones each grabbed an end and lugged her out to the limo. No one spoke directly to me, and I returned the favor."

I leaned back in the chair, which groaned in objection.

"I'm happy she's gone back home. Let her be Carmine's problem." I felt bad that Crum looked sad. "Bad girls are fun and exciting, until the police show up and there's a possibility that you might go to jail along with them."

"I'm old enough to know better," he snorted. "Got no excuse."

"Trust me, you'd hate jail." I smiled at him.

He handed me the keys to the truck. "It's got gas. You need a place to hide, you're welcome to stay here."

A couple of lights had come on inside the trailers. I had to get out of here before someone took their morning coffee outside and saw me. I left him standing there and slid behind the wheel. The interior was not as junky as I thought, the seats covered with faded out beach towels. I hung my hand out the window and waved as I shot out of the driveway.

Chapter Forty-Five

J S Auto Body showed no signs of life when I drove slowly by. I swung a U-turn and headed down to where he docked his boats. He'd be with Mother, so that meant they'd be on the houseboat or at her house. Walking down the ramp, I found the area completely deserted and both boats parked in their slips, in pristine condition. There was no police tape and no signs that there had been a kidnapping or that it had been reported to any law enforcement agency.

No sign of Jax on the speed boat, either, or that any work was in progress. I hoped he wasn't dead. I assumed that he would've found out we disappeared and hightailed it to safer ground.

Without going aboard, it was hard to tell if anyone inhabited the houseboat. I slipped my Beretta from my back holster and climbed the stairs. The outside clear glass door was locked, so I laid my finger on the bell. I checked out the spot where I'd last seen Billy sprawled, finding no blood or stains; surely that was a good sign. I'd like to think Billy wasn't dead, but chances were not good with the amazon involved. After annoying even myself with the shrill sound of the bell, I sat back in a deck chair.

Growing bored within minutes and tired of waiting to be invited in, I picked the lock and walked around, prepared to shoot the first face I didn't recognize. Spoon kept a clean house, not even a glass or utensil in the sink. In fact, it didn't look like anyone was currently staying in residence. I crept along the hallway, approaching the door to the stateroom I used—open and empty. The bed was made, nothing in the closets or drawers, everything I'd left behind had been cleaned out. Same with the room Fab used. I reassured myself that I was the only one on board and that there would be no unpleasant surprises.

I ransacked the refrigerator and returned to the deck, making sure the door was locked before settling on a long bench. I was out of sight, but from my vantage point could see anyone boarding. It felt weird to not have a plan of action, but I felt safer here than at my house, which I decided on the way over that Bonnet and company would check out first. I know I would. It annoyed me greatly that no one seemed to be looking for me. Maybe when we disappeared again they figured we just went rogue.

Wake up time! I took my phone out of my pocket and called Mother first. I missed her and wanted to launch myself into her arms.

"Madison is that you?" Mother asked.

She sounded worried. I assured her that Fab

and I were both healthy and safe. I didn't say anything more, knowing that any information Spoon gleaned, he would've kept her informed.

"Where's Spoon?" I asked before she could get in any more questions.

I felt ridiculous at being uncomfortable catching them together, since I knew that would be the case, but I tried not to delve too deeply into Mother's love life.

"You know we thought…but I never did," she sniffed. "He's right here."

"Where the hell are you?" Spoon growled. "Tell me that piece of shit Bonnet didn't hurt you? We thought you were dead. So where have you been?"

I held the phone from my ear until he finished yelling and hurling questions.

He finally slowed to catch a breath. "Where are you? I'm coming to get you two."

"Not while Bonnet is lurking around."

"So you don't know? Bonnet is dead."

I paced the cabin and smiled. I relaxed, just knowing I could go outside and sit, without having to worry about random bullets making an appearance. I jerked my attention back to what Spoon was saying.

"His yacht cruised out about twenty miles yesterday and blew sky high. Law enforcement knows there were four men and one woman on board because a small fishing boat passed them on the water. The yacht caught their attention because of the loud partying."

"That's sad," I said with no sincerity. I wanted to dance around, but I'd save it for Fab so she could wrinkle her nose and mumble, 'ludicrous attempt at dancing.' "We'll be back at the house this afternoon."

That would give Fab time and we'd skip the grilling as to why we split up.

"Where are our cars?"

"I'll have them delivered to the house. You damn well better be okay," he grouched.

"Let's celebrate. I'll cook dinner."

"Cooking, as in that loose way that your mother defines it, as in ordering take-out?"

I laughed at him. Most people thought because I didn't cook, that I didn't know how. I excelled at dinner for twenty, for two, not so much. Besides, I knew Mother would never tolerate anyone taking over her job.

"I'm telling you up front, I don't like microwave food."

I heard Mother laugh in the background and say something.

"Or frozen waffles," he added.

"See you later," I said and hung up.

It felt anticlimactic to be informed Bonnet was dead. It seemed too easy. For a second, I thought for a second, Spoon—possibly Creole—had a hand in the timely explosion, especially if they thought we were dead. I had a few questions for Mr. Spoon when I saw him.

Next call — Didier.

"Why are you using your phone?" Fab demanded.

"Get your ass back here, Bonnet's dead. Blown to bits," I said. I took a perverse delight in relating the news. "Call Mother and let her know you're okay. She doesn't know we're not together, so fake annoyance that I didn't let you talk."

Chapter Forty-Six

On the drive to The Cottages, I decided I wanted the fiftyish red Chevrolet pickup. I could horrify the neighbors and park it out front, maybe plant the flatbed with flowers. It made me smile that in a short period of time, I had become as eccentric as the neighbors. My aunt would be proud that I fit in, knew almost everyone in the neighborhood, and had the patience to be friendly to most.

I sent Mac a text to get her behind to work and said that she'd better have my cat. I worried he'd be a disheveled mess and would never forgive me for leaving him.

Two heads poked out from behind the blinds when I pulled in and parked in front of the office: Mac and Shirl, wondering who the truck belonged to. Once they figured it out, they appeared disappointed, and their heads disappeared.

The door opened, thanks to Shirl, who sat where she could see down the driveway and had a partial view of the street.

"I'm baaa-aack," I smiled.

All thoughts of Jazz hating me flew out of my

head. He was curled up in between Mac's legs as she reclined in her chair, feet on the desk. He looked up, barely acknowledged my presence, and went back to sleep.

Big Devil!

I took Fab's seat on the couch and put my sore feet up; afraid to take my shoes off. I'd never get them back on.

"Do we get details?" Mac asked.

I gave them a shortened version. They stared back in awe.

"We should do a girl lunch. Fab can tell you how amazing she is in a crisis," I said.

They both squealed.

"Let's hear it. Anyone die or in jail right now? Any jail runs while I was gone?" I asked.

Mac took an interest in her tennis shoes, banging them on the desk, not realizing they weren't the light up ones. She wore a cotton beach dress, covered in seashells. She didn't look her hippy self today.

"Just spit it out—tell me our two star tenants didn't die." I'd never be ready for Miss January and Joseph to croak.

"They're fine. We, uhm…" she hesitated, then blurted, "have a new tenant. I bent your rule on not renting to locals. I can promise you he won't be a problem."

"We always think that," I struggled not to yell. "Give him a week's notice and then call Spoon."

"Can't do that."

Shirl smirked, arms across her chest.

"Ba-loney. Get him out. They behave for a day or two; next thing, the driveway is full of sheriff cars," I said.

"I can guarantee you the sheriffs will be here all the time, probably using the pool," Shirl smiled big.

"The pool!" I shrieked.

Mac pointed at Shirl. "You can leave."

"I'm not going any damn where," she yelled back at her friend.

I slid off the couch. "I'll take care of it. Spoon's coming for dinner. Sooner is better when ridding the place of a felon."

"It's Kevin," Mac blurted.

"Julie's brother? He hates this place." I knew this was a joke. He'd never move in here. He barely tolerated me, although we'd come to an unspoken agreement to make an effort to get along.

"His duplex burned down and he was desperate. I wasn't going to be the one to tell him *hell no*," Mac said. "It was your brother's idea."

"Kevin introduced himself to his new next door neighbor at the duplex," Shirl said. "It spooked the man, thinking the sheriffs were on to his drug business and he went in and threw a lit cigarette on the sheets and left, destroying evidence," she snorted. "Now he claims it was an accident."

Shirl was a nurse on staff at Tarpon Cove

Hospital, and befriended all the sheriffs on the force. She got the latest and most accurate information.

"Put the word out, we're looking for another duplex. I'm sure he won't want to stay long." I grimaced. "Now give me my cat."

"Jazz is a great cat," Mac said. "I promise I took good care of him."

"I can see that and I appreciate it—a lot." I smiled at her.

He hated the cat carrier, but too bad. I couldn't drive while he was climbing in my hair. I waved to them.

* * *

I dropped Jazz off at home and ditched the pickup at Jake's, left the keys under the seat and texted Crum. It was a little worrisome that no one noticed that I snuck in the back door of the bar and rolled out my bicycle, but this time it worked out in my favor.

Pedaling down the beach, the wind in my face, I enjoyed the ride. For the first time in too long, I wasn't consumed with thoughts of how to stay alive. I scanned the backyard before stepping off the path, all was still quiet. Hurrying inside, I made sure the furniture and everything was in the same place as when we left for the safe house. No one needed to find out I'd stayed here alone last night.

Chapter Forty-Seven

Behind the wheel of the Mercedes, Fab blew into the driveway. Didier must have taken her car, which meant that only my SUV ended up stashed away. I whooshed out a sad sigh, feeling melancholy as I watched them from the kitchen window. Didier held the driver's side door and as Fab's feet hit the ground, he hugged her and kept his arm around her shoulder.

"We're back!" Fab yelled, throwing the door open. "We want details."

"Spoon wasn't forthcoming on the phone, so we have to wait. He and Mother are on the way here."

"I heard you offered to cook," Fab snorted. "We took a vote — unanimous for take out."

"You, too?" I frowned at Didier.

He laughed and shook his head at Fab. "Where's Creole?"

I ignored the question and focused on Fab, who slowly checked out the living room. She turned to me. "You stayed here last night, didn't you?"

I glared at her. "I didn't feel I'd be welcome at Creole's, so I hid out somewhere else."

"Cherie…" Didier soothed as he put his arm around me, giving me a hug. "You two will work this out."

Fab flung my bed pillow into the corner of the daybed.

She's so good. Anyone else wouldn't have noticed.

I continued to give her the evil eye. "What are we going to tell Mother?"

"The truth! She won't like it, but she'll be happy we didn't skimp on the details. She's not stupid; she knows we water down most of our stories."

"I'll let you tell her."

My brother burst through the front door. Slamming a stack of paperwork on the counter, he scooped me off my feet and twirled me around.

"Let me go, this clench is claustrophobic." I pushed away. "Don't say anything sweet, or I'll start crying."

We stared at one another for a long moment.

"I love you," I whispered.

"Yeah, me too." He pulled me into another hug.

"I'm going to tell on you. 'Mother, he touched me'." I gave a long, drawn-out whine.

"Go ahead, she'd love to send you to your room and lock you in," he laughed.

"Miss me, bro?" Fab hugged him. "Where's your girlfriend?"

"She's at Liam's track meet. He doesn't know

anything that happened, and she wants to keep it that way."

I shook my head. "He won't hear it from me but, when he does find out, he'll be mad."

"It wasn't my decision." Brad shook his head.

Didier handed him a beer and they talked about the next bike ride. Brad had his back to me. I settled onto a bar stool and opened the leather portfolio, crammed with paperwork that had been with him since college and looked worn out.

A real estate contract lay on the top and I scanned the contents.

"What the heck is this?" I held it up. "Don't tell me it's none of my business. That doesn't apply in the Westin family."

Fab looked over my shoulder. "What about my lighthouse?"

"My new gift shop is fine and not going anywhere," I told her.

The look of disbelief on her face was priceless, and I had to contain my laughter.

"We're selling the Trailer Court. Initial in the circles and sign on the last page," Brad informed me.

"Hold on a second. How is this going to work? I'm not willing to give up any part of the rest of the property. How am I going to share with new owners?"

Fab whistled and pointed to the sales price.

Didier motioned Fab to his side and she

ignored him, earning a glare and a few choice words in French.

"As you can see, I got us top dollar. The property was sub-divided long ago; the new owners will fence it off, making the current front entrance the back, thereby separating it from your other businesses. The dirt strip that runs along the far side will be paved, and the new entrance will be at the end. There's a clause that there can be no building of condos."

"Are you sure about this? I thought you liked your new venture."

"The fun was in fixing up the property and getting top dollar," Brad said. "Besides, we need the money for another real estate deal I'm looking at in Miami. You have The Cottages — do you want to run the Trailer Court? I know I don't."

I took the pen he held out and signed in all the appropriate places.

"Does this mean less fishing?"

"I'm keeping the business. Thinking about taking on a partner who will handle the trips."

"When do I get to hear about the new project?" I asked.

"We'll have a meeting," he smirked. "I'll pitch the deal. I realize I sprung this on you, but I'm not taking on a new project without your approval."

Mother rushed through the door, leaving Spoon behind to carry in a mountain of food. She grabbed Fab and me in a group hug.

"You two better be okay!" She kissed us, sounding relieved. She had tears in her eyes.

"Don't cry," I whispered. "We're fine.

"You're both grounded," Mother said, looking us over for cuts and scrapes.

"Good luck on that," I laughed. "In a tight spot, second daughter here is the best tool ever. She never backs down and doesn't accept defeat."

"Guess who walked in?" Fab nodded toward the French doors.

I turned and tall, dark, and devilishly-handsome Creole filled my eyes. I felt my cheeks warm, having been caught staring.

"You be nice," Mother warned as she pinched my arm. "Be sweet, distract him, and he'll get over his anger. You two will get back together."

"What are you suggesting, Mother?"

"Probably not cooking," Fab smirked.

Mother and I stared at her.

"You know what they say about men and food," Fab defended.

I watched out of the corner of my eye as Brad offered Creole and Spoon a beer. The guys unloaded the shopping bags: Mexican from Jake's. I kept waiting for the pitcher of margaritas but it never came. Instead there were all the makings for Spoon to blend them himself.

Creole and I made eye contact. He nodded and I smiled back at him.

An assortment of food was laid out on the countertop. Didier got out plates and utensils. The men worked well together, laying out the veritable feast.

We helped ourselves to the mountain of food, while Brad brought in extra seats. We crowded around the island as I sucked down half of my margarita. I needed to calm my nerves, but not get drunk and do something inappropriate.

"I suppose eating and talking about body parts isn't appropriate, but we're all here, and I'm sure we all have questions," I said. "Is Billy dead? Last thing I remember, I saw him lying on the floor."

"A bullet can't keep him down," Spoon smiled. "Lucky bastard, his dog tags saved his life. Never knew he did a stint in the Army. He's been discharged from the hospital; his girlfriend took him home with her. I know he's better, because he started milking the sympathy before he got to the car."

I stirred uncomfortably in my seat as Creole slid into a seat across from me. I couldn't help myself and stole another glance; he caught my stare, his lips quirking up.

"Did you blow up Bonnet?" Fab asked Spoon.

Didier said something in her ear and she jerked away.

"Well, did you?" Fab demanded.

Spoon grinned at her.

"No, and you know why? I thought you and

Madison might be on board." He hugged Mother. "Hence the reason we thought you might be dead."

"We thought you were in negotiations. Why no big rescue off the island? Did you figure we could fend for ourselves?" Fab continued to grill him.

"It wasn't the first time you two broke your word and took off," Creole reminded us, an angry edge to his voice.

"When was the last time we took off and left a man behind with an almost bullet hole in his chest, especially after he made us a yummy dinner?" I grouched.

"When Billy didn't answer my call," Spoon said, "I went to my boat and found him lying on the floor. You two were gone without a trace of a disturbance. Next day, I motored out to Bonnet Island."

Mother smiled up at him, patting his arm.

Spoon continued, "Billy told us you were in trouble as they wheeled him away on a stretcher. Me and my posse took a trip out there and confronted Bonnet, threatening him with war. He looked me in the eye and swore he had nothing to do with your disappearance, told me to have a look around. We searched the house and property and found no sign you'd ever been there."

"That's why the redheaded Amazon escorted us to the dungeon room," Fab said.

"So you met Lethal Lexie. Rumor has it she's a contract killer. Made her services exclusive to Bonnet a year ago. She's tougher than any of her ilk in male form that I ever met. Not an ounce of empathy, narcissistic to the extreme, her allegiance is to money. She is high-dollar talent."

"They kept us in a horrid cement room on the downstairs level," I said. "Didn't seem like anyone was looking for us, and we were on our own."

Mother leaned over and kissed my cheek. "I know my girls. I knew you two would be back."

"What's your side of the story?" Creole asked, eerily calm except for the look on his face.

I briefly glanced up at him. Although his tone sounded neutral, he didn't expect the truth. Fab and I exchanged glances.

Fab gave an evil smile.

"We were chloroformed. Did you notice the scratch on Lexie's face? That was a present from me." She apparently paid attention when I relayed stories; she recounted the details like bullet points, headline style. She embellished some, but stuck mostly to the truth.

My favorite was about how, kicking and screaming, putting up the fight of our lives, our abductor had to smoosh that rag over our noses to get us off the boat. Not a word that we were caught off guard sleeping. She turned us into super girls, sneaking past our captors, out of the mansion, overpowering the boat steward so we could jet ski to Key West. Mistaken for hookers, we lucked out running into a wannabe john that turned out to be an old acquaintance, and he gave us a ride back to the Cove.

Mother hung on to her every word. When she looked at me, I flashed her a small smile and winked. Everyone accepted the story. Creole held back; due to his experience, he didn't know what to believe.

Brad laughed. "I wish this was a story I could brag on about my sister."

"Fab deserves the credit," I said. "She never gave up, always had a plan. I did my best not to whine and show fear, believing she'd get us home in one piece, and she did." I smiled at her.

"Don't sell your contribution short." Fab smiled back. "The fun part happened when we finally got back on the mainland. For a while, we switched personalities and I was the calm one."

"Where's Jax?" I asked.

"When we found Billy, I checked on him," Spoon said. "Your mother insisted he relocate immediately. Thinking more about my boat repairs than his health, I wasn't happy. But it worked out better than I could have hoped. Jax got me an introduction to a friend of his. He's towing my boat to his shop and finishing the repairs."

"Got Jax a fishing gig out of Clearwater. When he's done, he has the option of signing on again or using the airline ticket I got him to go anywhere he wants," Spoon said.

"When he finds out about Bonnet, he'll probably head back home," Mother said. "We had a long talk before he left. He misses his family."

Brad's phone rang. He looked at the screen and laughed. After a minute, he responded, "Congratulations old man."

"Yeah, good luck," he hung up.

"Congratulations," he looked at me. "You're a step-mother to six."

Confusion written on my face, it took me a minute. "Harlot? Six kittens?"

"All different colors. You know what that means?" Brad raised his eyebrows.

"Yeah, she was banging every tom in the neighborhood," I said in disgust.

"Madison," Mother hissed. "Banging," she mouthed.

Fab and I laughed. Didier shook his finger.

"I know other, more colorful words," I said sweetly.

Mother held up her nearly empty margarita glass. "To family," she toasted.

Mother, Fab, and I sat at the island polishing off our drinks while the guys did dish duty.

Everyone drifted into the living room for more comfortable seating. I wanted to sneak off to my bedroom and avoid Creole. I just survived near death, I reminded myself. How bad could the brooding detective be?

I just didn't want to hear the words "we're over."

Creole lounged against one of the French doors, watching my every move like a hawk. I could feel his stare, finally getting up the courage to meet his eyes. I wanted to run to him, less chance of changing my mind. Scooting around my Mother and Brad talking, I inched my way to his side.

"Who invited you?" I asked, staring up at him.

"I don't need an invitation." He filled the small space between us, standing in front of me.

"You're welcome here anytime." I wanted to lay my head on his chest and ask if we could turn back time to pre-dead bodies and skip everything in between.

"Are you still mad?" I asked softly.

"Yes!"

"I could apologize, and then I'd gracefully accept yours for hiding us in that dreadful place." I hoped for a quick laugh, which I didn't get.

"Hypotheticals aren't helpful in this situation. Would you mean it?"

"Most of it."

"Hmm…"

"I have a second idea. We could drop our hard feelings and go straight to make-up sex. We haven't done it very often, but when we have, it's been spectacular."

His fingers wrapped around my arm, and he dragged me out to the patio. Suddenly he bent down and scooped me up and over his shoulder.

"The best thing I can do is to keep you where I can find you, a good way to make certain you never get away from me again."

~*~

PARADISE SERIES NOVELS

Crazy in Paradise
Deception in Paradise
Trouble in Paradise
Murder in Paradise
Greed in Paradise
Revenge in Paradise
Kidnapped in Paradise
Swindled in Paradise
Executed in Paradise
Hurricane in Paradise
Lottery in Paradise
Ambushed in Paradise
Christmas in Paradise
Blownup in Paradise
Psycho in Paradise
Overdose in Paradise
Initiation in Paradise
Jealous in Paradise
Wronged in Paradise
Vanished in Paradise
Fraud in Paradise
Naive in Paradise

Deborah's books are available on Amazon
amazon.com/Deborah-Brown/e/B0059MAIKQ

About the Author

Deborah Brown is an Amazon bestselling author of the Paradise series. She lives on the Gulf of Mexico, with her ungrateful animals, where Mother Nature takes out her bad attitude in the form of hurricanes.

Sign up for my newsletter and get the latest on new book releases. Contests and special promotion information. And special offers that are only available to subscribers.
www.deborahbrownbooks.com

Follow on FaceBook:
facebook.com/DeborahBrownAuthor

You can contact her at Wildcurls@hotmail.com

Deborah's books are available on Amazon
amazon.com/Deborah-Brown/e/B0059MAIKQ

Made in the USA
Las Vegas, NV
22 April 2023